Finding Jessica

Alan Grainger

Finding Jessica

Finding Jessica

Also by Alan Grainger

The Tree That Walked

The Klondike Chest

The Rumstick Book

Forestland Stories

The Learning Curves

Father Unknown

The Legacy

It's Only Me

Eddie's Penguin

Deadly Darjeeling

Deep & Crisp & Even

Box Of Secrets

Short & Fat & Dead

Good Intention, Bad Result

Blood On The Stones

Ω

Copyright © 2020 Alan Grainger

Amazon Edition

All rights reserved

ISBN-13: 9798669460051

Finding Jessica

For our many friends
in
Old Connaught House
who have kept us going
throughout the Corona Virus epidemic
and in our sunset years.

With very special thanks to
Pat and Edel, Susie, Derek and Natalie, Micheál,
Tony and Mary, Emma and Michael, Sam, Charlotte,
Edwin and Pat … and Caitriona.

Without your help and generosity,
we would never have survived.

Finding Jessica

'Do as you would be done by'

Charles Kingsley
The Water Babies

Finding Jessica

Prologue

The offices of Parsons and Ogelvie
Solicitors
68, George's Street, Sydney, NSW. Australia.

Gareth Parsons, the smartly dressed son of the partnership's founder, rose from his black leather chair and leaned across his desk to shake the hand of a man who'd just come into his office; a rugged, tanned, casually dressed old man, with gleaming silver stubble.

'Ah … Mr Townsend,' said Parsons, 'how nice to see you again after all this time. You're looking well.'

'For my age you mean … I wish I felt it?' the man replied, taking the seat, to which Parsons was pointing. 'And you'd better make it Oscar because, if you don't, I won't know who you're talking to!'

'Point made, right, Oscar it is,' said Parsons, grinning; 'and I'm Gareth. But you really are looking great. In fact, you haven't changed at all. How long ago is it since you were last here?'

'Must be fifteen years … it could be more. And what about you, Gareth … and how's that brother of yours … and your father … I suppose he's been put out to pasture by now. He had place on the coast, as I remember; a place to retire to? Give him my best when you see him.'

'I will of course, he moved there a while back. As to my brother … well he's set up on his own up in Port Macquarie these days; I never see him. You've a good memory.'

Oscar smiled; something he didn't do often. 'Yeah, not bad, but then again that's not always to my advantage. There are things I'd like to forget and can't. And things I want to remember, and don't. It's a funny old life.'

Gareth, by the nod he gave, seemed to agree. 'And what brings you here today?' he said, 'Something about your will, my secretary told me.'

The old man brightened up as Gareth spoke. At last his long-held wishes were about to be put in place. 'That's right,' he said, 'I'm going to alter it; I want to take care of a couple of things from my past that have been troubling me. Things I need to sort out before it's too late; before I'm unable to look after them myself if you know what I mean! I'm getting on now, I've a few difficult health problems to deal with, and … anyway … what is it they say… 'Time and tide wait for no man.'?'

Gareth smiled again They hadn't met in years; hadn't had the need to but, with Oscar's health failing, he could see why a meeting to review his affairs and make some adjustments to his will had been requested. Once a strapping six footer with the build of an Olympic athlete, Oscar had also been known for his nerves of steel. But now … well into his seventies and not at all in control of a debilitating illness, he was only the shadow of what he'd once been. Mentally, he appeared to be as sharp as ever … but, even if he was, how long would he be like that? Not long he reckoned and, if he was to do something to right the wrongs that were gnawing at his conscience, a meeting with his solicitor was a pressing need. Hence this one, booked a few days earlier.

Once the initial pleasantries were over, Gareth got straight down to business. 'So,' he began, 'you want to review your affairs *and* your will, with a view to bringing them up to date. Is that it?'

'Yes, it is; that's exactly what I intend to do.'

Gareth nodded, 'You've been retired from active business for some years, haven't you?'

'I have.'

'And, until recently, you've enjoyed good health?'

'Hardly ever had day of sickness …'

'But now …'

'Now I'm going down hill with no brakes, Gareth, and I want to ensure everything is in order before I hit the buffers.'

'Huh … you have a great way with words Oscar, a great a way. So, what exactly do you want us to do for you?'

'What do I want *you* to do? Hmm … that's the trouble.

I'm not sure. Alright, this might appear to be an odd request, but I want to make certain a few people I hurt in my early life, people who've probably been hating my guts and cursing me for years, get something, a legacy if you like, a gift that'll not only ease my conscience, but heal some of the wounds I caused.'

'I see. You're not married, are you, I can't remember?'

'I'm not married *now*. I was, sort of, once … in fact, I was sort of married twice … but I've been on my own for years; both before I arrived in Australia and since. The people to whom I'm hoping to give these bequests are more than likely living somewhere in Britain … though I'm not sure of that. Part of your job, if you decide to help me, will be to track them down.'

'And you came to this country … when?'

'Oh … back in … the seventies.'

'That's a long time ago, over forty years. Are you still in touch with any of the people you want to recompense?'

'No, I'm not. One way or another I walked out on all of them. Cleared off and left them in the lurch. At the time I just wanted to get away … I was being stifled in Brighton, where I lived, and I didn't give much thought to their feelings … didn't give a fig if I hurt any of them. And now, as I've got older, my conscience has opened my eyes, and I can see what a self-centred bastard I was. If I could turn back the clock, Gareth, I would. If I'd the guts to go back and find them, I'd …. Ach I don't know what I'd do … what I did before I suppose … run away from them all … just as I did the last time.'

'Them *all*?'

'Well, three, actually; my brother, my son, and my daughter, people whose lives may well have been ruined by my indifference. I abandoned every one of them.'

'So, the people concerned live in England, not Australia; and you don't have addresses for them?'

'I've no idea where they are.'

'Tracking them down isn't going to be easy - or cheap.'

'Will you try?'

'I'll try, yes, for you, Oscar, I'll try. But, as to whether I'll succeed or not, is another matter. Let me have whatever names and addresses and other information you *have*, and I'll take it from there. I'll get onto our English agents and ask them to make a start on finding them. In the meantime, you and I can sort out your will. How does that sound … OK?'

'It sounds like I was hoping it would sound, Gareth.'

'There you go then.' the younger man replied. 'When do you propose we make a start on this intriguing manhunt?'

'As soon as possible. I've got notes made already; jottings that cover my knowledge of the people concerned right up until the day I left England. And, as I've never been back, and not one of them has ever come here looking for me, I can only assume they've written me off, erased me, removed me from their memories. And, I assure you, I have never been in touch with any of the people I wish to compensate.'

'So you've some notes made?'

'I have them with me,' Oscar replied, pulling an envelope from his pocket and handing it to Gareth, who opened it and withdrew two or three folded sheets of paper, which he laid on his desktop. From a quick glance, as he did so, he could see they were abbreviated pointers to Oscar's early life, running from the day of his birth, to the one on which he emigrated to Australia, and right up to the present day. 'My Goodness,' he said, 'you *have* been busy, haven't you? It's going to take me some time to get my head round this lot. Leave them with me. We can meet again next week to set something up. Alright?'

Oscar said nothing; he just rocked his head from side to side. It'd taken him weeks to make up his mind to initiate these moves to salve his conscience and he wanted to get on with them, not put them off to another day. 'I was hoping we might make start now.' he said. 'Get a few ideas down on paper.'

'I see.' Gareth answered. 'Let me look at my appointments book again then ... but I'm pretty-well tied up all day today.'

Oscar nodded.

As he did so, Gareth couldn't help reflecting on how compliant the old fellah had become; a few years back he'd have banged on the desk demanding they start immediately. 'Alright,' he said, 'I can spare you an hour if we skip the lunch I was about to offer you. Why don't you wait in the canteen while I switch a few engagements round and read your notes? When you come back, we'll make a start on setting things up. O.K.?'

Oscar looked up with the start of a grin on his face. 'That's alright by me. But what about *your* lunch?'

Gareth chuckled. 'Look at me,' he said, patting his stomach; I eat too much. Go on, grab yourself something in the canteen; it's on the next floor. Tell 'em you're with me and they'll see you right.'

Oscar rose from his chair and turned for the door. 'Are you *sure*,' he said, 'only …'

'Yeah, yeah, I'm sure. Just remember to say who you're with.' Gareth answered, picking up the papers Oscar had left.

A quarter of an hour later, and having digested as much as he could from the first page, Gareth glanced through the jottings he'd made. What a story this was … what a life! He poured himself glass of water and, sipping it slowly, sat back to let what he'd read sink in. Such extraordinary revelations, with none of them showing Oscar in a good light. Were they exaggerations? Maybe they were … but every word had the ring of truth. He leaned forward, picked up the page again, and re-read every word of the sheet of paper Oscar had boldly headed:

BEFORE AUSTRALIA.

It was quite brief; all Oscar said was that his parents: George and Freda Townsend lived in Brighton, in the county of Sussex, England, and that he'd been born there in 1945, on the day the Second World War finished and four years before his only sibling ... his brother Everett. That he'd left school at seventeen, much against his parents' wishes, and that he'd never appreciated the sacrifices they had made in order to send him to a private school, hoping they'd both end up as bankers or civil servants. How, despite the ridiculous ambitions his mother and father held for him, he'd taken a job on a building site, where he was moved around, helping whichever of the tradesmen needed a hand. How, eighteen months after starting the job, he 'knew it all' and, brim full of confidence, he'd quit what he was doing to become a self-employed, cash only, 'builder', taking on small building repair jobs, and attic conversations, for folding money. There'd been no shortage of work and, before long, he'd been flush with cash *and* confidence; a young braggart who believed he was ready to take on the world.

Gareth put the paper down as he tried to imagine Oscar as he must have been at that early stage of his adult life. A cocky young man with no fear of hard work, or risk ...and no thought of settling down to lead what everyone else would have called 'a normal life', whatever *that* was, *in* Brighton, *in* the nineteen seventies. As he read on, the picture of Oscar as a young man became clearer ... and Gareth found him not unattractive. Wild and irresponsible, here was a man who, constricted when living at home, 'jumped ship' and went to Australia to do 'his own thing' ... and stuff everyone else. No surprise then that, under these circumstances, the next few lines of his pre-Australia information came out more like a list than an explanatory note.

Massive row with my father over my lifestyle.

Constant bickering with Everett over his, probably well intentioned, if somewhat sanctimonious, criticism of the way he said I was irresponsibly wasting my life.

Left home with no regrets, and moved in with Doreen, a timid girl I'd known at school, who'd a bed/sit of her own and a crush on me. It turned out to be a disaster for her for, while I never saw it as more than an expedient, but she'd taken it seriously and treated my living with her as some sort of 'marriage'. I'm ashamed to say I used her only for as long as it suited me.

A few months after moving in with her, she told me she was pregnant. I wasn't ready for that; I bailed out, shifted my gear into bed/sit I'd rented in Worthing, and found a new pub. Not long after that I learned from a friend that she'd had a child and named her Jessica.

I'd got to know Yana Choudrey by then, a fabulous looking and very bright Lebanese girl, a second year medical student and a part time waitress in a pub in Chichester. One night, after the pub closed, she took me back to her sea-front flat. Next day I moved in. Things went well for a couple of years but then, one day, she told me she was pregnant, that we were going to have a baby and that, if it was a boy, she was going to call him Hari, after her father. I was not happy; I'm not a baby man …. not a father … except in the physical sense, of course. I moved out the day the baby was born, left them, and went up north. But, after eighteen miserable years up there, I still hadn't found a decent job so I went back; back to Brighton and back to her and the kid. It still didn't work out, she never stopped grumbling and the child never stopped crying. I stuck it for a while but it was driving me up the wall so I took off again and got a building job in Dorking. It that lasted a year or so and it paid well, but I still couldn't settle. In the end I came to the conclusion I needed a complete change and, as I'd few pounds in the kitty by then, I thought I'd give Australia a go … *on my own*.

Even then I never said 'goodbye' to anyone, and I never regretted anything I'd done … until now that is; now I can't get my selfishness out of mind.'

Through the window in his door Gareth saw Oscar approaching; he had a slightly anxious look on his face and it didn't get less when entered and resumed his seat. 'I've never given much thought to the people I now want to compensate,' he said, 'now I can think of nothing else. I have to find a way of making up for the upset I caused in the lives of Hari and Jessica, the children I fathered, before I die. And I want to say 'sorry', in some way, to my brother; he always seemed to be left 'picking up the pieces'. Each of them will get a decent amount of money, but I'm going to leave something to both my so called 'wives' as well and, this time, it'll be more than the envelope full of fivers I shoved through their letterboxes the day I left for Australia.'

For a full minute before he put the paper down, Gareth sat staring at it; envisaging the tearful faces and angry exchanges Oscar had brought about, and he shook his head in near total disbelief. How could the harmless, grizzled old so and so, sitting in front of him, have been so blind to the cruelty he was handing out? What he'd just finished reading was a catalogue of selfishness, the like of which he'd never seen before. He shook his head again and, thoroughly exhausted by his roller coaster ride through Oscar's early days, took another sip of water and picked up the second sheet of paper.

From the start, it was obvious his new life in the antipodes, was going to be mighty different to the one he'd left behind; his move to the other end of the world didn't blunt his drive, it sharpened it and, before long, he was making money again. Not that it made him less self-opinionated, or more aware of the unhappiness he'd left behind him.

The next page began with the second leg of Oscar's outbound Qantas flight. It was entitled:

AUSTRALIA

'En-route to Sydney, via Hong Kong, I met man who

kept rattling on about Opals and opal mining,' the notes said. 'At first I thought him boring and wished he'd shut up. But then I realised what he was saying was interesting and, before long, I was listening to every word. Here was real adventure, just what I was looking for and, on his advice, after a day or two in Sydney, I made my way to Lightning Ridge, an area in north western New South Wales where, he told me, the best opals were mined. Within a day, I got a job as a temporary replacement for an injured member of the famous Lunatic Hill Syndicate, who happened to be working the Ridge. It was a move that set me up in my new life. I made enough money that year to buy a quarter share in small, abandoned, short tunnelled claim, only a mile away. On the tenth day, following our re-opening of it, part of the entrance tunnel wall collapsed, trapping me in the blind end. It was a terrifying experience but, ultimately, it also turned out to be a lucky one.

As the mass of fallen stone and compacted gravel and clay was being removed by my team mates in order to get me out, the glint of an opal was spotted coming from a fractured nodule embedded in the newly exposed wall of the tunnel.

Over the next four days, two other fist sized craggy nodules, or 'noddies' as the miners call them, were recovered from the rubble and the newly exposed seam, most of which was still trapped in the mine wall.

The chunkiest, a much prized rarity, being basically black, would hardly have fitted into a teacup, while one of the others, also black, was as big as a pigeon's egg. There were a dozen or so smaller ones too. The unexpected and highly unlikely haul was deemed, by those in the team who knew more about opal mining than I did, to be a fluke. They were probably right because, apart from that first day, no opals have ever been found in the area. The partnership was dissolved afterwards, and the lucky finds sold.

My share was enough to set me up, in a small way, in property development, as I had always intended. I moved back to Sydney, borrowed whatever additional cash I needed, and started with one dilapidated bungalow, renovating it in eight weeks, and selling it for twice what I'd paid for it. And so it went on, year after year, one run down 'uncared for' house after another, and all in the south western suburbs of Sydney where I still live, on my own, in a villa that could house an army. I ought to be pleased with my life, and I am. But not entirely; those early days in Brighton keep coming back to haunt me, and will probably do so every day until I put a few things right and clear my conscience.

Gareth put down the page and, rocking back in his chair, eyes closed, tried to picture Oscar in his prime. 'Some man.' He thought. 'But what a swine.'

It took half an hour and a deal of cross examination for all the information to sink in and, twenty minutes after that, they had the rough outline of a plan. It was set out in a series of steps, ones they'd need to take if they were to open up the possibility of permanently irradicating the guilt Oscar was feeling.

'That's it then.' Said Gareth, standing to shake Oscar's hand when they'd finished. 'I'll be in touch the minute I hear from our associates in England.'

Already looking younger, Oscar smiled again. He'd done so more times that day than he had in the previous month. And he was happier, more content than he'd been for a long, time. Soon he'd be putting down his burden. Soon he'd be able to look himself in the face again.

DAY ONE

Crackstone Manor Hotel and Country Club
Brighton

3 months later, at 5.22 p.m.

There was only a handful of players out on the course, so late in the afternoon. In half hour, if the light held, the numbers would build again as 'golf mad' members, on their way home from work, stopped to 'hit a few balls' before their evening meal.

One of the few people playing and, apparently, doing so on her own, was a woman. She'd been on the elevated fourteenth tee for the previous ten minutes, practising her swing and preparing herself for the course's most challenging hole.

An observer might have thought her behaviour odd, and wonder why she seemed to have such an obsession with this one particular element of the course but, as far as she could tell, there wasn't anybody in sight, no 'observer' to take the slightest interest in what she was doing. Which was just as well for, without being too obvious, she was also trying to work out what was happening on the other side of the hedge dividing the fourteenth fairway from a narrow country lane she'd never noticed when standing there previously.

Her attention had been caught, as she was about to climb the rough-hewn granite steps to the tee hoping that, for once, she might hit her ball onto the green first time. But, hardly had her foot left the ground than she heard the yell. Someone was shouting instructions to someone else on the other side of the hedge. What was going on? The lane didn't seem to lead anywhere, as far as she could see, other than to what looked like an old barn. What had really prompted her curiosity though, wasn't the barn but the car; of which she'd got an occasional glimpse through the hedgerow's branches. It was a big shiny black BMW, and it was partially covered with a tarpaulin as it was being slowly backed down the ramps of a low loading trailer.

She watched until both vehicles disappeared from sight; the car towards the barn, and the tow vehicle towards the main road. 'That's odd.' she thought, turning back to face the hole.

The fourteenth at Crackstone is the member's favourite, it's a real tester for anyone, and especially for players, like her, who loved a challenge. In her eagerness to achieve victory before the rain came though, she'd failed to notice a man, who was watching her from behind a nearby gorse bush.

The clouds had been threatening since she arrived on the course and, as she looked down the fairway to the green, lining up her shot, she could see a shower wasn't far off. Was there time for one more go? She looked up at the sky again and laughed. 'What am I doing here anyway? This is ridiculous; I ought to be at home getting ready by now, not standing around here waiting to get soaked, thinking about shiny black BMWs, and wondering if I should use a seven or a nine.

It's a seven … definitely … or is it? Every time I play this flippin' hole I'm faced with the same question; is this the ball that's finally going to land in the centre of the green? Huh. I wonder. It probably isn't going to land on the green at all … it's never done so in the past, it's always been short, and why … because the club the Pro keeps insisting that I use, a nine when I'm sure it ought to be a seven? 'Anyway, one more and I'm off,' she muttered, putting the nine back into her bag and pulling out the seven … all thoughts of strange activity in the lane well to the back of her mind. And then, carefully, she placed the last of her practice balls on the tee and stood back, waving her club threateningly as she composed herself to make the shot. 'Right,' she said to herself, '*this* time!'

She never heard the man creep from the bushes and steal up behind her; had no idea she was in any sort of danger when, with one final squiggle of her hips, she drew back her club to power up the stroke. As her club began to descend, the man raised a mallet-headed putter he'd plucked from her bag, lying on the ground at the foot of the steps and, with all the force he could muster, brought it down on her.

Luckily, and for no obvious reason, she moved her head slightly a second before the impact, turning his heavy, possibly fatal, blow into a glancing one that nearly took off her ear.

For a split second, it looked as though she'd not been affected at all. But then she began to crumble; lurching sideways until, losing her balance, she dropped to her knees and tumbled head first down the steps to the fairway. The man paused; it was as if he was working out what to do next, and then, barely glancing to check if she was alive, he raced off into the bushes and disappeared.

She *was* alive … but only just, and she might have been there all night had it not been for the joggers - brothers - two of them - James and Alistair Forrester, members of a health club attached to the hotel that owned the course. She'd seen them in the distance earlier, when standing on the tee watching her first ball land short of the green; their pale blue track suits standing out against the dark green foliage of a clump of rhododendron bushes. And then, when they'd got to the point where the track crossed the fairway at the back of the tenth, they'd spotted her, draped, upside down, on the steps to the fourteenth tee, their attention caught by the brightness of her yellow pullover. What could have happened? Had she stumbled? Was she alright? They raced across the course fearing the worst

14, Malvern Gardens,
Brighton.

5.58. pm

Detective Superintendent Foxy Reynard, Sussex Criminal Investigation Department's most experienced and successful detective, wasn't in his customary good mood. In fact, he hadn't been in it all week, for this was the day of his retirement, his last day in a job he'd loved so much it had all but consumed him. Now, approaching the final moments of his career, and with no plans for the future, the changes that were looming were making him more and more morose. Surprising really, for Foxy had always been well known for the way he meticulously planned *his* life, and scorned those who didn't do the same with theirs. Six more hours though, and he'd be gone ... shoved out to grass with no appetite ... a prospect to which he was not looking forward.

Nor was Cathy, his wife, though, wisely, and from long experience, she tried her best to keep her thoughts to herself.

'I hate these flamin' do's,' he said, 'I wish it was damned-well over and done with.'

She grinned. 'Don't be silly. You'll have a great time.'

'It's a waste of money.'

'Of course it's not; it's just your friends wanting to give you a night to remember. They want to send you off with a bang ... it's their way of saying 'thank you'.'

'A bang? Dear God, d'you think so? I reckon it's the free drink they're after; they don't give a damn about me.'

'Of course they do. Come on this is not like you.'

'All they're concerned about is how they'll come out of it ... what's in it for them ... promotion and so on. They won't give hoot about me sitting at home twiddling my thumbs; bored out of my mind with nothing to do.'

'Nothing to do! I've plenty lined up for you to do; you can start with the sitting room.'

'No Cathy, *you* can start with the sitting room, I'm going to start looking for a job.'

'A job ... you must be joking. Doing what?'

'I'm not certain, but it won't be painting the bloody sitting room, that's for sure. Anyway, that's for the future. Tonight, I'll stick to the norm and pretend I'm liking it.'

Cathy smiled; he was going to go quietly. At sixty, with his close cropped curly hair still only showing the odd streak of grey and his body on the lean side of stout, he looked more like a banker than police detective. No bomber jackets, torn jeans and Doc Martin's for him; he was always dressed in a well-cut dark grey or navy blue suit, which'd be worn with a white cutaway collared shirt and a Paisley tie; his shoes polished like a Grenadier Guardsman's boots. It's a mode of attire known throughout the force as 'Foxy's Uniform', one that aspiring members of his team have to adopt if they have even the remotest thoughts of promotion into it, one of benign amusement for everyone else in Sussex's Criminal Investigation Department. His attitude to those who serve under him is unusual too; for a start, he mostly addresses people by their rank and name, in a very formal sort of way, whereas others generally prefer first names or nicknames.

Regarding the way he wishes others to address him, he is equally pedantic; requesting them to use his rank and name though, in more recent times, he's relaxed this a little, allowing his team members to call him 'Guv' or Governor; a London cockney's mode of address that is popular within The Force.

He glanced at his watch and began to walk towards the door. 'You're not driving, I hope.' Said Cathy.

'No, I'm not; young Riggs has organised a minibus through a pal of his in the rugby club. and one of the duty drivers is bringing the 'Top Brass' in a squad car. It's all been taken care of, don't worry.'

'Alright then,' she said. 'have a good time … and don't drink too much.'

He didn't answer, he glowered. How could he possibly have good time when he was on his way to the gallows?

Crackstone Manor Golf Course.

6.01.pm

James, the shorter of the two men, got there first and, dropping to his knees, gasped when he saw how much blood was oozing through her hair, trickling steadily across the back of her neck, and dripping down onto the steps.

'Crikey,' said his brother, Alistair, when he got there, breathless, a few seconds later. 'Is she alright?'

'Alright? I don't think so; far from it, I'd say. She seems to be breathing ... just; but I've no idea if she's *really* badly hurt ... life threateningly hurt.'

'Christ, that's bad. What'll we do?'

James sucked in a breath through his pursed lips, and shook his head again. 'Damned if I know ... move her I suppose, raise up her a bit. The bleeding won't stop until her head's above the rest of her body. See if you can find a towel in her golf bag - something to get her head higher. I'll try to get her more upright.'

Alistair obviously didn't agree, and gave him a doubting

look. 'Are you sure you know what you're doing?' he asked. 'You're not supposed to move an injured person until ...'

'Oh come on Alistair, if we don't get her head higher she'll bleed to death. Get out of the way I'll do it myself ... *I'll* hoist her up ... *you* can check the golf bag. See if her purse is in it - or her phone - anything to tell us who she is. But first, I need a pullover or a towel to prop her up.'

Still unhappy at what his brother was planning to do, Alistair stood his ground and didn't move.

'What're you waiting for? James snapped, struggling, on his own, to manoeuvre the woman into a more upright position. 'Find me something ... *anything* ... I need something to shove under her flippin' head.'

Alistair still didn't answer; his attention; had been drawn to the top of what looked like a leather wallet sticking out of the breast pocket of the woman's sleeveless fleece. He leaned forward, plucked it out and opened it.

'So?' asked James.

'So, you won't believe this; of all things, she's a copper!'

'A copper? ... what d'you mean ... a police woman?'

'A detective inspector.'

'Crikey ... you'd better get help as quick as you can then ... I'll stay with her.'

Alistair nodded, then took off at a pace, leaving James with the injured woman and checking her pulse occasionally.

There'd been no sign of a mobile phone when they'd

gone through the rest of her pockets and golf bag and they weren't carrying one but, as a result of the speed Alastair ran to get help, an ambulance, was soon tearing up the eighth fairway.

The golf professional, trotting along behind it, had his fingers crossed in the hope the turf hadn't being too badly churned up.

They found James, together with two other men, who'd been out on the course trying to squeeze nine holes in before the light went. All three were crouched over the inspector's body arranging their jackets over her to keep out the cold breeze but, once the ambulance got there, they gladly handed over.

Twenty minutes later, and having raced in a straight line across five different fairways to the road, leaving the 'Pro' tearing his hair out, Detective Inspector Lucy Groves was being loaded onto a trolley at The Royal Sussex Hospital, Brighton.

The Marquis of Granby

6.52.pm

The informal 'few drinks' get-together that had been arranged to mark 'Foxy' Reynard's retirement was just getting underway. The Chief Constable *had* asked Detective Chief Superintendent Colin Bradshaw, head of Sussex CID, to set up an all 'bells and whistles' lunch to mark the occasion in the Epicurean Room at The Lord Nelson, but Reynard had said 'No', he'd rather something less ostentatious. Such affairs, he reckoned, always wound up as 'a beano' for high rankers, who the retiree hardly knew, while people he worked with every day were left out 'to keep the numbers down'. He wasn't going to have that. If there was to be anything to mark departure, it was going to have to be a quiet evening with those he regularly slaved away with - they were the people he was going to miss - and they were the ones he'd want at his farewell 'do' ... if he *had* to have one at all.

Bradshaw wasn't surprised, he knew Reynard of old,

knew pomp wasn't up his street, knew his respect for those worked for him far exceeded that which he held for most of his superiors. There were a couple of exceptions ... Scotland Yard's Commander Bill Simpson, National Criminal Investigation Coordinator for instance, and Colin Mustard the Chief Constable of Sussex. Years ago, when Simpson, a Brighton man, had been a raw recruit, fast tracked to detective work, he'd been put into Foxy's squad. It turned to be the first of his steps to high office, but it was also the start of a lifelong friendship. The connection to the C. C. had sprung from their meeting in the course of Foxy's investigation into the murder of one of the C.C.'s neighbours, a tea merchant called Nelson Deep. It had become a bond of some importance, though it never developed into what might be called a friendship. Apart from these two they were still waiting for a couple of other C.I.D. officers to arrive; D.I. Lucy Groves, until recently Foxy's second in command, and currently in the process of building a team of her own; and D.C. William Riggs, 'Riggsy' or 'Lanky', who was on his way back to Brighton after spending the day in the Public Records Office in Horsham.

Reynard had been dreading his retirement party almost as much as he'd been dreading retirement itself. Why he was being jettisoned when he was still not yet at the peak of his investigative powers was beyond him. But 'rules are rules' his Chief Super had told hm and, though he'd scorned taking early retirement after banking twenty years, with thirty-eight on the clock he had no choice, he was obliged to go. A lifetime's experience destined for the scrap heap. He couldn't understand it. As he stood, steeped in his past, he saw the minibus had just pulled up at his gate. He sighed, kissed his wife goodbye and, as he headed for the front door, called out 'Don't wait up for me; I could be quite late'.

'No chance of that.' she whispered to herself, reaching for the gin and tonic he'd just poured for her.

'The Marquis' is an old fashioned pub conveniently situated, from Foxy Reynard's point of view, half way between his quiet cul-de-sac home in Malvern Gardens, and Sussex Police HQ at Sussex House, Brighton. He's been dropping into it on his way home ever since he was transferred to Sussex House from John's Street, all of nineteen years ago. Once retired he might be seeing more of it for, with no hobbies, no interest in DIY or gardening, and seldom seen with anything in his hands more enlightening than a Sunday newspaper, he's still not got any idea as to how he'll fill his time in. It was beginning to look as though he was heading for a 'pipe and slippers' retirement, and he couldn't think of anything worse.

In the run down to the dreaded moment at which his life would end and he'd no longer be a copper, he'd handed over the squad's cases to recently promoted, D.I. 'Dessie' Furness, a long standing member of the team who, in the short term, would be backed up by D.I. Mathews, another long serving detective on the verge of retirement, who'd been drafted in from his back office job to help Furness ease himself into his new responsibilities.

'Handing over' for Reynard was proving difficult. Listening to someone else taking the decisions and issuing the orders was worse. He'd sit at the back of a meeting trying to look interested, trying not to interfere when he saw things being done the way he'd never have done them … and he felt guilty … he knew Furness was trying his best.

Not being in charge during the previous few month, when meetings were taking place and plans were being drawn up, had tested his patience. But he stuck it out for Furness's sake. Soon it would be over …only a few hours to go … not much left bar the party and few 'goodbyes'.

Everyone, including Reynard, had hoped to see Lucy Groves, recently promoted to Detective Inspector, take over. Indeed, he'd been grooming her for the job from the start but, as luck would have it, an opportunity to head a new mobile CID squad, on permanent stand-by to be rushed anywhere in the county, cropped up, and she couldn't resist applying for it. The interviewing board had no hesitation in choosing her; she was the most experienced of all the candidates by far, and, despite the fact she'd walked in Foxy's shadow for many years, her name and achievements were well known.

Reynard had been disappointed, but he knew opportunities, such as heading this new 'flying' squad, rarely came up and, with it being such an obvious route to other future promotion, he swallowed his feelings and advised her to take it.

She'd telephoned him earlier in the afternoon to say she'd be 'a bit late' getting to the party, and that she was looking forward to telling him how she was getting on in her new position. He was pleased she sounded happy, and even more pleased the skills in which he'd so carefully groomed her were now about to bear fruit.

All in all, Reynard reckoned, a 'few beers in The Marquis', with his team and a couple of bosses, was the way to mark the end of his career. Yes …some drinks, plenty of laughs, mostly at his expense, and a few outrageously exaggerated stories of the team's investigations would be more than enough. No speeches, no presentations, and, with a bit of luck, an early night.

It had been in anticipation of such an evening that he'd kissed his wife 'Goodbye' and gone out to the minibus.

Furness was already there, talking to D.I Archie Lawrence, leader of one of the other teams in the division; Sgt Geordie Hawkins, from SOCO, and Dr Emil Vladic the police surgeon were with them. Best and Riggs, who'd just arrived, the two most recent recruits to the team, both D.C.s, were chatting to each other at the bar; and Jack Crowther, another CID squad leader arrived minutes later. He was followed by Detective Chief Superintendent Bradshaw, the head of the division. With him, and in civvies to make everyone feel less intimidated, was Foxy's one-time trainee - Commander Bill Simpson.

Maybe it was going to be a good evening after all, Foxy thought, as he looked around the smiling faces; a night of leg pulling and laughter … and a damned sight better 'do' than any posh bloody dinner at The Lord Nelson.

As he'd entered and walked across the room, those who were there before him stopped talking, and Best and Riggs, already into their second drink, began to clap. It stopped him in his tracks; he hated being the centre of attention other than when he was using his authority.

Bradshaw, sensing the embarrassment of the silence that ensued, reckoned it might be the right the moment to deliver the Chief Constable's apology for not being able to be present, and to pass on to Foxy his best wishes for a happy retirement.

'Gentlemen … *Gentlemen … please,*' *h*e began. 'While you're still all sober, I'd like to take the opportunity offer Foxy the apologies of the Chief Constable, who cannot be here with us personally, to say 'Happy Retirement' to a man who's brought the division nothing but praise. Praise we have all enjoyed as much as we have enjoyed working with him, may I say. He's put this division to the forefront in the field of criminal investigation and we're now well-known where it matters. Ultimately, this is all down to him and the C.C has asked me to particularly emphasise Foxy's singularly …'

Before he got any further Furness, who'd slipped from

the room when his mobile phone began bleeping, rushed back in with his hand held up.

'Sorry Sir,' he said, 'this is important … there's been a serious incident on the golf course at Crackstone Manor and D.I. Groves … *'our'* D.I. Groves … has been seriously hurt.'

The Royal Sussex Hospital

6.15 p.m.

The moment the ambulance drew up it was surrounded by helpers waiting to take the injured policewoman from the paramedics. And, for the next few minutes, there was a flurry of activity which only ended when the victim was safely hooked up to all manner of pipes and drips in the intensive care unit. At the same time, she'd been undergoing a preliminary examination by the resident chief neurosurgeon and his assistant, who'd been hastily assembled while the ambulance, bearing the unconscious policewoman, was still racing through Brighton's streets.

Based on the surgeon's assessment, a decision to make a fuller investigation in one of the operating theatres was agreed and, half an hour later, Detective Inspector Lucy Groves (patient 12759) was being wheeled in to be met by Professor Dickenson, and his waiting surgical team.

144, Peabody High Row

6. 35pm

The tiny two story Edwardian terrace house in a complex of buildings at the back of Brighton Station is the home of the minor, and often flamboyant, criminal, Barney Truscott.

It had originally been constructed by a charitable trust in 1905, with the objective of providing affordable housing to less well-off Brighton citizens and, in this role, it had served the community well for nearly a hundred years until 2002, when it was taken over by the council. They modernised it to its present standard and rented it to the existing tenants, including the Truscott family, consisting of Barney, his wife Doris, and their two sons 'Rocky' and Ronnie.

Rocky, who'd actually been named 'Rockwell' by his mother (so her family name could live on) was a quiet boy who visitors hardly noticed. Ronnie was the exact opposite - a boisterous tearaway visitors couldn't possibly miss.

Three years previously, Rocky, by then 19, had moved to London, reverted to his given name of Rockwell, and begun to work his way through a teaching degree course at Brunel

University. He'd set it all up himself, financing his course costs with a 'Peabody' scholarship he'd won while at the Dorothy Stringer Secondary School in Brighton, and his accommodation and living expenses with the wages he earned as a waiter in an Uxbridge Bistro. His mother was immensely proud of him, but Barney, was even more proud of twenty four year old Ronnie ... gradually working his way into the world of glitzy night clubs and luxury cars ruled by Norris Scorton, a local petty criminal and an idol of Barney's.

Scorton stirred many illegal pots in Brighton without getting caught, because he employed men like Barney to do his dirty work. If Ronnie could wangle himself into Scorton's good books, Barney reckoned, he'd be well on the way.

Progress in this respect had started unexpectedly when 'out of work' Ronnie, in a moment of unlikely gallantry, rescued Scorton's daughter from an intoxicated man who was pestering her one summer's evening on the promenade. Ronnie didn't actually know who she was until an hour later when, having escorted her home, she introduced him to her father. A day later he was working as a barman in Scorton's Flamingo Club and hoping it was the first step on the ladder. Barney couldn't believe it when Ronnie told him ... Doris daren't.

A moderately successful man in his own small way, Barney Truscott is a curiosity to most people ... a man whose day generally starts long after midday, and ends long after midnight. He'll tell you he's a dealer in job lots, a trader in factory rejects and 'seconds'. And he is ... indeed every bit of spare space in his house is packed with what he calls his 'stock', hardly any of which has clean provenance, and none of which has an associated receipt. He is smart though, in every sense of the word, a dapper little man who wears Bengal striped shirts and plain colour matching ties under one of his well-pressed suits. Short and tubby, he struts around like a well trained soldier, despite being barely five and half feet tall; a cocky, barrel-chested bantam, with bags of presence.

Doris is the complete opposite; she's taller than Barney, by six inches, a shy, retiring, humble sort of a soul who treats him like a god, slavishly giving in to his every wish.

Rocky, being away in London, is seldom seen in Brighton, but Ronnie, still notionally living at home, is getting progressively more like his father in appearance, while leaving him trailing far behind as far as ambition and determination are concerned.

Barney has worked on and off for Norris Scorton for years, as the police well know; but he's never managed to capture the gangster's complete trust, never managed to get right into the centre of his empire. Ronnie has, and Barney is extremely jealous.

Foxy Reynard, needless to say, has always known of Barney's connection to Norris Scorton, the one gangster he's never managed to nail, though he has trimmed his feathers from time to time. Ronnie's deeper involvement with Scorton and the rest of his gang has not yet come to his ears though.

If Reynard was to somehow 'nail' Scorton, he thought, it'd be a grand way to wind up his career; a sweetener to alleviate the bitter taste of retirement, a monumental grand finale, that would send him out to grass on a high note.

Ronnie Truscott, in the meantime, hardly aware the minor skirmishes his father and Reynard have had in the past, is confident without being too cocky and, since going to work for Scorton, walking taller. In his spare moments, and he doesn't have many, he works alongside his dad doing 'little favours' for people who'd rather not get their hands dirty. One day, he reckons, he'll be able to go freelance too but, in the meantime, he's happy working his way up the ranks in the Scorton organisation by undertaking occasional jobs over and above his barman's duties in The Flamingo Club.

The extra employment he gets is generally in a 'steal to order' racket called Kontinental Kars owned by Scorton and a shady car salesman called Declan Murphy. D.I. Groves has had her eye on them for months but, so far, has made no progress in determining exactly how their operation works.

Not that Ronnie is troubled by any of this. In fact, he doesn't know the police are sniffing around at all; he's concentrating on shaking Harvey Wallbangers and looking busy, so he'll catch Norris Scorton's eye and get moved up the scale in The Flamingo Club.'

Sussex C.I.D. Headquarters, Brighton

6.40.p.m.

Furness's shock announcement, to the group assembled in the Marquis of Granby celebrating Detective Superintendent Reynard's retirement had at first stunned everyone to silence. But soon everyone was talking at once, with Reynard's voice all but drowning the rest ... 'Shut up everyone ... *please* ... the party's over and, if you'll permit me,' he said to the Commander, 'I'll take over from here. Lucy Groves is not only one of us, she *is* us. I want no stone unturned until we find why she's on her way to hospital in an ambulance, instead of being here as expected. I'm going to the hospital, once I know for sure which one she's in. The rest of you can head back to HQ, clear your desks, and wait there for me. I am *not* retired yet!'

D.C.S. Bradshaw, Reynard's immediate boss, grabbed his arm. 'Take the duty car Foxy, it's outside somewhere, waiting to return the Commander and me back to the station after the 'do'. You can have it; we'll go back in the minibus with the others. I hope you don't find it too bad a scene when you get there. I'll see you later … back at the station, O.K.?'

'Nothing will be O.K. until we have the so and so who's done this locked up.' Mumbled Reynard, thinking ahead.

'I agree … pity about the party though … and I'm sorry you're leaving us, just when we need you.'

Reynard smiled. 'I haven't gone yet.'

'I know, but you will have by tomorrow.'

'Will I? You know what they say about tomorrow, Sir… it never comes.'

Bradshaw grinned and turned to the Commander. 'Can't you do something about his man; he won't listen to me?'

'I doubt he'd take any notice of what I say either;' Simpson replied, winking, 'not once he's got the smell of a case.'

By the time Bradshaw had thought of a suitable response Reynard was half way to the door … he had to know the severity of Groves's injuries. Before he left for the hospital though, he got the address of Lucy's next of kin from a clerk in the records office. It turned out to be that of her sister, Beth, a lady he didn't know and, as he was going to pass her place on his way to the hospital, he decided to call on her to break the news of the incident, and to tell her what he knew of her sister's situation.

Nobody answered the door when he rang the bell, so he ripped a page from his note book and hurriedly pencilled a note, giving his number, and asking her to ring him as soon as possible.

Finding Jessica

She must have been on her way home as he was scribbling, for she got caught him on his mobile a few minutes after he'd arrived at the hospital, where he found Lucy was about to be wheeled out of the operating theatre. He got a brief glimpse of her in the distance, as she was being transferred back to the ICU, but he couldn't see enough of her to make any deductions regarding her condition.

A moment after she'd disappeared from sight, two men, who he assumed were part of the surgical team, emerged from the theatre, talking. He told them who he was, and asked them about her, but they said little in reply other than … 'It's too early'. He wasn't going to be brushed off with that though, and kept pressing them for an answer, calling on them to be more explicit. It made no difference … they refused to elaborate on the brief statement they'd already given him.

Before leaving the hospital, he bought himself a coffee, found himself a quiet seat in the waiting area, and sat down to put what the doctor had told him in his note book so he could tell the Super and the rest of the team when he got back to the station. It wasn't much.

He'd just re-read the notes he'd made and decided to head for home when his mobile began to ring in his pocket.

'Now what?' he thought,

It was a woman.

'Hello,' she said, 'are you Superintendent Reynard?'

He replied with a cautious, 'Yes'.

'Sorry to trouble you, but I'm worried'

'Who did you say you are?'

'I'm Lucy's sister, Beth,' the woman said, 'and I've just got back and found your note. Can you spare a minute to tell me what's going on? I've telephoned Lucy countless times since six, but she doesn't answer. I was supposed to pick her up from her place to drive her to some sort of party on my way home.'

'Huh, that'd be my retirement 'do', but listen Beth … Lucy's been in an accident and she's in the Royal Sussex; I've just come from there myself. Like you, I wanted to know what was going on this afternoon that has left Lucy the way she is.'

'Is she alright?' What happened?'

'As to what happened … I still don't know. As to how she is … well they're determining that now. It seems she was hurt on the golf course at the Crackstone Manor Hotel and taken to the hospital with a head injury. I've no idea how it happened. All I know is that she's a nasty cut and she's unconscious. There's no point in you rushing there; they've already told me they won't know much until the morning. She's in good hands, the best, I've checked that. We'll just have to wait and see how she is tomorrow.'

Apartment 208, Princess Court,

East Shore Road, Hove.

7.20 p.m.

Back in her home after a day visiting friends in Shoreham, and following the telephone call she'd had with D.S Reynard a few minutes earlier, Beth was trying to come to terms with the shock she'd received, and wondering whether she should call her other sister Connie, on holiday in Portugal and due to return the following morning. In the end she decided to say nothing until they were face to face; after all there was little Connie or anyone else could do, except wait to see how the medical situation developed.

As Beth pondered on Connie's return, the doctors, back in the hospital, were discussing their findings regarding their patient, and hoping the action they'd taken would start to put things right. The preliminary assessment they were preparing would have to emphasise the severity of the wound; point out the hairline fracture they'd discovered in the victim's skull and report the severe bruising to her brain that had shown up in a precautionary scan. All of which would have been bad enough if, in addition, it hadn't been accompanied by the partial excising of her right ear.

The opinion of the principal neurosurgeon, Professor Dickenson, was that there was a high probability the patient would recover completely, though her long term prospects relative to those of a normal person were not clear. The report would also have to note that, thanks to the rapid response of the Forrester brothers, the patient's outcome was likely to be generally positive with her final position depending on the extent of the damage within her skull. A fuller investigation of this would have to wait until the bleeding had stopped and the swelling had become much reduced.

As to re-attaching the de-gloved skin above her right ear and dealing with the two bare patches caused by the weapon when it scraped down the side of her head, Dickenson said they would look at them later. Finding a way to permanently fix the position of her ear, that was cosmetically acceptable, was reckoned to be a minor issue; one that could be attended to at some time in the future. Praying he'd done enough to save his patient, Dickenson came back to earth when the anaesthetist, said. 'That was a tricky old job, wasn't it?'

'Indeed it was Brian; it was enough to make me wish I'd chosen dentistry!'

Reynard's office

8.15. pm

Except for the chief super; who was in the canteen with Commander Simpson, they were all in Reynard's office, waiting for him to arrive from the hospital. Each was hoping to hear Groves was alright, that she wasn't seriously hurt and was recovering, and that they might soon see her back with them ... but it didn't take long for Reynard to disillusion them.

'So how is she really, Guv?' asked Riggs.

Reynard, mouth shut and teeth clamped together, rocked his head from side to side delivering a message nobody could possibly have misinterpreted; a message he was too upset to put into words ... and everybody's face fell.

'She *is* alive though isn't she?' asked Best, 'I can't get my head round it; Lucy attacked on a bloody golf course in broad daylight. What the hell was she doing there anyway?'

Riggs stuck up a finger to attract Reynard's attention, which brought frowns from the others, but didn't quieten him. 'I know the answer to that one, Guv,' he said, 'she's getting ready for her new job ... good as told me last week ... advised me to do the same actually, though I thought she was joking at the time. 'I'm taking up golf' she said, 'All senior officers play golf. That's how they get on.'

'Really … that *is* interesting,' said Reynard, unable to resist making his response sarcastic. 'And are you considering taking a similar fast route to the top yourself. Get real young man … hard work and dedication to the task in hand is the only way to get ahead in this job.'

'Oh, I know that Guv; of course I do.' Riggs replied, 'it just seems an odd coincidence that the Sarge and I should be talking about golf and the next thing is she's found lying, unconscious, on a golf course.'

Reynard, still staring accusingly at Riggs, was about to tell him he was wasting time when, to everyone's surprise, he changed direction. 'Alright then, yes,' he said, 'I suppose you might have point. Did she say anything in particular that might … ?'

'Lead us to what happened? No. We were just chatting about the clubs she'd bought. I'm battling with a ton weight bag full of old pre-war ones my uncle gave me, while she's very sensibly just got herself a few really good new ones - a driver, a couple of irons, and a putter. I wish I'd done the same.'

'My Dad always told me …' Best began …

But Reynard halted him immediately; rapping on the table and telling him that, interesting as this conversation about golf clubs is, he should stick to the point and not waste their time going down side alleys that led nowhere. And,' he continued, 'we can begin with what's been learned during this evening's interviews. There may be indicators in some of the conversations you've had, that could point us in the right direction. D.S. Furness you'd better start …. but, before you do, let me remind you of one thing. We're making enquiries about what appears to be an unprovoked attack on a victim who, as far as we know, will recover. We mustn't let our outrage at what has happened to 'one of ours' dilute the effort we're currently employing on other cases. Had D.I. Groves lost her life it would be different matter; death will always elevate an enquiry to a higher level. But she didn't lose her life, so let's not give anyone the opportunity to accuse us of favouring one enquiry over another. Right?'

'Ah we know that, Guv,' said Furness. 'Shall I start?'

Reynard nodded. 'Yes, let's get on with it and, once we've completed the conversations with those who were on or near the scene at the time of the attack, two of you will have to return to what you were on before this all happened. Is that understood?'

Nobody answered, but it was clear from the earnest expressions on their faces, that they all appreciated what he was saying, and he smiled. If anyone could get to the bottom of this unexplained attack on Groves, this team surely could.

So bound up in his thoughts was he, that he nearly missed Furness's opening remarks. 'OK, here we go then. D.I. Mathews and I have been out to Crackstone Manor and spoken to the people who were either in the hotel or the restaurant, and D.C. Best and D.C. Riggs, although it was nearly dark, went out on the course checking the area around where the incident had taken place, which was being protected by uniformed officers from John's Street nick. With nothing obvious to see, they returned to the hotel and clubhouse to join me taking statements from those who were being held in the ancillary buildings. 'None of the people I spoke to saw anything that could be tied to the incident.'

'Same with you and me, wasn't it Riggsy? Said Best.

Riggs nodded 'Yeah, I drew a total blank. Mind you, there'd only have been a few out on the course at the time of the attack, according to the Pro.'

'What d'you mean by 'a few'?' asked Mathews.

'Half a dozen. He showed me the bookings: three twosomes and a single, the latter being ...' L. Groves' ... Lucy obviously ... I saw her signature. The other players were all members and, the Pro told me, they played there regularly. The last of the twosomes came off the course while D.C. Best and I were there, and we interviewed them first. They'd seen nothing unusual. The other pair were the ones who'd stopped to help the two brothers when they were tending to Lucy while she was on the ground at the fourteenth. They'd returned to the clubhouse with the brothers once the ambulance had left. All they could think about,' one of them told me, 'was the sight of Lucy's blood dribbling down her neck and trickling down the steps. Other than that, they said they'd seen two women and a little boy walking an Alsatian, and a man with a stick, who was probably doing the same, though they didn't spot his dog.'

'Other than that!' Exclaimed Furness. 'What were they expecting, for God's sake?'

'Gentlemen, gentlemen … that's enough. I think we might pack it in for tonight; we could have a long day in front of us tomorrow. I want to see you're here at seven thirty a.m. sharp. I'm off to brief the super and the Commander now, if they're still in the building. See you tomorrow.'

They *were* both there, the Super and the Commander, when Reynard walked in, and they started cross-examining him and hurling questions before he'd even *got* to the seat to which Bradshaw was pointing. Eventually he had to hold up his hand to stop them in order to give them a verbal interim report.

'I'm sure you know D.I. Groves is a very popular woman in this division,' he said, 'and it'd be easy for us to drop everything else so we can concentrate on finding her attacker. However, we will *not* be doing that. As of tomorrow, half my men will return to the other enquiries upon which we are presently working, and the remaining men, two of them, will be aimed solely at bringing D.I. Groves's attacker to justice. This evening though, in the hope of securing pertinent information that might disappear if it's left too long, I've had the whole squad interviewing all the people who were in the vicinity of the incident at the time it took place: that is to say … the hotel, the clubhouse and course, and so on.'

Sitting back in his chair with his arms folded, the Commander asked what part in the investigation Reynard was intending to play, bearing in mind he'd be retired in 'something under four hours' time.'

'Ah … Blast it … I knew there was a catch somewhere." Reynard replied, grinning like an errant schoolboy. 'Fancy me missing a little thing like that; I'd better look at this from a different angle then … suppose I don't retire?'

The commander burst out laughing. 'Suppose pigs can fly!' And then, almost as an afterthought, and with more than a hint of mischief in his answer, he said 'Maybe, just maybe … in *very* special circumstances … pigs can be *made* to fly?'

Bradshaw was nodding as the commander spoke. 'Of course they can, Sir … I'll get onto it first thing in the morning.'

'There you are Foxy, leave it with D.C.S. Bradshaw,' said the commander; 'he'll sort something out … 'You get on and catch your villain.'

Reynard left them immediately afterwards, confident that, one way or another, he'd have a free hand to solve what would surely be his last case. As he was crossing from the bottom of the stairs to the front door, the desk sergeant called him. 'I've a man on the phone, who wants to talk to someone about the attack up at Crackstone Manor Hotel. He says he saw something that might be of interest to whoever's running the investigation. That's you, isn't it, Sir, … will you take the call or shall I tell him to ring later.'

Reynard looked at his watch, let out a long sigh of resignation and said. 'No … put him through to Interview Room One. I'll talk to him in there.

'Will do.' Said the sergeant.

Grabbing a chair with one hand, and picking up the phone with the other, Reynard swung into action as soon as he was in the room. 'Detective Superintendent Reynard speaking,' he said, 'I believe you've some information for us."

'Are you in charge of the inquiry into the…'

'The attack on the golf course? Yes, I am. Did you see something? The sergeant told me you were very near the hotel at the time? What's your name …we'd better have it first.'

'Fair enough … I'm Ernest Dussek, Ernie if you like, Ernie Dussek … and I live in Corville Avenue. Yes, I *was* near the hotel at the time. I was in my car actually, on my way home from work. I'd just passed the entrance to the hotel when my phone went. I didn't answer it immediately of course; I won't talk while I drive. No, I pulled into that long lay-by on the opposite side of the road to the hotel and about a quarter of a mile beyond it.

'I know where you mean,' said Reynard, 'it's heavily wooded on both sides of the road there, isn't it?'

'Oh yes,' Dussek replied, lots of trees, they're silver birches, I think, but, here and there, on the hotel side, you can still see bits of the golf course through them. Anyway, when the phone went, I was just coming up to the lay-by and, as soon as I got to it, I pulled in and took the call. It was my wife asking me to pick up some milk on the way home. Not that that matters.'

'Which is when you saw ... what?'

'A man throwing something into the trees.'

'Into the trees ...are you sure?'

'Yes, and there was only one car in the lay-by when I started pulling over towards it. The man was standing beside it. He had his back to me, and he was throwing something into the woods. I don't think he spotted me until I pulled up a few car lengths behind him. He scattered then alright. Into the car, and off he shot. If there'd been anything going along the inside lane, he'd have hit it.'

Reynard could hardly contain himself; it looked like this man had seen something of real significance, and he wanted more. 'Sir,' he said, 'I'd be grateful if you'd come here to see me in the morning ... before nine if that's possible. I'd like a couple of my colleagues to hear what you have to say. In the meantime, perhaps you wouldn't mind answering a few other questions. For instance, did you see what the man threw?'

'No, I didn't, unfortunately; the sun was going down right behind him and I was too dazzled to make out anything in detail. I just picked up the action of his arm as he hurled whatever it was into the trees. One thing though; I saw it flash, so it might have been something metallic.'

'That's helpful. Anything else?'

'Not really … it was the sun, you see; it was so bright all I could make out were silhouettes.'

'What about the man … can you describe him?'

'He looked tall … and pretty well built … I think.'

'And the car?'

'I couldn't make it out in any detail either. It was a big estate, dark in colour. And, before you ask me, I didn't see the registration number.'

'Anything else, Sir?'

'Not really … do you think I saw him … the man who attacked that policewoman?'

'It's a possibility. Thank you for calling us. Incidentally, how did you hear about the incident … and when?'

'About it half an hour ago on the local radio. I connected what the reporter was saying to what I'd seen, straight off.'

'Well, thank you again, Mr Dussek. 'you've been most helpful. I wish everyone was alert as you, and I look forward to our talk in the morning.'

Reynard sat so long thinking over the flood of events that had taken place over the space of three few hours, the desk sergeant was prompted to knock on the Interview Room door and ask him if he was alright. He said he was, but he wasn't; his world had turned upside down and, for the first time in his life, he felt helpless. His wife was aware of the retrospective mood he was in what he got home and, sensibly, said little. She just went to the sideboard, poured him half a tumbler of '10 year old'. With each sip, as he savoured it, he began to feel himself again; soon his brain was whirling with thoughts and, as the fiery liquor diffused through him, he began thinking of what might lie ahead, rather than of what was behind. Foxy was still Foxy after all … to hell with retirement!

DAY TWO

Criminal Investigation Dept. HQ

9.00 am.

The daily catch-up meeting in Detective Superintendent Reynard's office was about to start. He was at his desk ... his notes in front of him. Facing him, were the rest of the team; Detective Inspector Rory Mathews, only recently seconded to the squad, Detective Inspector Dessie Furness, a long time member of it, and Detective Constables Norman Best and William Riggs, the latter of whom, was pouring the freshly brewed Costa Rican coffee that was always evident at these meetings.

Mr Dussek had turned up at eight thirty and Reynard, accompanied by Furness, had interviewed him. The meeting hadn't lasted much more than fifteen minutes and, though Dussek had no more to add to what he'd told Reynard the previous night, it was enough to point to the conclusion he'd almost certainly seen the man who'd attacked Groves at the moment he was trying to dispose of the weapon he'd used.

Before this valuable new information could be put before the rest of the team assembled in Reynard's office though, Sergeant Hatton from the front desk could be seen approaching through the glass panel in Reynard's door, He had a determined look on his face and Reynard didn't hesitate; he beckoned him straight in.

'I've lady downstairs wants to talk to you, Foxy. She says she's Lucy's sister.'

'Ah ... Good' Reynard answered. 'I was going to try speaking to the sisters this morning; but I didn't get round to setting a time. I don't know much about them, but I guess the one that's downstairs'll be Connie; she was to fly in from Portugal early this morning. I spoke to the other one, Beth, when she rang last night.

'Do they share a house or what?' asked Riggs.

'No, they each have their own place.'

'And what about their parents? Did you manage to contact them?'

Reynard shook his head.

'We'll have to find out where they live, they must be told'

'It'll be difficult; they died a while back.' said Reynard, 'No, the only people we need consider are the two sisters and, thank God, I've spoken to one and the other's downstairs.'

'What'll I tell her?' asked the Sergeant.

'Tell her I'll be down in a minute. Put her in Interview

Room One and ask her if she'd like a cup of tea.

'I've done that already,' Hatton replied, 'and she didn't. I'll say you'll be with her shortly then, shall I?'

'Yes.' Reynard answered, smiling at Hatton as he left, and then getting up from his chair and turning to check the rest of the squad was listening. 'Right. Listen everyone. I'm going to slip down and have chat with this lady ... see what she has to say and so on. I was going to have to talk to the sisters this morning as I said, but, with one calling in last evening, and now this one downstairs, I'm going to save a lot of time. You can clear your desks while I'm interviewing her and, when I get back, we'll revue the position and work out how we're going to catch our villain. Oh yes, and in this connection, I've already been interviewing a man who rang here last night to say he'd seen someone throwing something into the woods running either side of the road skirting the golf course. I'll tell you about it after I've seen the lady downstairs.'

'You didn't say how Lucy was when you saw her, Guv.'

'You're right, and that's because I didn't see her, and I didn't get much in the way of information either, other than that she was comfortable and they'll know more this morning.'

'Just one minor point before you leave then, Guv,' said Furness almost apologetically ... are you retired or not?'

'Not.' Said Reynard, with a look so fierce nobody was inclined to challenge him. 'Not *yet* anyway.'

Heading for the ground floor interview room a few

minutes later, he began to wonder what Lucy's sister was going to be like. He'd never met either of them before, and he was curious to see if the one he was about to see looked anything like Lucy.

As he entered the waiting room, the woman stood up, her hand bag clutched to her chest as if was expecting Reynard was about to snatch it. She bore little obvious resemblance to Lucy.

'No, no … please sit down' he said, waving her back to the chair from which she'd just risen, and taking another, on the opposite side of the table, for himself.

Clearly, she'd she recognised him but, before she got a chance to say much more than her name, Reynard launched into the words he'd been assembling in his mind on his way down to meet her. 'Can I say 'er … from the start … 'er …'

'Connie,' she said, 'I'm Connie.'

'Oh, right, how d'you do? Beth told me you were coming back today, and that you'd be calling here to introduce yourself, but I didn't expect to see you as early as this.'

'It was on a 'Dawn Flight'. I landed at Gatwick three hours ago and went straight to the hospital.'

'And found she was still unconscious. I know. I rang an hour ago myself.'

'They're talking about inducing a coma if she starts to recover naturally. 'A better chance for her brain to repair itself, they told me'; I hope they're right,'.

'And have they done it ... put her under?'

'Not yet. A decision will be taken later this morning.'

With that response Reynard seemed to relax a little from the state of high tension that had been gripping him since he'd awakened. 'Yes ... well .... Connie,' he said, 'we're all devasted here by what's happened, and we'd like you and Beth to know how highly we regard Lucy. She's not only our colleague, she's our friend, and we want her back.'

'So do we. We're an odd family, Beth and Lucy and me ... compared to most that is. Our parents have gone and our children have yet to arrive but, despite all sorts of adversities the three of us have stuck together. Have you found who did it, who hit her?'

Reynard shook his head. 'No, but let me assure you we're determined to catch whoever's responsible. Unfortunately, as of now, we don't have any idea of what prompted the viciousness.

Connie smiled. 'All the same ... thank God ... we have you on the case. If anyone can succeed you will. You're Foxy Reynard aren't you and Lucy is always telling everyone you catch more crooks than the Mounties. We may never have met before Superintendent but, just speaking to you, has given me a great sense of confidence that the case will be solved and we'll get Lucy back, with us, where she belongs. Actually, I'm here for a purpose over and above finding out *how* she is, I'm here to tell you something you probably don't know; I'm going to tell you *who* she is in the hope it will direct you to her attacker.'

Reynard looked at her blankly. 'What d'you mean … '*who* she is … she's Lucy Groves?'

Connie smiled again. 'Ah, Superintendent, but is she?'

Reynard's blank look began to turn into a puzzled one.

'No.' said Connie, 'I'm here to give you a few bits of somewhat unusual personal information regarding her. Stuff of which you're probably unaware, but might find useful. A bunch of unlikely historical facts relating to her that, under normal circumstances, wouldn't see the light of day. Things she may never have disclosed, even to you. Things associated with a period of her life she's been doing her best to forget.

Reynard, even more puzzled, couldn't stop himself blurting out 'Gracious to me, you surprise me. So, Lucy has secrets. Ah well. I suppose we all do. I for one …'

'What I'm about to tell you,' said Connie, ignoring his interjection, 'are things she's always kept buried, and I'd be obliged if you keep *whatever* I say to you … to yourself.'

Reynard nodded, but slowly, as he mulled over what his visitor seemed to be implying. What could Lucy possibly have been up to that he'd no knowledge of?' What was there about her he didn't already know?' Was it even *possible* that a member of his team, his most trusted member, had dark secrets about which he knew nothing?

'Superintendent … *superintendent*.' Connie whispered, leaning forward and touching Reynard's wrist to get his attention when she saw the ever-increasing look of disbelief that was building on his face.

'Er ... sorry,' he said, as he tried to think of what might have prompted Lucy to keep things from him. She knew damned well he liked everything out in the open.

Connie saw he was drifting off into his thoughts again, and tapped on the table.

He came back to earth immediately and grinned. 'Sorry' he said, 'sorry ... go on.'

'It's alright Superintendent, you needn't worry ... she's not been *up* to anything ... it's just that I know there are parts of her life she likes to keeps private ... parts of it not known outside our immediate family.'

'I see, and d'you think they may be linked to the attack that was made on her?'

'Maybe. I'm not sure.' Connie replied. 'It'll be up to you and your colleagues to work that out. All I can say is that it's family stuff. I just want to make sure you know as much as possible about Lucy, when she was younger, it might be important.'

Reynard was lightly keyboarding the table with his fingertips as she spoke, and it seemed to be signalling his relief. 'I can't imagine her being involved in anything unsavoury,' he said, 'or that she'd allowed herself to get involved in anything of which she was ashamed. I know we all have things we'd rather keep private. Maybe it's just that. So, what is it you want to tell me … we're all on Lucy's side, y'know.'

Connie paused; it was though she was struggling to take in some profound thought. And then she drew in drew a big breath and leaned forward. 'I know you are,' she said, 'and it really is all family stuff. I'll keep it as simple as I can … but you'll soon see that it's far from that.'

Reynard nodded encouragingly and sat back, arms folded, ready to hear what she was about to reveal.

'Well, for a start,' she said, 'we're *not* sisters.'

'You're *not* sisters? I don't understand.'

'It's simple.' Said Connie, 'Lucy, and Beth, and I, all have the same mother … but we've each got a different father.

'Ah … I get it.' Said Reynard … 'Now I'm with you.'

'Yes, you see, Mum got married three times … the first time was to Lucy's Dad, Bruce Wilding. He was killed in a road accident when Lucy was eight. The second time she got married, was to a friend of Bruce's called Charlie Roberts. They had a daughter and …

'That'd be your sister, Beth … right?' interrupted Reynard, looking pleased with himself.'

'Nearly right,' Connie replied; Beth's my *half*-sister, as is Lucy. Anyway, Charlie, died … heart attack. He was only forty.'

'And then …?'

'And then … some years later again, she met and married Kevin Maxwell, my Dad. I was born a year after they met. At that stage, the family consisted of Mum and Dad, my half-sister Lucy, who was about sixteen I think, my half-sister Beth, who was eleven, and me; a new born baby.'

'Give me a moment, Connie, if you would;' Reynard said taking out his note book. 'I'd better get some of this down ... 'it's a lot to take in.'

Connie laughed. 'And a lot to keep secret!

'You're right there; it's certainly that ...'

'And who's to say she's wrong trying to keep that time in her life under wraps?' said Connie, 'I don't. By closing off her back-ground she's been able to keep clear of the long explanations with which I get bombarded. I envy her the position she's worked her way into by not telling anybody anything she didn't need to.'

'Like not telling me, for instance.' Said Reynard slowly swinging his head from side to side. Why on earth had she been hiding her background? Had she not trusted him?

Connie felt inclined to reach across table to lay her hand on his, but she didn't. She could see how put out he was though, and maybe how angry that the trust he'd had for her sister had not, been reciprocated. But she didn't move, instead she tried to alleviate his disappointment, to reassure him, by telling him she knew Lucy felt guilty about not being totally open with him ... hoping it would lift him.

Eventually it seemed to have done so and, after a short silent pause during which each was finalising their thoughts, he promised to find Lucy's attacker. 'She's the best detective I've got … and one of my best friends. I'll stop at nothing to catch whoever … you know … did it.'

Connie nodded understandingly while Reynard, a tad deflated after the intensity of their conversation, thought Connie was looking smaller. And then, just as he rose for his chair to signal the end of the interview, she whispered … 'Just find out who did it … *please* find out who did it.'

'We'll do our damnedest.' said Reynard; 'You can rely on it. We'll be going flat out until we have someone behind bars and, in the meantime, I'll be taking all these points you've mentioned into consideration. Yes … We'll need everything we can get, to track down this monster, so, thank you very much for coming in. You can ring me at any time.'

As spoke, he'd been edging his way towards the door. But Connie … who seemed not to have recognised his signal, remained sitting. 'Was there something else?' Reynard, asked reaching for the door handle.

She raised her eyebrows, noisily sucked in a deep breath through her teeth, and leaned forward, her elbows on table. And then, almost mischievously, said 'I don't think you've got the point yet, Superintendent. And you've certainly not got all the information. It's the names you see.'

'Names?' asked Reynard, returning to the seat he'd just left. 'What names?'

'*Her* names … Lucy's'.

'Ah yes; of course,' he said, slapping the table top with

the flat of his hand. 'She's called Groves isn't she, but her late father was called … what did you say his name was?'

'Wilding … Bruce Wilding?'

'Wilding, yes … Now … wait a minute … I can see what you're driving at.' said Reynard, sitting back and running his hands through his hair. 'Yes … of course … her name at birth would have been Lucy Wilding wouldn't it… *not* Lucy Groves? Yes … good point … so when we trawl through her life looking for reasons as to why she was attacked, we need to think of her as Lucy *Wilding* … *as well* as Lucy *Groves* … No, wait a minute, that can't be right. None of the men your mother married or lived with was *called* Groves … So where did she get that name from? Oooh …. yes, now I've got it … at some time before I met her, she must have been married. I wonder why she didn't tell me, why she didn't want me to know. Cheeky blighter. I can't get over it.'

Connie raised her hand to stop him. 'Lucy has never been married … not to anyone.'

'So?' asked Reynard.

'So, I told you it was complicated, didn't I? But we're nearly there. It was all down to my mother you see, she insisted that, in order to keep awkward questions at bay every time she married or moved in with a new man, she took his name, and changed her children's names to match it. When Mum was married to Bruce Wilding, for instance, Lucy was a Wilding. When Mum was with Charlie Roberts, she was a Roberts, and when …'

'Yeah, yeah, yeah, she changed her surname to Maxwell after your Mum and Dad married. All this would all have been done by Deed Poll, I presume.'

Connie shook her head, 'No, it wasn't done officially.'

'Fair enough.' Said Reynard, back to smiling again. 'So where does this leave us. Let's see if I can work it out again … the person we currently know as Lucy Groves; the woman lying unconscious in the Royal Sussex Hospital, my 'right hand man' as it were, has, at various times in her life, been known as Wilding, Roberts, Maxwell and Groves … no that's wrong … it still doesn't show us from where she got the name Groves if she was never married? Surely, she didn't just invent it. Good God, this is some tangle; I'm going to have to speak to as many of these people as I can. And, I think I'd better start with *your* parents, *your* mother and father perhaps.'

'That's not possible, I'm afraid, Superintendent … they're both dead. Dad had a stroke that killed him two years ago. And Mum … well her life was a mess at every turn, and she simply gave up.'

'What d'you mean … gave up?'

'Committed suicide; her life had been never been much more than a procession of disasters and she'd had enough; it's hard to blame her.'

'And Lucy?'

'Lucy decided to give herself a brand new start after

Mum and Dad died, and she set out to cut herself off from all the misery and death that had surrounded her since birth. When she was twenty one, a couple of years before she joined the police, she changed her name again, and yes, she did it by Deed Poll this time. The name she chose was Lucy Groves. And that's it … that's what I came to tell you.'

Reynard leaned back in his chair, his hands on his head and his fingers crossed. 'I can't see how this will impinge on our findings so far Connie, so I'm going to sit down on my own, somewhere quiet, while I try to get all this new information into my head. Now, are you sure you've told me everything? Shocks like this upset my thinking.'

Connie pursed her lips; she *had* omitted one other thing, a tiny but important bit of information she'd forgotten to include in the fusillade of revelations she'd just fired.

'There something else, isn't there? He asked, when he saw the hesitancy in her face. 'What is it? Surely it can't be worse than anything you've already told me.'

'Let's hope it's not then.' Said Connie. 'When Lucy changed her name from Maxwell to Groves after Mum died, she changed her first name too. Prior to that, as I told you, Mum had made us seem like a regular family by making sure we were all known by the same surname.'

'Yes, said Reynard, 'you told me that. She'd been Lucy Wilding, Lucy Roberts, and Lucy Maxwell; before changing her name to Lucy Groves, which she eventually did by deed Poll.'

'Correct, only that still isn't everything Superintendent, I forgot to say the name she was given when she was born wasn't Lucy, it was Mavis ... she started off as Mavis Wilding; I've seen her birth certificate. And she kept the name Mavis until she changed it to Lucy at the same time, she changed Maxwell to Groves. Lucy Groves is an entirely made up name. I'm sorry I misled you; it wasn't intentional.'

Reynard, his head spinning, was hard put to respond but, eventually, he recovered enough to disclose his thoughts. 'Connie,' he said, 'I'm flabbergasted.' Such a string of disasters for that poor girl to contend with, it's no surprise she ran away from them in the end. But thanks anyway for ... well ... telling me all these things. None of them'll weaken our resolve of course; I'll not let them do that. No, I reckon they'll goad us all the more in a way; give us extra impetus. We're going to find out who attacked Lucy, and we're going to bring them to justice. I'm going to get this villain if it's the last thing I do.'

Tears weren't far off when Connie left a few minutes later, leaving Reynard with a look of grim determination on his face and thinking the case might turn out to be the trickiest he'd ever undertaken ... as well as being his last.

After Connie had gone, he retreated back upstairs to join the team. Everyone went quiet as soon as he entered the room, and remained so while they concentrated on the wealth of detail regarding Lucy as he read it out. It took all of twenty minutes for him to work his way through the information contained in the notes he'd made, mostly because of the procession of questions to which they gave rise. Every man there, except Best, perhaps, was trying to understand how he knew so little of the life of a fellow officer and friend. She was a mystery alright, a difficult person to fathom. And, as to her family, of which they all quickly realised they knew little or nothing, it presented the greatest challenge. Before they got down to making plans for the day though, there was the matter of the new witness to deal with. Ernie Dussek had given Reynard and Furness a hopeful lead to what might be a critical piece of evidence, and it had to be followed up.

The slightly dazed look on the faces of the team, as they tussled with the details of Groves's life they'd just heard, had to be got rid of quickly. 'What better way,' Reynard thought, 'than to dish out the new and possibly relevant information he'd got from Ernie Dussek a while earlier?

He rapped on the table and Riggs, who was on his feet and on his way to attack the Cona coffee jug, sat down again.

'There's just one last thing,' said Reynard, 'Before we get down to allocating everyone's task for today, there's something *new* I want to tell you about. Something D.I. Furness and I got from a man called Ernie Dussek earlier this morning. It seems he might, and I emphasise *might*, have inadvertently witnessed a man ridding himself of what *could* be a weapon.'

Riggs jumped to his feet and punched the air.

'Yes, Constable' Reynard said, benignly waving him back to his seat instead of reprimanding him. 'We all feel a little bit like that, but for now let's go cautiously. We have no idea who the thrower is, nor do we know what he threw. I want you, Constables Best and Riggs, to go to the lay-by where the thrower was spotted, and have a good look around to see if you can find what he threw. D.I. Furness will give you the details. As soon as you have something, or at lunchtime at the latest, ring me. I want to know if this angle is worth pursuing.

Best half held his hand up 'Er Guv … will you join at the scene us if we find something?'

'Yes, I will, and make sure you don't touch anything you come across that could be used as a weapon. And have a look around the lay-by first, he may have dropped something.'

'We could help them.' Said Mathews. But Reynard shook his head. 'Later, maybe, as the situation develops, I don't want to give the impression we give special treatment to incidents involving our colleagues. No, you and D.I. Furness had better stick to our other jobs for the moment. We can't afford to give the impression we favour our own, especially when looking into cases in which one of us is the victim.'

'Fine,' said Mathews …'just thought I'd ask.'

Reynard nodded. 'O.K., everyone seems clear as to what they have to do, so where are we? We've dismantled Lucy's life and put it through a mincer. We've delved into her past and her privacy to a degree that's almost indecent. Now we have to justify our intrusion. Physical harm is bad enough but the mental problems, that are also on Lucy's horizon, are a much more serious matter. We're walking on glass here gentlemen, so let's tread carefully, let's not make things worse by blabbing out any of Lucy's secrets. Don't let me down. Don't let Lucy down … keep your mouths shut.'

As he finished, Reynard looked up from his notes. Every man there had his mouth closed, his teeth clamped tightly together, and a look of grim determination on his face. It brought a lump into Reynard's throat; even tough men like him have a soft spot, and leaving a bunch of men like those in front of him was going to be hard to swallow. All he said as they left though, was 'Think about what's been said, and be here at eight tomorrow morning. Understood?'.

'Understood', they answered, filing out and leaving Reynard on his own for the first time that day.

After they'd gone, he sat back and looked around. How was he going to cope when this was all over, when his lifetime of service was going to be shoved into a filing cabinet and forgotten? He'd spent the best part of forty years in the service, now it was about to end; in a few days' time he'd be plain William Reynard again. Even saying it to himself it sounded strange. Once Lucy's attacker's been caught, charged, and sent for trial … it would be the end, the end of everything. No more early morning starts and late-night finishes. No more delving into other people's secrets … no more anything. 'Silly old bugger,' he said to himself. 'the world's not going to stop going round just because I'm not there.'

Behind him, the water for his coffee percolator was going full blast … someone must have topped it up. He took a mug and the last pack of chocolate bottomed Hobnob biscuits from his desk drawer and, still ruminating, sat back again. 'This'll surely be the end of the line. Once I have the bastard who went for Lucy, I'm as good as gone, and it really will be 'Farewell Foxy'. … ah well, all in all it wasn't bad.'

D.I. Jack Crowther who'd served in Brighton as long as Reynard, and who was walking past on his way to his office, stopped at the open door. 'Putting your feet up already?'

Reynard hardly moved a muscle, he just winked.

In a lay-by on the A23 near Crackstone Manor

10.30. am

Best unfolded the A4 sheet of paper on which Reynard had sketched the map showing the location of the lay-by and the positions of the two cars parked in it; the man's and Dussek's.

'O.K. fingers crossed,' he said.

Riggs, being Riggs, had come prepared with a small aerosol can of water-washable white paint and, using the approximate positions Best pointed out on the map, he marked out where the cars had been the day before.

Best remained sitting in his car. He could easily see Riggs, crouched with the spray can in his hand, at the spot where the back of the man's car must have been.

'What d'you think?' shouted Riggs, as he stood up.

'I think Ernie Dussek's right;' Best answered, 'I can see you in detail now because it's cloudy. If it were sunny, I'd hardly be able to make you out. Try a few throwing gestures, pretend you're pitching something into the trees. And then try to envisage where it might have landed. If you start looking, I'll climb over and work my way through to join you. Maybe we'll get lucky.'

'Maybe won't be good enough for Foxy,' said Riggs 'we'll have to do better than that.'

'Let's get stuck in then,' replied Best, 'you get over the wall where you are, and I'll get over here. We can work our way towards each other, checking as we go.'

As Riggs dropped to the ground on the other side of the wall, he found himself knee deep in screwed up sweet wrappers, empty boxes, and bottles made of glass and plastic lying scattered amongst an amazing selection of household rubbish. He even found an old Singer sewing machine. It was just like the one he remembered his grannie using and it was lying half buried under an old and torn mattress.

Best found much the same when he hit the ground after scaling the wall. In fact, they were hard put to find anything but discards of one sort or another until Riggs, who'd been beating the long grass growing under the farther back trees, looked up. What he saw, made him shout to Best to come and see too.

It was a golf club; a putter of some sort with a weird shaped head, and it was caught in the branches of a Silver Birch tree about ten feet up from the ground. The temptation to jump up and try to grab it was almost overwhelming, but Best quietened his colleague down, reminding him of Reynard's insistence that anything suspicious they found, was not be touched by their hands.

In the event, all Riggs, at six foot nine in his socks, had to do, was shake the branch and let gravity do the rest. Best stooped and using his handkerchief, to avoid smudging possible finger prints, picked it up and the two of them scrambled over the wall and raced back to their car. As they jumped in, and were about to race back to HQ with their trophy, Riggs had sudden thought. 'I wonder if we're rushing this ... supposing the man also threw something else. Hang on mate, I'm going back to have another poke around ... make sure we haven't missed anything.'

Best laughed out loud. 'Don't be daft, Riggsy, but, if you really are in doubt, *you* go back and have another look; I'm staying where I am.'

Riggs *did* go, but he discovered nothing of further interest to them, just more jettisoned paper and plastic rubbish and they were back in Brighton by twelve.

Reynard found them drinking coffee when he returned at about three and straight away gave in to their insistence that he read the report of what they'd found. As he went through it, he could sense the excitement they seemed to be relishing, and it wasn't long before he was beaming himself.

A good start, as early as this in an enquiry, was rare; now it was down to the technicians in Forensics to make it even better.

Still beaming with the reception their find had attracted, Best and Riggs returned to their desks to run through their notes again. After that it'd be back to the lists Furness and Mathews had drawn up at the interviews. The ones conducted at the hotel and in the clubhouse the previous evening.

'I want a connection,' Reynard told them. 'No matter how veiled, no matter how unlikely. I want to know if any of the people interviewed last night might have had one with D.I. Groves, or her family and, if they did, I want to hear about it. Meanwhile I'm going to the hospital again, but I'll be back in an hour if anyone wants me.'

When he got to the hospital, he found Lucy had been given coma inducing injections and was slowly slipping into a deeper state of unconsciousness, one in which her brain would find it easier to fix itself. 'It might be days', the consultant told him. 'But, equally, it could be weeks before she shows any signs of recovery.'

Reynard's disappointment must have been showing when the medic went on to say; 'We're optimistic of course; at her age, and with her otherwise good health, she has a fair chance of a complete recovery, but it'll be slow, very slow.'

As the consultant left, Reynard looked at his watch. It was just on five so, as there seemed little point in going back to the office at that time, and as he was dog tired following the excitements of the previous day, he went home.

Little did he know what was round the corner.

Wyckham House
Rodean Road, Brighton.
Private Retirement Home.

5.00 pm

A 'sit at table' meal in the dining room, was in full swing. Sardines on toast had been served to everyone, except Hilda Goulding who said she couldn't stick the bloody things and had a boiled egg instead. The savoury dish had been accompanied by tea bread butter and jam, and the feast was in the process of being topped off with lemon drizzle cake (being a Tuesday). On Wednesdays a raspberry jam and cream sponge would have been served and, had it been Thursday, it'd have been chocolate eclairs. Each day brought a different extravagance. It was a signal in a way; one to jointly indicate the day of the week and the end of the meal. The elderly residents in Wickham House appreciated being in a regime that was so well ordered, particularly those who were struggling with memory loss.

All round it had been a fairly normal day up until then. One of boredom for those whose mental faculties continued to function, one of irritation for those who were struggling to accept their independence had gone; and one of singular worry for Mrs Rudd who spent her whole time calculating and re-calculating her funds hoping to confirm she'd enough to cover her fees at Wyckham House for the rest of her days.

Susie Knight, one of the three retired nurses who worked there as superintendents, came in to see if everything was alright just as the lemon drizzle was being handed round. It *was* alright *except* for Mr Townsend ... he wasn't there.

'Anyone seen Mr T?' she asked, looking around the room. Nobody answered.

'Right then ...' she said, turning and, with an exaggerated sigh, making for the stairs leading to the residents' bedrooms. 'I'd better go and see what he's up to.'

He wasn't 'up' to anything when she got there ... quite the opposite. He was lying on his bed with a deer's foot sticking out of his chest and he was looking exceedingly dead.

In most circumstances such a sight would have brought a scream or a shriek; but not from Sister Knight. After ten years in 'Casualty' at the Royal Sussex Hospital she'd become immune to the most grisly of sights. The deer's foot hadn't been the surprise to her it might have been to others either; she'd recognised it straight off; it was the handle of his letter opener. The rest of the knife - the blade - was buried deep inside his rib cage, and possibly into his heart. The front of his shirt, not surprisingly, was soaked in blood. She walked calmly over and put her finger to the side of his throat and felt for a pulse. There wasn't one. She grabbed a hand mirror from the dressing table beside his bed and held to his face There was no sign of misting. In fact, there wasn't any sign of life whatsoever, *and* he was stone cold. 'Oh dear, we've got a nasty problem here.' she said to herself, swinging round and glancing round the room before making her way downstairs to tell Doctor Neilson, what she'd discovered.

A practising GP before a road accident had forced her to take on a physically less-stressful life, Neilson was entering purchase invoices onto her computer when Knight walked in. She waved her to a seat and continued to type. 'I was just about to go looking for you,' she said, 'I want to talk to you about Mr Townsend.'

Knight almost smiled, 'Mr Townsend? I want to talk about him too.'

'Not another complaint ... What is it this time?'

'*It* isn't anything - he's dead.'

'He's what?'

'Dead. And it might have been for a while.'

'Dead!'

'Yes ... murdered ... unless he stabbed himself. He had that animal's foot thing of his sticking out of his chest.

'His letter opener ... the funny one with a deer's foot for a handle; I hate it.'

'So do I. Well it's not so funny now … you should see the blood; it's everywhere.'

'What? … Oh blast; as if I didn't have enough problems?' exclaimed the doctor, swinging round on her typist's seat.

'What'll we do? Call the police?'

Neilson, with her head beginning to droop, emitted a long sigh. 'Better check he's clinically dead first I suppose, come on I'll ring the police after I've examined him.'

'Right.' Said Knight, turning and heading for the door.

As Neilson slid from the seat, on which she'd been perched, to follow her, her trousers rode up revealing the business ends of her prostheses - metal and plastic where once there'd been flesh and bone. 'Have you told anyone?' she asked.

Knight shook her head. 'They're at tea.'

'Thank Goodness for that, you'd better come with me then ... let's hope nobody's stumbled into his room.'

'Oh I doubt anyone's done that; I think they're all still in the dining room.'

'Right.' Said Neilson, 'I presume you locked the door.'

Knight put her hand to her mouth

'You didn't?'

'I can't remember, sorry. I was more concerned about finding you to tell you what had happened.'

As they spoke, they were climbing the stairs, with Knight feeling progressively more and more guilty for having left the door un-locked, and Neilson worrying about the adverse impact a murder would have on her business.

When they got to Everett Townsend's door at the end of the West Wing landing, the one opposite it surprisingly opened … and Betty Forward came out. She'd just 'slipped' up for her book, she told them, and was on her way back down to the sun-room to claim the red velvet chair with the sea view before Hilda Goulding got there.

'Huh, you two!' said Neilson, 'you're as bad as each other regarding that chair!'

'What are you doing up here?' Mrs Goulding replied, ignoring Neilson's comment. 'Don't tell me Everett's in trouble again … what's he done this time?'

Neither replied; a chat was the last thing they wanted.

'Oh charming!' Said Mrs Forward. 'What's he been up to?'

'Sorry, we're just …'

'Alright, alright, no need to apologise; I know where I'm not wanted.' Said Mrs Forward, hurrying off to grab the red chair before Mrs Goulding got to it.

As soon as she'd gone, Neilson went to open the door, but she couldn't. 'I thought you said you didn't lock it.' She said, 'Give me your key.'

Knight dug in her pocket, pulled out her pass key, and handed it to Neilson, who tried to insert but couldn't.

'There's something in there,' she said, 'it could be the

key. Now what do we do?'

'We poke it out,' said Knight. 'I've a knitting needle in my hand bag my son's turned into a 'key poker outer'. I'll get it.'

'Are you serious … a 'key poker outer'?

'Of course I'm serious, we use it all the time.' Knight answered. 'I'll pop down to my locker and get it.'

To Neilson's surprise, the strange homemade implement worked, and soon she was opening the door and entering Mr Townsend's room.

Knight didn't follow; she was trying to work out how the door could have become locked in the short time that had elapsed between her going downstairs for the doctor and the two of them coming back. Had she surprised the killer when she came up looking for Mr Townsend the first time? Had the sound of her footsteps on wooden floor alerted him so much he'd hidden himself under the bed, or in the en-suite, or even in the wardrobe, seconds before she entered the room?

Her thoughts were cut short when she heard the doctor gasping with horror and she raced in to see what had happened. Nothing had happened … everything was the same; Mr Townsend was still lying covered in blood exactly as he'd been when she'd left … on his back, with his mouth open, and a deer's foot sticking out of his chest.

Neilson, clearly still in shock, had to hang onto the ornate headboard to steady herself leaving Knight to carry out the re-examination.

'There's definitely no pulse … and he's not breathing, but you're the doctor, you'd better confirm this yourself.'

'Is he cold?'

'Cold? … he's like ice.'

'Right ... well ...' Neilson replied, reluctantly moving to Mr Townsend's bedside to confirm the findings, while trying to hide the fact she couldn't cope with the sight of so much blood. 'There's not much *we* can do,' she said, 'so we'd better lock him in here until the police arrive; I'll ring them now on my mobile, and then we'll go downstairs and wait for them. And ... listen ... this is important ... say nothing of any of this to anyone.'

'Yes ... right.' said Knight. But she felt far from it.

14, Malvern Gardens

5.25p.m.

'Riggs was like a dog with two tails' Reynard told his wife, Cathy, when he got home.

'I'll bet.' She replied, 'and did the golf club turn out to be the weapon?'

Reynard paused; it was the question that was utmost in his mind too. 'I believe it will,' he said, 'but it's with Forensics at the moment; they're checking it for prints. If Lucy's are on it, then it probably is hers; and if his are on it, and he's been in trouble before, we'll soon know who he is.'

'Fingers crossed then.' Said Cathy. 'Who's going to take over the enquiry, now you've retired?'

'Nobody; my retirement's been deferred. '

Cathy started laughing, in part because she thought he was joking, and in part when she realised he wasn't. But he stopped her. 'Why not? Surely you don't think I'd walk off leaving that menace loose on the streets; he might go for Lucy again.'

'O.K. ... but what about me ... am I retired?'

'No, darling, you're my wife.'

Wyckham House

6.15pm

Doctor Neilson sat looking at the phone in her hand, her mind racing as she tried to work out what she'd say to whoever answered the 999 call she knew she'd have to make. In the end she only required one word - 'Police' A simple answer that brought a menu of searching questions requiring her reply. Once that had been done and, in no time, it seemed, a police car, with flashing lights, was pulling up at the front door.

When the residents saw it, they abandoned their drizzle cake, left their tables, and crossed to the window in case they missed anything.

Had they known what had brought 'the law', they might have stopped chattering, or shut up completely. But, as they were ignorant of the reason, they were left to speculate and, in a place where nothing ever happens, speculations can be wild and fanciful. Not that wild or fanciful would be enough to explain their presence in this case though, for *they* didn't know Mr Townsend had been found, fifteen minutes earlier, with a knife in his chest. Had they been told: they wouldn't have believed it anyway; such things don't happen in Wyckham House, a well sited Edwardian seaside villa with tremendous views, that had been cleverly converted into an old people's home some years earlier.

It is, undoubtedly, a fine looking building, but the thing that really distinguishes Wyckham House from other retirement homes in the same category, is the exceptional care given to its residents who are renowned for letting others know they're more than 'comfortably off'.

The owner, creator, and chief executive of this up-market enterprise is Renata Neilson, a 50 year old female medical doctor of Italian/Danish descent. A determined single woman, she has managed to make a new life for herself by investing the proceeds of a compensation package she was awarded as the result of a road accident - one in which she lost both her legs. A determined woman and a 'doer', rather than a 'watcher', she took on the challenge of being self - sufficient when the odds seemed stacked against her. As a young GP working in a jointly owned practice of medical men, she'd seen the average survival age of the practice's patients increasing at a rate that pointed to problems in the future. She'd even gone as far as suggesting the partners might look at ways of bolstering their income and their pensions by investing in a small 'care home' adjacent to the practice. But they'd said 'no'; they were happy the way they were. The awful life changing car accident that happened to her not long after that, and the pile of money she got as a result of it, helped her to where she is today - the sole owner of a very solid business that makes money while helping to satisfy an ever increasing demand.

The house, built in 1905 on a large plot facing the sea on Rodean Road, has all the architectural characteristics of the period, while in more recent times, in order to improve and increase the functionality, two single story extensions have been added at the back. One contains six single en-suite bed sitting rooms and the other has four similar doubles. Across the front of the house, at ground level, there's a sun room; a full width half glazed extravagance furnished with comfortable chairs that look out to sea. This room is the most popular place in the house and it's where the majority of residents congregate at any time of the day if they're not in their own quarters. The rest of the original building is much as it's always been, with the kitchen, dining room, sitting room and study (doubling as the office) on the ground floor; and the whole of the upstairs, apart from two single bedrooms and shared shower room for the house maids, set out as Dr Neilson's private quarters.

Three single men and three single women live in one of the extensions ... the so called East Wing: Everett Townsend, a retired man in his seventies who had been the headmaster of a Private Secondary School in Hove; Rueben Platz, 81, a retired banker (he says), whose wife, because of her own infirmities, is no longer able look after him at home; and Frank O'Leary, also 81, a widower, and a relative newcomer to Wyckham House, who told Platz, when asked what he used to 'do', said he'd 'dabbled in finance a bit', but he wouldn't elaborate further.

Dispersed among the three men's rooms, are those of three women: Hilda Goulding, 90, a divorced retired hotelier; Marianne Rudd, 79, an unmarried woman who'd once owned a fashionable boutique in Ship Street; and Betty Forward who never told anyone how old she was, or anything about her background, except that she'd spent her life 'abroad'.

The East Wingers, other than Marianne and Betty, who were seriously self-centred, always seem to be at odds with each other and had little in common with those living quite harmoniously in the West Wing.

Wyckham House, it is acknowledged, is well run and, though expensive, secretly considered good value by those who dwell there.

Dr Neilson manages the business, does the accounts, and provides emergency medical care. And she's supported in this by three Superintendents; Judy Blackstone, 60, retired married nurse, Susie Knight, 58, retired staff nurse, and Diana Wheeler, 52, also a retired staff nurse who, together with the other two and working in shifts, keep things moving. There are also a pair of 'live-in' eighteen-ish year old Kurdish girls, Citra Karim and Kemala Bhutto, who cook, clean, and generally do pretty-well everything else. All in all, Wyckham House is more a lifestyle than a home, a lifestyle that's well cushioned from drama; definitely not the sort of place, one would think, in which a murder might take place.

The two policemen, who'd arrived in the car with its blue lights flashing were greeted at the door by Dr Neilson, who conducted them straight to her office, where Susie Knight was waiting. A brief conversation then took place during which Susie told of finding Mr Townsend, of how she'd seen straight away that he was dead, and of how she'd hurried downstairs to report the tragedy. Dr Neilson told them she'd taken over then, and she and Susie had gone back up to the room, where she'd no hesitation in confirming Mr Townsend was dead, which had prompted her to ring the emergency services on 999.

The senior of the policemen, recognising the importance of C.I.D. getting on the job as soon as possible, didn't waste time cross-examining the staff or residents, by then crowding the hall in the hope of finding out what was going on. Instead he telephoned C.I.D. HQ in Sussex House.

Riggs and Best were side by side at Best's desk, working through the previous day's first interviews at Wickham House, when the phone rang and, a few minutes later, Best, on the strength of the resumé of the happenings at Wyckham House, rang D.S. Reynard, at home.

'Right. You'd better go, straight there and wait until I arrive.' Reynard answered, kicking off his slippers and pulling on his shoes again.

'You're not going out surely.' Cathy said, 'Have you forgotten … you're on the verge of retirement? Let one of the others deal with whatever it is, go on … put your feet up again.'

She might as well have been talking to the wall.

Wyckham House
The Office,

9.45 p.m.

Doctor Neilson was restless. Reynard had noticed how she'd begun to fidget even before they'd settled in the staff room's only two comfortable chairs, but he'd said nothing, not wanting to be side lined by whatever trivial concern was troubling her. In the end he asked her if there was a problem. Her answer embarrassed him; how could he possibly have missed something so obvious?

'It's the residents' she said, 'they're old and they're not used to excitement such as we've had this evening, they've not even had their cocoa. One of the things that makes this place manageable is routine … what you think boring, is a lifeline to them, and I don't want it broken. If it is, they'll never settle down and the staff, including me, will be run off our feet.'

Reynard thought for a minute before answering. She had a point; he could remember his own mother in her later years. If she got too excited, she'd not sleep properly for days, and the resulting period of tiredness she had to endure got everyone on edge. 'Yes, I know,' he said, 'and we'll be as quick as we can, but the longer it is before we get on the trail of whoever committed this disgusting crime, the harder it will be to track him down. The two officers I have interviewing the residents and staff are good at their job ... we'll not keep anyone a minute longer than necessary.'

Neilson seem satisfied at that, and asked Reynard what he wanted to know.

'For a start,' he said, 'tell me about this place. I need to know its status, its ownership and how it's run. General stuff so I can get a handle on it. The medical people will find out how Mr Townsend died, as if it wasn't obvious, but they won't be able to help regarding all the other people who might be involved, residents even, and about any currents of discontent circulating within or without this house.'

Neilson looked at him aghast. 'There's nothing going on here, Superintendent,' she said, having looked again at the card with his details on it that he'd given her; she wanted to ensure she was addressing him correctly. 'Not a thing that would explain such atrocious behaviour. No this was an outsider, of that I'm sure.'

'And you might be right.' Reynard answered, 'indeed I hope you are, for if it turns out that one of your other residents, or one of your staff, is involved ... trust in the whole establishment will be destroyed,'

'And we'll be finished, yes I know ... but it won't be one

of us ... so what do you want to know?'

'We'll start with you, and then move on to the staff. Thumb-nail sketches only for now; we can get down to greater detail tomorrow. So ... over to you ...'

Neilson had obviously been preparing and making notes for this moment ever since Susie Knight had rushed in to tell her what she'd found when she'd gone to look for Mr Townsend, and she handed them over.

Reynard took the long list of well marshalled information in his hand and sat back to read ...

1. Wyckham House, Limited, a private limited company, wholly owned by Doctor Renata Neilson who lives on the premises and manages the company. No significant debt. Net assets 1.8 million pounds.
2. Staff includes Dr Neilson, for medical and admin duties. Caring is provided by the three Supervisors (all former staff nurses) working on shifts, and two Kurdish domestic girls; Citra Kamin. and Kemala Bhutto, who live in and look after everything else.
3. Residents: three single men: Mr Townsend, now deceased, Mr Platz, and Mr O'Leary; three single women, Mrs Rudd, Mrs Forward, and Mrs Goulding; and two couples; the Armitages and the Wilberforth-Watts.

'I'm impressed,' Reynard said, when he'd finished. Just a few questions then. Have you been aware of any tensions amongst the residents, especially lately; any disagreements, arguments or fights?

'Oh Superintendent, we've arguments all the time, but not fights. No, they're usually just silly tantrums over minor issues.'

'Like what?'

'Like who gets to the red armchair chair in the sun room first, or who's turn is it to help pass round the cocoa we have each evening ... that sort of thing ... petty stuff that's so childish it makes me laugh.'

Reynard smiled, thinking of his own mother in her old age again, and the stupid and sometimes tetchy squabbles he used to have with her over issues that were utterly trivial. 'I know what you mean,' he said, 'and I know how frustrating life can get when faced with someone else's intransigence. Maybe we'll be the same one day; I suppose we will.'

'We'll be following a well trodden path if we do, that's for sure;' Neilson answered, 'but back to your question ... No, I've not heard of any upsets between our residents or between them and the staff. So where w do we go from here?'

'I'm going to see how my two officers are getting on and, when they're through, we'll be off. But we'll be back in morning ... mid-morning probably... we've a few things to do in the office first. If you're worried about what's going to happen between now and when we get back … don't. I've arranged for a couple of men to be here all night. They'll keep an eye on things, especially on the crime scene, the section we've taped off.'

When he joined D.C. Best, Reynard found the questioning of the staff was nearly over. Several sheets of paper covered with handwritten notes were lying on the desk at which Best was sitting. 'We're all done here, Guv,' he said, as Reynard took up and began to read the top sheet.

'And the staff?'

'They're in the kitchen drinking tea.'

'O.K. Any idea how D.C. Riggs is getting on?'

'He's done too, I think. I saw him walking towards the hall a few minutes ago. He was with the SOCO men who're just off. I think they're coming back in the morning. And, oh yes, a couple of uniformed men have just arrived in squad car.'

'They'll be part of the overnight team. Any idea where Constable Riggs is?'

'Gone upstairs, I think. He's finished his interviews.'

'He'll have finished his blinkin' career if he's poking around in the room where the incident took place.'

'Which he isn't!' said Riggs, who'd come into the room unobserved and was standing behind him. 'I told the Supervisor woman …'

'Mrs Knight?'

'Yes Guv, her; I told her I was finished interviewing and

that you'd probably ask me to have another look inside Mr Townsend's room next; to see if I could spot anything the S.O.C.O. team might have missed.

Reynard answered with a bemused smile 'Oh I see, is that what I'm supposed to do … ask you to check S.O.C.O.'s findings? Alright you'd better do it then, but ask Mrs Knight to see if the people who have the adjacent rooms can be moved elsewhere for a day or two so we can completely close off the area.'

'Oh, that's done Guv, and the landing's taped off too. I was just about to poke around in the victim's room to see what I could find … any idea what we're looking for?'

Reynard stood in silence for a second or two trying to work out whether Riggs constant attempts to push his views at the expense of everyone else were misplaced enthusiasm or downright cheek. '

'Anything that looks out of place,' he said in the end. 'Anything you wouldn't expect to see and especially any letters, papers, photographs and so on … I'll come with you.'

They spent an hour going over what S.O.C.O. had already checked in Mr Townsend's room, but found nothing, that seemed pertinent to the case except for a box file they discovered tucked out of sight under his armchair.

'Not much to help us here except this file then, it's only got his current paperwork, bills and so on, in it.' Said Reynard, 'I'll put it back where I found it.'

DAY THREE

D.S. Reynard's office, CID HQ.

8.00 a.m.

They were all there, sitting grouped round Reynard's desk when he arrived, after spending the previous half hour reporting progress to D.C.S. Bradshaw, his immediate boss, head of CID for West Sussex. It was a normal start to the day and Reynard was hoping it would remain that way. In fact, it looked as though it might do so, when he noted the four navy blue or charcoal grey suited men with pristine white cutaway collared shirts, Paisley ties and highly polished shoes sitting before him.

In the background another of his idiosyncrasies bubbled away, his percolator. Yes, Foxy was just as well known for his Cona coffee and his Hobnob biscuits as he was for solving crimes. One thing was different though, glaringly so … the chair to Reynard's right, occupied for the previous four years by Detective Inspector Lucy Groves, stood vacant. By common consent they'd decided to leave it that way until such time as she'd recovered from her injuries and returned to work, a reminder, if they needed one, of what a vital part she'd played in the team. Her return, when it came, would be short-lived though, for her promotion from Sergeant to Inspector was linked to a change of job and location. Soon she'd be leaving both the squad, and Brighton permanently and, with Reynard on the verge of retirement, big changes in were about to take place. The competition to secure one of the most prestigious vacancies that would arise in consequence of Groves's and Reynard's departure, was becoming more evident daily.

'Right, Gentlemen;' said Reynard, 'let's start. I've updated the Chief Super regarding D.I. Groves, who, incidentally, is still in the induced coma we heard about yesterday,' 'And I've given him the latest on the situation at Wyckham House, having called there at half seven this morning, on my way in. Now let's hear where we are with the other cases we're involved in … D.I. Furness what have you got for us?'

'Not much, Guv. Nothing new at all really as we were all bound up with Wyckham House. I do know though that the ATM machine stolen a couple days ago has turned up with its back blown off. Kids found it in a ditch. It was empty of course. SOCO have got it back to their workshop and are working on it today. We might know something later. Nothing new on the car scam that D.I. Groves was on either, but that's not surprising. The only thing new that's turned up is a complaint about the apparent increase in shoplifting that several stores have reported. I'm putting something together on that which I'll give you tomorrow.'

'Is that it?'

'Yes Guv. Not much to get our teeth into, is there?

'Anyone got anything to say?' asked Reynard, who wasn't the slightest surprised when Riggs held up his hand.

'I'll continue with the Millennium Cars enquiry D.I. Groves was on if you like. I've listened to the reports she's been giving and while I know she's been interested in the guys that run it Norris Scorton, Declan Murphy senior, and his son, Declan junior, both of whom have records as I remember, I can see she's come to a halt. Maybe new eyes and a fresh approach might nudge us on a bit. What d'you think?'

What Reynard thought was that he hoped one of the others might get in first one day. Riggs was impulsive, inclined to take risks, and deaf to criticism, but he was a good, a damned good, detective … with a much livelier imagination than any of any of the others. 'Alright,' he said 'you can familiarise yourself with the details D.I Groves has assembled, but then come back to me so we can discuss possible action. Do not go racing out stirring up trouble with the crowd we think are involved; they're a dangerous lot and with these two new cases to handle and being without D.I. Groves who knows the ins and out of where we are, we'll need to tread carefully. Right?'

'Yeah, right.' Said Riggs, grinning from ear to ear.

With Riggs likely to be quiet for the next few minutes, and with Reynard's news of Groves present situation quelling any further queries regarding her, he turned to the situation in Wyckham House. 'So,' he said, 'as to the murder of Mr Townsend I think we can go to the allocation of duties. We were all there up until late last night, and you've had plenty of time to exchange information this morning while I was with the Chief Super so we must all be fairly well up to date. What we must now do is ...'

'Before you start Guv,' said Furness, 'there was a call for you from one of the uniformed men who was there all night. I took it. Apparently, the body's been taken to Doctor Vladic's lab at the mortuary in Worthing. The victim's room is still locked though, and the guy I spoke to wants to know if he can let the Wyckham house staff in to clean up, and whether the tapes can be removed and the owners let back into their rooms.'

'I hope you said No',' Reynard replied. 'everything must be left as it was when we went home last night.'

'Which is what I told him. I also said some of us would be there again soon, that we'd probably be there for most of the day, and that you'd be the one to decide when the staff could get in to do the routine cleaning as well as tend to the victim's room.'

'Fine, let's hope they do as you asked, particularly with regard to Mr Townsend's quarters. OK, it seems to me we might all move over to Wyckham House today. All except

Constable Riggs of course, he'll be acquainting himself with D.I. Groves's Millennium Cars file on stolen 'top end cars' and sketching out a plan for us to look at tomorrow. All done? Good. I and those who're going to Wyckham House had better travel in our own cars; we'll be more manoeuvrable that way.'

Wyckham House

09 15. a.m.

Best arrived first, went straight up to the taped off area, and was chatting to the uniformed man who'd arrived the night before when, shortly afterwards, Reynard got there, having, stopped at Connie's flat on the way to give her an update, and to explain that the murder at Wyckham House was likely to slow down the hunt for her sister's attacker.

She wasn't there, as it happened, so he pressed on and joined the others, grouped at Mr Townsend's door talking to Doctor Neilson and Susie Knight, who just come on duty.

'Can we have a room for our exclusive use d'you think, Doctor?' he asked.

'We've a vacant one you can use, one with much more space than Mr Townsend's. You get to it by turning left at the top of the stairs instead right as you did when you came here. It's empty at the moment because it's just been painted ready for a couple who are moving in, in two week's time. I'll have a table and a few chairs put in if you like and, before you ask, there are ample power points and a telephone line in there."

Ten minutes later they were in and ready to continue

their meeting where they'd left off at Sussex House. Hardly had the others gone than Riggs was off too. With no intention of following Reynard's advice, he was on his way to give Millennium Cars the once over. The traffic had been light all along and, in no time, it seemed, he was driving along the A27 in the direction of Lewes. Millennium Cars forecourt came into sight just after he'd driven past the turning into Morpeth Road, and he could see straight off that it was a small enterprise. Six immaculately presented saloon cars of various makes were parked in a single line before the window of the glass fronted showroom in which there were two other magnificent vehicles; a sparkling cherry red vintage Bentley Continental, and a dark grey metallic Porsch 911.

    He carried on driving past it, as slowly as he could bearing in mind he was in a stream of traffic, until he came to the roundabout around which he drove until he was facing back in the direction from which he had just come. Short of the garage by fifty yards, and on the other side of the road to it at that stage, he pulled into an empty space and settled down to watch. For a long time nothing happened, and he was beginning to think he'd wasted his time, let alone risk the fury of D.S. Reynard, who, he knew, would not have approved of what he was doing.

    And then, out of nowhere it seemed, a sallow complexioned black haired man of about thirty or thirty five with a beard, and wearing a dark suit, came out from the showroom. One of his arms was held out to shepherd a grey haired man on crutches, who'd an enormous surgical boot on his lower leg. They made their way between the parked cars, slowly crossed the road to the pavement on Riggs side, and continued along until they got to a big Mercedes estate, two vehicles in front of him, where the younger man opened the passenger side door and assisted the grey haired man into the front seat.

Riggs, keen to take advantage of the situation, but terrified he'd be seen, switched the phone in his hand to photo mode and risked a couple of quick un-aimed shots. He'd taken them so hurriedly he didn't even know if he'd captured the men at all. Once the 'Merc' had driven off, he remained where he was; quivering with apprehension lest he'd been spotted. And then he started to chuckle … 'so what', he said to himself 'there's no way they'd have had me down as a copper, even if they saw me, and I don't reckon they did.'

The older, grey haired, man hadn't seemed to have much to say to the younger man who, Riggs thought, was more than likely one of the salesmen rather than the old man's chauffeur.

After the car drove off, he waited for his heart to return to its naturel rhythm, and then, thankful for having flaunted Reynard's orders and got away with it, he drove back to Sussex House. His brief visit to Millennium's site, had left him with a favourable image of Millennium Cars business so, if they *were* involved in car smuggling, as Groves seemed to think they were, where was the dodgy bit, the 'Steal to Order' bit, the mysterious outfit called Kontinental Kars?

Back in Sussex House twenty minutes later, and with his heart beating normally, he pulled out the notes and newspaper cuttings Groves had been assembling before her attack. There wasn't much to look at; the cuttings referred to reports of luxury cars being stolen and sold on the continent and nothing else.

There were at least a dozen of these excerpts and, bar one, they'd all come from local newspapers circulating in towns along the south coast. The exception being a half column taken from the Daily Express.

The hand written notes were sparse too, and varied from a couple of sheets of A4 covered in Groves's spidery handwriting, to fragments of paper torn from a notebook on which had been recorded a number of addresses and telephone numbers, including those of Millennium Cars. Two lists of vehicles that were for sale had been stuck to the inside of the file cover. They looked as though they'd been cut from a fairly current issue of a motoring magazine. All in all, Riggs reckoned, the file and its contents suggested some interesting lines to follow.

Twenty minutes later, after adding a few thoughts of his own, he shoved the paperwork to one side; it was time to start making a plan he could put before Reynard.

Before he could do that though, he needed to assemble everything he'd learned and have it clear in his own mind. 'O.K. … Lucy's discovered there are two elements involved here; one,

Millennium Cars, a well-known local car dealer and another, Kontinental Kars; an outfit that may ultimately turn out to be no more than one or two men, who aren't even be in the motor trade.'

Assembling other scraps picked from Groves's notes, Riggs then began to think about the various ways it might all work out and, soon, he was scribbling down his ideas … mumbling to as he went.

'Right then, according to Lucy, Millennium Cars seems to secure orders for 'up market' cars from agents in France and Belgium. To satisfy these requirements, the men who do the stealing are contacted and asked to locate, steal, and then store a specific model of car until the paperwork for its new owner is 'ready', which probably means forged. A driver from the continent having crossed on the ferry, then collects the car and drives it to its new owner via whichever of the channel ports is most useful.

The points he'd written down, when enumerated so specifically, made it clear to Riggs that unravelling the connection between the two parts of the scam had probably been Lucy's principal first objective, and she'd made some progress by identifying Millenium Cars, or a some section of it, as being involved, though a lot of the other stuff she'd written was probably guesswork rather than anything else.

The question was, where should *he* start looking? He'd have no chance of locating the two men whole stole the cars when he didn't know who they were, or where they were. And he hadn't a clue where to look anyway. Millennium Cars may only be part of the system but it was all he had. How could he penetrate their secrets without giving the game away? Not easily. He pulled a new sheet of paper from his desk drawer and, with a freshly sharpened pencil clamped between his teeth, sat back, eyes closed and began to plot.

Reynard found him sitting there, happily asleep, twenty minutes later, and slammed his hand on the desk to awaken him. The resulting noise not only woke Riggs, but almost frightened the life out of him.

'Feeling tired?' Reynard enquired, almost mischievously. 'Maybe I'm giving you too much to do?'

Riggs shook himself awake and grinned sheepishly. 'I was thinking Guv that's all ... thinking.'

'Ah, of course ... well think out loud next time. Now, tell me, what you've been up to; I saw your car was missing earlier ... calling on someone without telling me first, were you? You need to get a grip on yourself, Constable, we're a team here and I don't want any maverick actions ... I find they usually go wrong and I'm left clearing up the mess.'

Riggs, unsure as to whether Reynard had guessed what he'd been up to and where he'd been, slowly shook his head. 'I'm sorry, Guv, I just wanted to see the lie of the land ... I went to find out where Millennium Cars were.'

'Were you spotted?'

'No Guv. I was too far away for that.'

'Did *you* see anything; anything of interest?'

'Not really Guv, I only saw two people in the ten minutes I was there, they came out of the showroom and drove off. They looked like salesmen to me Guv; they were wearing suits.'

'Really? Policemen wear suits too … even a few of 'em round here, or hadn't you noticed?' said Reynard, swinging round to make for his office.

Riggs never saw the smile on his boss's face … or hear the spluttering laughter that followed it once he was in his office, Reynard was thinking the young man he'd just left might be a good lad … but he was a lousy liar.

The sigh Riggs gave out was one of relief. Not describing the two men more thoroughly was dangerous but, on the other hand, if he could progress his enquiries a bit further without asking for help, he might score a point or two.

Wyckham House

Midday

It had been a fruitless morning as far as progress on the enquiry into the murder of Mr Townsend was concerned, which would not have been considered unusual, for the first twenty four hours after a murder has been committed are often spent on gathering information. Action only follows once the data has been put in order and analysed. An exception, of course, would be if the killer had been recognised or seen. In such instances early apprehension becomes the focus. Mr Townsend's killer had not been seen, as far as he knew, so information gathering was still the team's principal task and, when Reynard arrived, he went straight to the room that had been set aside for his use. He wanted to see how Furness, Mathews and Best were getting on.

They'd been getting on fine, and were all but finished bar checking over their notes, knowing that Reynard would be questioning them closely as he probed through the data they'd amassed. Furness and Mathews had each interviewed about half of the residents and Best had spoken to the staff excluding

Doctor Neilson, who Reynard had instructed them to leave for him to question. An easy morning all round then, for Furness had only been left with Rueben Prozanski, Sam O'Leary, Marianne Rudd and the Armitages to interview, while Mathews still had Hilda Goulding, Betty Forward, and the Wilberforce - Watts. Best had had it even easier; he'd only seen three people: the duty Supervisor, Susie Knight, because of her involvement the previous day, and the two young Kurdish domestics; Citra Kamin and Kemala Bhutto.

Doctor Neilson, who'd been impatiently hovering around all morning, descended on Reynard the minute he arrived, and asked if he'd be long as the presence of so many strangers in the house was unsettling for the residents. Reynard smiled at her indulgently while explaining that he'd have police officers there until an explanation for Mr Townsends death had been found. 'We cannot leave you and your residents exposed to danger now … can we?' to which he'd received a reluctant 'No I suppose not … but you will keep out of sight as much as possible won't you.'

Reynard didn't see much point in letting her irritating response get under his skin, so he settled for saying 'We'll try.'

She started to walk away at that but, before she'd got any distance from him, he called her back.

'I hope to conclude the interviews this morning Doctor, and I'd like to do yours as soon as you have a free half hour. In the meantime, I want to see how my men have been getting on.

Let me know when you're free.'

It took but ten minutes for him to check with Furness, Mathews and Best and discover they'd nearly finished and were getting their notes in order after which he told them Dr Neilson had arranged for sandwiches and tea to be sent into them at twelve thirty, after that, they should finish editing their notes. He'd join them as soon as he could. Everyone seemed happy at that but, before they said anything, Dr Neilson appeared and said she was ready for him.

'Fine, we'll do it now, shall we? He said, following her to her office and taking the seat she'd got ready for him, facing her across her desk on which there was a tray bearing tea and sandwiches.

'I presume you eat!' she said, clearly in a better mood once she'd seen 'something definite' was happening.

C.I.D. HQ

2.00 pm

It had been a near thing for Riggs. If he'd been spotted at Millennium Cars, Reynard would have had a fit. As it was, he seemed to have got away with it, but he wasn't happy. Nor was he much further on. Lucy's notes were neat and comprehensive but, when all was said and done, they didn't amount to much. He spread them out again and, one by one, tried to commit the information written on them to memory.

Millennium Cars was a limited company, a legitimate family owned enterprise that employed ten people including the two owners, and was moderately profitable.

The shareholding, according to the balance sheet submitted at the end of the previous year's trading, was split eighty/twenty between father and son: Declan S. Murphy and Declan P Murphy, who were directors as well as well as being employees. The profit of the year submitted was £21,000, half of which had been paid out in dividend and half transferred into the reserves. The premises on the A23 had been leased to the company for twenty five years in 1995.

Finding Jessica

All in all, Millenium Cars looked like a well-run, profitable, if small, enterprise. Assuming the Murphy's were also able to take a reasonable salary out of it, where was the evidence it had any sort of connection to a car smuggling business?

The facsimile school wall clock fixed over the door to the division showed two. Plenty of time for another little recce before anyone was likely to return from Wyckham House, plenty of time to see where the Murphys lived and check the style in which they did it. Lucy had several postal and email addresses and telephone numbers written down on one bit of paper, the Murphy's was one of them. Another, to Riggs's surprise, was that of Barney Truscott, what could his connection be? He was no car thief, he wasn't a thief at all, he was a swindler a small-time conman and occasional snout, and everyone in Brighton CID knew him. With the note in his hand, Riggs sped down to the car park; he had to be back before there was any chance D.S. Reynard beat him to it ... which gave him an hour ... just ... it was leg crossing time and he knew it.

Bella Vista was well named, Riggs thought. Looking at it from a distance, having driven past once and deciding he'd be too exposed if he stopped too close by. It was very impressive; the home of a wealthy man, a sprawling double fronted bungalow on about half an acre and views, well ... they were staggering, sloping down across an area of common land and Western Parade to the sea. It didn't look much like the home of the owner of a small car show-room. How on earth could Declan Murphy afford to live in this style? Groves, from her notes, had obviously come to a similar conclusion so she must have been here too.

'Of course', he thought, 'she might have got directions to the house wrong, for she hadn't given it a name, she'd only described it as being a big bungalow on Anscombe Road, with a huge bay fronted sea facing sun room across its front; and a free-standing garage for three cars at its side.

As he sat, he slowly began to think she must have got it wrong ... but how could that be? Lucy Groves was meticulous in everything she did. If she said this was the Murphy's bungalow ... it was. And then, as if to confirm it, the front door opened and young Declan Murphy accompanied by the Middle Eastern looking guy, who'd been driving the man with crutches, came out and went over to the car parked at the open door of one of the garages. It was a Mercedes estate.

'Bullseye, Lucy.' thought Riggs, and then, wary of being accosted because he'd been there so long, he started his car and drove back to Sussex House.

Wyckham House

03.15.p.m.

D.S. Geordie Hawkins of S.O.C.O. was waiting for Reynard when he arrived at Wyckham House, and he grabbed him before he'd started to collect the interview reports. 'We'll be off soon,' he said, 'I'll drop my report on your desk later today but, for now, there's just one thing you might look at further.'

'Further? We've hardly started; my boys are still talking to the residents and staff. What have you dug up?'

'Very little. This place is so clean there's damn all to find. We might get lucky with that miserable little bit of a finger print we found on the hoof segment of the knife handle, the one I told you about yesterday ... but that's about it. Or it was 'it', until about half an hour ago when we were packing up.'

'You came across something else after all ... what?'

'Another fairly good fingerprint that, at first sight, looks remarkably similar to part of one we found on the hoof. I'll be checking it more closely when we get back to the lab.'

Reynard, wanted to smile but held back, asking if a part print would be good enough to be used as evidence of identification. Hawkins said he thought it would be in this case, because it had a distinguishing scar running across it, a souvenir of some minor accident probably.

As they spoke, they moved, through French doors, out onto the balcony/fire escape where they immediately saw how the metal structure might not only provide an opportunity for a resident to sit out in the fresh air or use as an escape route, but permit an outsider to get into the building without passing through it.

'The really interesting thing though, Foxy, is where we found the 'new' print. It was on the rim of a big glazed pot full of geraniums, sitting on the fire escape, the same as half a dozen others. They'd obviously been spaced out to mark the portion each resident could use as a balcony. The pot under examination looked as though it had been shoved to one side, the S.O.C.O. man told them. And, it was on the assumption the killer had moved it, that it was being scrutinised.

Reynard and Hawkins pushed past the man crouched at the pot, and went down the steps to the ground. Looking up they could see the balcony/fire escape was a relatively recent addition, and had probably been added when Wyckham House was converted from a private residence to a Care Home. An ornate wrought iron structure, it looked very attractive from the ground, and they marvelled at the way it so cleverly performed its two functions. 'But said Reynard, with a laugh, as they walked round to the front door. 'Is it a joined up series of balconies you can use as a fire escape, or is it a fire escape you can use as a row of interconnecting balconies'

'I'll leave you to sort that out,' replied Hawkins, 'my boy's going to check it all from the glazed double doors of the victim's room, to the steps that go down to the backyard. He's also going to have look at the doors and the woodwork surrounding them.'

As they'd been speaking, they'd slowly returned to Mr Townsend's room and Reynard, much happier by then, summed their conversation up. 'There's little doubt in my mind, Geordie, that the killer entered via the fire escape and left the same way having locked the main door to the room from the inside. There must have been a little pantomime moment when he hid in the en-suite, or the wardrobe, in between Susie Knight's first visit to check if he was OK, and second when she returned with Doctor Neilson. We looked everywhere for the key, with which he locked the door prior to leaving, but we couldn't find it; he probably took it with him and chucked away later. Mind you, if it turns up, it'll be a vital clue.'

'I agree, I'll have cast around before we leave,' said Hawkins, 'If I find anything, I'll let you know.'

Ten mutes later, Reynard, having joined Doctor Neilson in her office, was about to take a seat when the phone on her desk rang. She picked up the handset, listened for few seconds, and passed it to Reynard. He said almost nothing to the caller, who seemed to be passing him information. When the call was finished, and the handset was back in its cradle, he told Nelson it had been from the hospital. 'One of my team is having a bit of trouble,' he said.

'Ah yes, you told me yesterday, Is she alright?'

'I hope so … they say there's been no change.'

'She's the one who was attacked a couple of days ago on Crackstone Manor golf course isn't she? I play there myself sometimes; my friends say I'm the only one they know who can do eighteen holes when they're legless!'

Reynard tried to smile, but he wasn't really in the mood for joking … he wanted to get on.

'What I need from you,' he said, 'is an outline of Everett Townsend's life before he came here. If you can help me with that, I might be able see a way forward. I can't imagine him being involved in anything that would attract a killer since he's been here. No, I'm sure it's something from before that, something from his previous life. So it's a summarised account of what he was doing before he took up residence here that I'm looking for.'

'I was expecting you'd want something like that,' she said, 'so I've made some notes for you, d'you …'

'Good, the notes will be just the thing, thank you,' he replied, taking the sheet of paper she handed him on which she appeared to have written a lengthy essay, instead of a short summary.

'I hope it's not too much,' she said, when she saw the expression on his face, 'but Everett was such a talker if he sensed he had an audience. Anyway, I think I know enough about him to write his biography.'

'Fine,' said Reynard, 'give me few minutes to run through what you've given me and, once I have the hang of it, I'll probably want to ask you some questions.' He made no comment on her tiny writing which was so minute and closely spaced he had a hard job reading it. As it progressed, however, a picture of a very strange and lonely man began to appear.

'Everett Townsend told me,' she'd written, 'he was four years younger than his brother Oscar, a lively boy who'd turned into an irresponsible tearaway by the time he was in his early 'teens. 'I don't 'need a third level education to succeed', he told his father, on his seventeenth birthday and, much to the dismay of both parents, he left home the following week, moved in with a girl called Doreen Makins ... a girl he'd met at school, who was two years older than him and had a bed sitter of her own. He left school around then too, and got himself a job as a plasterer's mate. They both had been ridiculous and impulsive moves, and they only lasted long enough for her to get pregnant. When she told him she was 'expecting', he abandoned her and moved in with another girl he'd just met; a twenty one year old foreigner. A year later, she had a child, and she told everyone, it was Oscar's.

Everett was at university by then and, encouraged by his parents and his good exam results, was aiming for the teaching profession. Oscar, on the other hand, was working his way through a whole series of jobs, none of which he liked, all of which he hoped would come in handy one day. At various stages and in various locations in England, he'd been a plasterer, a bookie's runner, a roofer and a barman and he still wasn't twenty five. With a foreign wife who bored him and a child who wouldn't stop crying, he decided he have to break out. The last anyone in the family heard of him,' Doctor Neilson said, 'he'd walked out on the second girl, the foreign one, and his child, and emigrated to Australia. They never heard of him again.

On top of the way they'd been treated, the notes said Oscar's complete disappearance had hurt his parents deeply and; in truth, according to Everett, his mother 'never got over it'.

Following his father's death a few years later, he became the sole prop upon which his mother began to lean and, so dependent on him did she become, he found himself abandoning his own life to support hers. He told me he'd never fully realised the effect her clinging existence was having on him and how, by continuing to live at home, he'd never had a separate existence, or a true friend he could call his own. He'd never married, and never swerved from his ambition to teach, at which he was outstanding, eventually achieving the headmastership of a Brighton Private Secondary School at which stage he was forty. It was a post he held until he retired. In short, Neilson said, He was a dull, friendless man, who only seemed to find peace when he moved into Wickham House.

Reynard put down the paper. 'Wow,' he said, 'you *have* been busy. I know you weren't joking when you said you had enough to write his biography. But you were right, this man's story, and that of his brother, are so bizarre, you might even have the bones of novel.'

Neilson laughed … despite the fact she'd secretly, been thinking the same.

'O.K. I'm going to see how the others have been getting on,' Reynard told her. 'and then I'll come back to ask you a few questions concerning issues that weren't covered in this excellent report you've assembled.'

'I missed something?'

'Not missed, no … it's just that I want more, so I can get a more balanced picture of his recent life. I need as much as you can give me regarding the visitors he had here, and the friends, business and school colleagues he had from *before* he came here.'

Neilson looked disappointed, she thought she'd covered everything but, on reflection, she realised she'd ignored huge chunks of Everett's life about which she knew nothing.

As she pondered on this, Reynard set off to find Best to see how he was getting on with Susie Knight, Sam O'Leary, and the two Kurdish domestics and it didn't take long for Best to enlighten him when he found him.

Sam O'Leary, who he'd interviewed first, had only taken up residence in Wyckham House a week previously, and didn't know anyone. He'd spent most of his life at sea as Master of a series of oil tankers and, as a result, he'd spent more than three quarters of his married life away from his wife.

Surprisingly his marriage had stood the test, and he'd retired early with the happy intention of buying a house in Ibiza for his wife and himself, from which he could still see the sea. It had turned out to be an aim that never came about, for she died of cancer before the sale had gone through. He'd struggled on for a while on his own but with no other family he eventually gave up trying to defeat loneliness, and moved into Wyckham House.

The girls, immigrants from Sinop, a Black sea port in that part of Turkey known as Kurdistan, were seen next. They'd told him they hardly ever came out of the kitchen unless they were cleaning or serving, and they'd little in the way of relationships with the residents because of the language barrier. Both said they'd been frightened of Mr Townsend as he always seemed grumpy and stern. The likelihood of either having anything to do with his death, was so remote Best reckoned it impossible.

Reynard was inclined to agree, but decided not to say so until Furness and Mathews and had submitted their reports.

As to Susie Knight, Reynard wasn't so sure what to think as he read through Best's notes. That Knight had been first on the scene and discovered Mr Townsend dead was not in dispute, but who was to say she wasn't the *last* to be on the scene *after* she'd killed him. She seemed a very unlikely candidate to fulfil that role, but her relationship to Townsend was rumoured to be a cool one, and had to be investigated. As a result of this doubt, Reynard asked Best to go and find Knight so he could ask her a few clarifying questions.

She bounced in a few minutes later, full of confidence her interview would be a short one. It was in the end, but only after several anxious moments. The impression of tension between her and Mr Townsend was real enough, but the reason for it was more obscure, and dated back to a difficult time for both of them twenty years earlier. The incident, that had inflamed the temper of one of the senior boys at the school of which Townsend had just become headmaster, was the theft of the senior boy's cricket bat. He said he saw a junior taking it and, having grabbed it from him, hit him with it so hard he broke the young boy's wrist. The boy said he'd only been passing through the changing room, had nothing to do with the senior boy's bat, or even touched it. Everybody denied everything when they were hauled up before the headmaster, Mr Townsend, and, to avoid being accused of favouritism, he taken the easiest way out and suspended both boys for a month. The younger one was Susie Knight's son, and she'd never forgiven

Townsend for what she'd seen as a breach of trust and gross unfairness. The issue, she'd told Best when he'd asked her, had never been mentioned by either of them during Mr Townsend's time in Wyckham House but, every time she encountered him on his own, she admitted she felt inclined to kick him. Ironically, both boys subsequently became friends after learning the real culprit, the boy who'd actually taken the bat, had admitted to doing it, some months later, to a hugely amused audience in saloon bar of The Dog and Duck.

Best saw the Armitages next, but they had little to contribute when he'd asked them if he could put a few questions to them. Mrs Armitage, having taken on the responsibility of 'mothering' Mr Armitage, more and more as his Parkinson's worsened, told Best they seldom left their room other than to go down for meals, or sit out on their balcony or on a bench in the front garden looking at the view. They'd never spoken to Mr Townsend, she said, other than to say 'Good Morning' or 'Good Afternoon', when they encountered him at meal times.

Once he felt he'd got as much as he was going to get, Reynard, with Best's reports added his own and those of Dr Neilson, went looking for Mathews, eventually finding him in the staff room drinking coffee.

'All finished?' he asked.

'All but.' Mathews answered, handing him a sheaf of papers covered in American style sloping hand writing.'

'Who have you got left to see?'

'No one; I just need to tidy up my notes up a bit.'

'Right, ten minutes,' said Reynard, 'I want one last look around the room while SOCO are here, and I must ring Doctor Vladic to see what he has to say; assuming he's finished the P.M.'

He rang Vladic first, but he was no wiser at the end of the call than he'd been at the beginning. Mr Townsend had bled to death having been stabbed in the heart with a paperknife that was still stuck in his chest when he was found. Vladic had removed the knife and passed to D.S. Hawkins, of S.O.C.O., for examination in the forensic laboratory.

'I don't suppose they've found much,' Said Reynard to himself, 'though the knife might just yield something.'

It hadn't yielded anything worthy of note though, other than one indistinct finger print on the hoof, as the fur had prevented any possibility of prints being left anywhere else on it. The examination of the room had produced nothing either; Mr Townsend had been a tidy man, and they couldn't find anything out of place.

Disappointed at the dearth of information gathered at that point, Reynard moved on to talk to D.I. Furness, who'd been holding forth in a small room beside the office in which he'd been seeing Betty Forward, Hilda Goulding, Rueben Prozanski and the Wilberforce-Watts. The interviewing was nearly over with only the Wilberforce-Watts left to be tackled.

The talk he had with them proved fruitless; they were a couple who kept themselves very much to themselves when in the house, and most of their time out of it looking after one, or more, of the twenty one grandchildren their four daughters had born for them. They had a busy life with so much family commitment and, when at home in Wyckham House, they were happy enough to put their feet up in their room, or sit out on their balcony sipping coffee or Prosecco, depending on the time of day. Their room, being on the opposite side of the building to Mr Townsend's, meant they hardly ever saw him except at mealtimes, where they had many conversations, as their tables were adjacent. Other than this occasional contact, they said, they really didn't know him well enough to suggest any reason for the attack on him.

Betty Forward, who Mathews had seen first, 'is,' he said, 'a mysterious and shifty sort of a woman, who'd fidgets all the time, and whose eyes keep darting about when she speaks.' She'd not seen anything different or in any way unusual the day Mr T, as she kept calling him, was killed. After lunch she'd walked up the stairs to her room alongside him. She'd even asked him if he'd like to watch a short video clip she'd just received on her lap top from her daughter, showing her at Niagara Falls. But he'd said 'No, he needed a rest and was going to lie down for an hour'. Later, after the tea bell had gone, and she'd not heard his door closing, she'd knocked on it in case he was asleep, for he'd missed his 'tea' a few times that way.

But she'd got no answer. It was only some time later, coming up to teatime, she thought, when she'd noticed the anxious looks on the faces of Susie Knight and doctor as they came up the stairs. Only then did she begin to feel concerned.

'She was wondering if she ought …'

'If she ought to say anything … did she?'

'No.' said Mathews. 'Realising she was going to be late for tea, she stopped knocking on Everett's door and went down to join the other residents who, she told me, were already on their first course.'

'Fair enough … did she think Mr Townsend friendly?'

'She said he wasn't anything, bar being the quietest and most introspective man she'd ever met. She quite liked him, she said, and she couldn't imagine why anyone would want to kill him. She even wondered if the killer was after someone else.'

'Like who, for instance?'

'She didn't know … herself maybe. She told me she's 'quite well off', and then jokingly added. But I'm not the sort to keep my money under my mattress!'

Mathews sensed her remarks hadn't been made entirely in jest but he didn't pursue the matter; he kept it for D.S. Reynard. He'd be the one to sort out silly comments like that.

Betty Forward disappeared down the corridor to the stairs when Mathews had finished with her and, hardly had she gone than Marianne Rudd tapped on the door. He invited her in and asked her to take a chair, which she did, once they'd introduced themselves. But, having barely settled herself, she was up again; pacing about, clenching and un-clenching her fists.

Mathews seeing the state she was in, chose his opening remark carefully. 'It's a difficult time for everyone,' he said, 'and I can see you're upset. But we have job to do, we have a bad person to catch, so will you please concentrate and answer my questions?'

Ms Rudd, screwing her hanky into a tiny ball, nodded, and Mathews, well aware of how nervous she still was, laid his hand on hers for the briefest of moments. She tried to smile in appreciation but it didn't quite come off, so she leaned forward towards him with her hands gripping the edge of the desk, 'I'm sorry,' she said, 'I'm frightened.'

'It's alright, Mrs Rudd,' Mathews answered, 'take your time … all I want to know is if you knew Mr Townsend well.'

'No … and I didn't want to; he was rude to me the day I arrived … called my boutique a 'dress shop' … ignorant man … I didn't answer him then, and I didn't speak to him afterwards. I've no time for people who put you down. Huh! … Dress shop! Would you believe it? And he was supposed to be a teacher; I'm glad I wasn't one of his pupils.'

'Yes, that must have been very distressing Mrs Rudd, I can see that. So … as to the day he died?'

'I can't remember if I saw him that day, I left here at about half past eleven in the morning and got a bus into town where I had a midday meeting with …. Have you ever tried to sell a business Inspector? I've been in the process of selling mine, the Boutique Classique … it's near Bentall's. I've been trying to finalise the sale of it for the last six months and, that lunchtime, I had an appointment with my solicitor to finalise everything. I was in Brighton all day actually, and I did a lot of things I'd put off due to the fact I don't drive. Seeing my solicitor was the most important thing, but I also had my hair done, did a bit of shopping, and had lunch with a friend. I got a taxi back, arriving just in time to go into the dining room for tea. I never saw Mr Townsend all day.

Hilda Goulding was the last to be spoken to. An explosive character who 'knew everything', Mathews told Reynard, adding that he'd found her to be the type of woman who went into a situation with the intention of dominating it. Her single purpose seemed to be to implant her point of view and, Mathews confessed, he found that hard to deal with without being outright rude. Eventually Reynard, who'd got the report in his hand, put it down and said; 'I think this lady's got under your skin hasn't she? Let's abandon your report for the moment, and talk me through your findings.'

Mathews looked relieved. 'Thanks Guv, with so many years before I joined this squad spent in the office, I'm not used to this intensity of questioning; talking it through will be better.'

'Good. Fire ahead then.'

Mathews cleared his throat, nodded, and, with his eyes

closed to aid his concentration he began … 'Mrs Goulding is a difficult woman to deal with, and I found it hard getting the answers I was looking for because she kept going back to herself and issues that have nothing whatever to do with our case. For a start she'd fallen out with Mr Townsend weeks ago over the noise coming from his television late at the night; a perfectly understandable reason for complaint. Dr Neilson sorted it out, and that should have been the end of it, but Mrs Goulding wouldn't let it go and continued to make snide remarks whenever she got the opportunity … even as recently as the day he was killed. She said something to him that lunchtime that must have really irritated him for his mumbled reply, according to Mrs Rudd, who was at the same table as Mrs Goulding, just made things worse. He stamped off, and she left the table and went to her room with her lunch untouched. Was the remark he made to her the trigger that, ultimately brought about his death. I don't think so Guv; these people aren't killers.'

Reynard was about to say he agreed but, before he got a chance to do so, Mathews was talking again. 'I realise, none of this has anything directly to do with Mr Townsend's death, but it does point to an animosity that might have got out of hand sometime during that afternoon. Personally, I think it's unlikely. For what it's worth I believe Mrs Goulding's claim that she'd not been anywhere near him once lunch was over is a true one. I just cannot see her going into his room and stabbing him … no matter what the provocation. She's out as far as I'm concerned.'

'Excellent and to the point.' Said Reynard. 'And I agree … whoever killed this man must have done it after lunch and before the end of tea. I dare say the lab will confirm this.'

'I asked her if, at any time prior to his being found dead, she'd seen anyone on the stairs or the landing … anyone who ought not to have been there. But she said she didn't, nor did she hear anything unusual.'

'Right … that's all then …'

'No guv, I also spoke to Mr Platz.'

'And how did you get on with him?'

'Famously. Mr Platz is the most likely of all the people I spoke to who has information that might help us. As far as I can see, he's the only one who genuinely liked the victim.'

'Ah, so we might see things from a different perspective if we see them through his eyes. O.K. tell me about him, paraphrase your report. We can go back and read it in full later, when we consider it alongside those coming from D.I. Furness and D.C. Best.'

'O.K … Mr Platz.

'First name? asked Reynard.

'Rueben … Mr Rueben Platz … he's an Englishman, despite his name, because he was born here of parents who'd fled to London from Warsaw just before the German invasion of Poland in 1939. They remained Polish throughout their lives but he took advantage of his birth and has been an Englishman virtually since he came here. He's short in stature and grossly overweight … a happy man despite the many the adversities he's had to face. He has no wife or children and, at seventy six, he's alone in this world without being lonely. He has many friends; a jolly man … who always looks on the bright side.'

'Not Mr Townsend's type one would think.'

'Oh no, he wasn't anything like Townsend, yet they were great friends. I couldn't understand this until he told me they were both backgammon enthusiasts. They played every day, and for hours on end if the weather was poor.'

Reynard began to giggle. 'Good weather stopped play, eh?' he parodied, before going on to ask 'What's the weather got to do with it?'

'I said they both loved backgammon.' Mathews replied, 'Well they both loved reading too and, on fine days if it was warm enough, they'd spend hours reading out on their balconies. Joining up for a whiskey, in Townsend's case, and vodka, in Platz's, before going down for their evening meal.'

'Very matey, I must say,' said Reynard. 'So, our victim had one friend at least.'

'He did, Platz was the only one in Wyckham House who seemed to make any effort to include a man who was so obviously lonely. Townsend may have been a headmaster, a man with a high profile, but he had no friends except Mr Platz.'

'So … anything else?'

'Only that the reason for this came up one day, and Platz reckoned it explained Townsend's sense of not belonging'.'

'Oh. What's the point you are trying to make?'

'The point I am trying to make, Guv,' said Mathews, 'is that Townsend's only friend, the only man who knew how he ticked, is convinced he wasn't killed because of anything he'd done, but because of something someone else had done.'

'Are you suggesting mistaken identity …and if you are who, for God's sake, is the real target?'

'I asked him that, but he held out his hands as a beggar would, and said that was 'for me to find out'. I couldn't work out what he meant,'

Reynard took a deep breath and sat back. 'Great,' he said, 'we'd better get our skates on then. I just want a word with Doctor Neilson and I'm finished. We'll meet at the office tomorrow at eight, and start putting a plan together.

Mr Townsend's room in Wyckham House

5.15pm

Doctor Neilson found Reynard waiting for her when she entered the room where murder had taken place. He was standing at the open door to the balcony and looking thoughtful.'

'Are you finished here yet, Superintendent? Only I want to get this room stripped of everything in it, and then I'm going to have it re-decorated and re-furnished ready for the first person on the waiting list who doesn't feel intimidated by what's happened. If I can't find anyone, I'll move in myself and offer my room to the next applicant. It won't be a very satisfactory situation, or a convenient one, but what else can I do?'

'Well that sounds like good idea but I'm afraid I can't let you have the room yet; we might need to come back again. Tell me do many people use their balconies?'

'Oh yes,' she answered. They all do if the weather's nice. Do you think that's how he got in?'

Reynard nodded, 'It seems a high probability; the room was locked from the inside, Mrs Knight told me. She had to poke the key out to get her pass in, and that's not easy.'

'Not for you maybe, but it is when you've had the practice our staff get; our residents are always locking themselves in and then going down by the fire escape, forgetting they've left the key in the lock. If they return to their room through the house they can't get into their quarters so they ring me to get them in. Old people do funny things.'

'They certainly do … O.K. … so, if the door was locked from the inside, he may have *entered* via the landing but the presence of the key on the inside tells us he didn't *leave* that way. However, I'm fairly convinced he came in from the balcony; there's no other way. Do all the rooms have balconies, and are they all really just one long structure that doubles as a fire escape when required?'

'Clever isn't it?'

'Clever yes, but is it legal? Does it fulfil all the health and safety requirements we have to obey these days? No, forget I said that; someone else can worry about how you use it.'

As they spoke, they'd been edging towards the door to balcony which was open. When they got outside, Reynard could see, as he and Hawkins had seen the day before, how the cleverly placed pots of geraniums fulfilled a double purpose … decoration and segregation; attractive features that marked out the length of balcony available to each room.

'Is it possible to get onto this balcony/fire escape from every room.' Asked Reynard, 'I mean what about the rooms on the other side of the building?'

'Of course, the balcony/fire escape, as you call it, runs right round the building at balcony height, except at the back, where two flights of steps lead down to the ground.'

Reynard could see the possible ways of entering and leaving the room were growing, and it was going to be more than a chat with Doctor Neilson that would be needed to work out which one had been used to get into and out of Mr Townsend's room the day he died, so he begged to be excused and drove back to HQ, stopping at the hospital on the way.

There was still no change but the doctor told him they were considering allowing D.I. Groves to start recovering.

By the time he got home it was seven and his meal was on the table. It had been a long wearying day and, all he could think of as he swallowed the last of his liver and bacon, was how much he was going to miss days like the one he'd just had.

As if she could read his thoughts, Cathy told him he was looking tired. 'You shouldn't be rushing from one place to another like you do. You ought to leave it to one of the others in your squad.'

'And what'll *I* do?' he asked, 'Retire?'

She didn't answer; she poured him another cup of tea and picked up her book.

DAY FOUR

D.S Reynard's office in C.I.D H.Q.

8.15 am

They were all there and ready to go when Reynard, accompanied by the boss of Sussex CID, Chief Superintendent Colin Bradshaw, appeared.

Riggs, by then used to being responsible for the making of coffee had filled the Cona jug and switched on the machine. Best was reading the notes he'd taken the day before, and Furness and Mathews were quietly chatting. The only one missing was D.I. Groves, but she hadn't been forgotten, her chair, by common consent, would continue to remain unused and in its usual place until she returned

'Before we start,' said Reynard, 'Chief Superintendent Bradshaw wants to say a few words … Sir …'

'Good morning everyone,' said D.C.S. Bradshaw, who'd remained standing in the partially open doorway behind them. 'D.S. Reynard has been filling me in, and I have to say you've covered a lot of ground since I last spoke to you yesterday. From what he's been telling me just now, you're going to have step it up even more today. We have to find who killed this man in Wyckham House, and we have to nail whoever it was who attacked your colleague and mine … D.I. Groves. I'll say no more, except to re-assure you your efforts have not been unnoticed. Keep it up … find these bloody villains and let's get them where they belong … behind bars. The press are onto me constantly; an attack on a serving member of the police force and the murder of a pensioner in a Care Home like Wyckham House, are like manna from heaven to them, and the public will be clamouring to buy their damned papers so they can lap up the half-truths they contain. Don't let me down. Maximum effort again today and as long as it takes. Let's catch these so and so's and lock 'em up.'

'Blimey!' said Riggs as the Chief Super departed.

Reynard, a smile on his face, tapped on his desktop. 'Right Gentlemen,' he said, 'you heard the man. Now let's get on with it; we have a long day ahead of us.'

Reynard's measured words brought them back to earth after the Chief Super's surprise intervention, his suggestion they had their usual coffee and Hobnob biscuits before starting the meeting went down even better though.

It was nearly nine before the meeting eventually got under way. It started with Reynard telling them D.I. Groves might soon be allowed to slowly emerge from the induced coma she was in. Everyone looked so pleased to hear it, one might have thought they were congratulating themselves on making the decision. 'It's just a step on the way,' Reynard said, 'so don't build up your hopes too soon; I find that often leads to disappointment. I'll keep you informed daily … let's hope the news gets better every day.'

Best, who, apart from Reynard, had known Groves the longest, said what they were all thinking; 'Thanks be to God."

With their minds eased regarding Groves recovery, Reynard asked Furness to let them know what progress, if any, had been made in their older cases.

He had little to say, as almost nothing had been done due to them having put the emphasis on finding the perpetrators in the Groves and Townsend cases. 'The exception, Guv,' Furness added, 'being our investigation into Millennium Cars, about which I expect D.C. Riggs will have something to say in due course. All our other live enquiries, including the robbery of the ATM machine and the shoplifting business in the city centre, have been handed over to D.I. Crowther's team on your instructions.'

'Which,' said Reynard, 'came from the top. The brass want us to concentrate on the attack on D.I. Groves's and the murder at Wyckham House. I took it on myself to put D.C Riggs on Millennium Cars which, as you know, was the case D.I. Groves's has been working on and I don't want to see her efforts wasted. D.C. Riggs is helping me make sure it isn't.

O.K.? So now we come to the first of the two cases that are our main concern - the attack on D.I. Groves.'

The debate that followed Reynard's introductory words began after they'd defined what they needed to look for on their way to identifying the attacker, and after they'd talked in depth about the information they'd already gathered. Furness, the senior member of this section of the team, led the discussion, leaving Reynard to watch.

'O.K.' Furness began. Let's first all read the reports you took and all the lists you compiled that first evening at the clubhouse. I want to you pass round them round so we all start from the same place. When you've digested them, I'll give you the statements of the runners who found Lucy, together with those of the two golfers who helped them. Lastly, I'll tell you what came out of the search made in the woods near Crackstone Manor.

We might need a breather after that so, if nothing more urgent has come in, we'll proceed to working out our next moves. Hopefully we'll be through all that by midday, after which, I assume, we can talk about Wyckham House.'

'What about Millennium Cars?' asked Riggs, who was feeling left out. 'Lucy was on that … maybe one of them, one of the Murphy's, beat her up to frighten her off. Maybe she was getting too close to finding out what they're up to?'

Reynard was inclined to smile … but he didn't. Impulsive and often badly misjudged leaps into investigation possibilities that had been seen by enthusiastic and inexperienced young coppers occasionally did solve cases that were otherwise stuck. All he said though, was … 'Later, D.C. Riggs … later.'

With the morning laid out, they got down to work and, for the next hour or so, all that could be heard was the scratch of pencils on paper, the turning of pages, and some whispered queries. Reynard looked on them, his team, his squad, with a mixture of pride and sorrow - the one because he'd chosen, and then shaped, these smart young men who he was going to miss badly when he retired - and the other because, for the moment, it looked as though he'd be with them much longer. For a brief moment he saw flashes of river banks and fishing flies and he smiled. But it didn't last; retirement was coming, and fast, and there was nothing he could do to stop it.

With the clock showing ten thirty, Furness tapped the desk with the end of his pencil and, when they all looked up, he pointed at Mathews and asked him what his thoughts were.

'I've kept it simple,' Mathews said, 'because I'm new to this squad, and still not quite sure of the way you work. But take the first set of interviews; nothing more than names and addresses came out. None of the names or addresses rang a bell, but then again, I'm new to the area.

The second set of interviews didn't involve me at all. Knowing I was passing Forensics, D.C. Riggs asked me to call in to see how they were progressing with the golf club he and D.C.

Best had found in the trees near the lay-by. Luckily the guy who'd made the examination was there, and he told me they'd found it had been wiped clean of prints. On taking a second look, after I'd asked him to do it however, he said he'd spotted an indistinct part of a print that might help to identify the man who threw the club and, thereby, connect him to the attack on D.I. Groves.'

When he'd finished Mathews sat back, grinning as if he was waiting for a round of applause.

The others present, bar Riggs who was still scribbling on his note pad, waited to see what Reynard would say.

He said nothing; he sniffed, folded his arms and gave the newest recruit to the squad a stern look.

Poor Mathews, confident when reading his notes, was unsettled by the lack of response and sat with his fingers crossed waiting to be demolished.

They all looked at Reynard, sensing an outburst, but his answer surprised them all ... 'Well done Sergeant,' he said, 'better news at last.'

Mathews's relief could be felt all round. 'Thanks,' he said, 'it's my first bit of solo work since joining the squad and I didn't want to make a mess of it.'

'And you haven't ... not so far, but where's the rest of it? Where's your plan, your suggestions for our next move? Maybe D.C Best can tell us ... go on Best ... your turn.'

Best knew Reynard inside out so, with a smile aimed at

Mathews, he didn't waste time repeating what had been said about the first and second interviews, except to point out that they'd provided nothing worth following up. The essential thing that had come out of those interviews, that had been done on the night of the incident involving D.I. Groves, had been that no one had seen anything. As most of those spoken to had either not been on the course at all, or not been on it at the time of the attack, Best reckoned they could strike out them off the list. After all, if they hadn't been there, they couldn't have seen anything.

That idea was too much for Furness, who glared at Best and said; 'Nobody's getting ruled out at this stage; we don't know enough about them. Tomorrow I suggest …'

'What about motive?' Riggs all but shouted.

Reynard was hard put not to laugh when he saw how determined Riggs was to get his view heard. 'Clever at times, that young man can be a menace;' he thought, 'he just has to be involved in every aspect of every case we tackle and, even if his interventions are pertinent, incise, and, to the point; they more often than not upset the others.

'I'm coming to that.' said Best, testily. 'Motive's next on the list. I went through Lucy's desk, as you suggested, hoping to find something D.C. Riggs had missed but, I came across nothing new in her desk diary, her pocket book, or her laptop. The reason for the attack on her remains a mystery. It might be something personal of course, and her personal stuff will all be at her flat. D'you think we ought to have another look round it to see what we can find? I was going to ask you if you thought it'd be alright last night, Guv, but, somehow, I didn't get round to it. Going through a complete stranger's personal effects is one thing; I don't mind doing that. But raking through your mate's stuff in their own home, when they're not there seems, well, bloody intrusive.'

'Intrusive or not, it has to be done.' said Reynard, 'We may find some little, relatively inconsequential, thing, that could lead us to the attacker. So, whether you feel uncomfortable or not that flat has to be searched. I'll go myself once I've spoken to Connie and asked for the loan of a key. You'd better come with me D.I. Furness ... and I'll ask her to be there as well.'

'I'll go with you if you like, Guv.' said Riggs, eager to be involved, as usual. But, when he saw the expression on Reynard's face, he backed off adding 'Yeah ... maybe not.'

Mathews, who'd been silent and contemplative since his report had been belittled a few minutes earlier, suddenly seemed to come to life again. 'I've been thinking, Guv, Mr Dussek told us he couldn't see what the man who threw the golf club looked like, didn't he? And, when we asked him for a description, he said the sunlight had prevented him from seeing any facial details so he wouldn't be able to identify the guy if he saw him again. We didn't press him though, didn't get much of an idea of the man's height or build. I'd like to try talking to Mr Dussek again, maybe he's remembered something by now.'

Reynard pushed his cup forward, and Riggs, chastened by Reynard's refusal to let him go to the flat, filled it.

Ten minutes later the meeting broke up, with Reynard and Furness heading for Connie's to borrow a key and, hopefully, to persuade her to go with them, and with Mathews setting off to find Mr Dussek and the two golfers.

'I'll buy you a pint when we're done.' It was Best who, seeing Riggs look of despondency, decided to help him back to his natural ebullience with the aid of a glass of bitter ale and a ham sandwich. As the two youngest members of Reynard's squad they were natural allies and well used to their share of ups and downs. Most of Best's strength came from his slow and deliberate way of going about his job, a tactic which left him either missing something obvious or unexpectedly coming up with piece of startling evidence everyone else had failed to see. Riggs was quite different; he nearly always, rushed in regardless of the consequences … which quite often turned out not to be in his favour. Balancing his sometimes embarrassingly badly judged 'bull in a china shop' behaviour, with his occasional inspirational guesses, indicated a talent that was yet to be fully developed.

Earlier, in the office, the conversation had mostly been about the attack on Lucy Groves and the fact her flat had not been searched. As a result of these deliberations, Reynard and Mathews were on their way to pick up Connie and then, with her, go and have a look around it. Furness was on the hunt for Mr Dussek and the two golfers, to wring more out of them if he could. Which left the two least experienced members of the team; Best and Riggs, to go to Wyckham House in order to go over some of the statements again and also to try to work out which, if any, of the approaches to the building were in full view from the ground floor windows, a critical bit of information that should have been checked the day before.

It was all a question of access of course, 'How *did* the killer get into the building without being seen and, if *that* was not found to be possible, did anyone actually see him and then deny they'd done so when questioned? Nobody had admitted to having seen anything amiss when interviewed, but what pressure, if any, might have they been under to say this? Why had they not disclosed what they'd seen if they *had* seen something? Finally, the biggest query of all … was one of the people in the house at the time the killer?

The Governor had dealt them a great hand despite their relative inexperience, now it was up to them to play it.

Mr Dussek's House

11.55 a.m

'So, Mr Dussek,' said D.I. Mathews,' thank you for seeing me without notice; I just wanted to check something. You reckoned that, without the sun, you'd have been close enough to see the man clearly, to gauge his build, pick out his features and so on?'

'Probably … yes I think I would.'

'But the sun was behind him?'

'Right behind him.'

'You'd have had pretty good silhouette then?'

'Yes, exactly. I told the other officer last time. Why are you asking me all these questions? I wasn't able to tell him anymore, because I didn't see him properly …what else can I say?'

'Was he tall; a silhouette would show that?'

'Erm … Let's see … standing beside his car … yes I suppose he was, and he was pretty hefty too.'

'Hair … was it long, short, black, grey?'

'He didn't have any … oh, I see what you mean.'

'So he was a tall and hefty and bald. You didn't by any chance take a camera shot of him, did you?'

Dussek didn't answer; he looked down at the ground, clearly to avoid Mathews stare. But Mathews wasn't to be put off; he knew Dussek was trying to avoid a straight answer so, in an effort to encourage a response, asked he him again.

'I tried to,' said Dussek, his face reddening with embarrassment, 'but I didn't want him to see what I was doing, didn't want the metal bits of my phone flashing in the sunlight and alerting him to what I was doing.'

'Have you still got any pictures?'

Dussek nodded, took his phone from his pocket, gave it to Mathews who, on the verge of receiving a valuable bit of evidence, had begun to smile. He might as well have kept a straight face though, because the three pictures were all blurred with only a bit of the man's silhouette showing down in one corner of the frame.

'They're no good, are they? said Dussek. That's why I said nothing.'

Mathews rocked his head from side to side before answering; and then, with a loud laugh, said. 'You'll win no Oscars with these Mr Dussek but, luckily for you, and even more luckily for me, the top of the man's head has the sun beaming on it in one of them … and it's shining like a beacon. I'd buy you a pint if I could, you've made my day.'

Dussek drove off after that, but Mathews, just four hundred yards from the entrance to the golf club, chanced his arm and drove there hoping to find the two golfers were present. They weren't of course; they were more than likely at work, but the Pro said they came in most afternoon for a few holes before going home for their supper and, being a Friday, he was sure they'd turn up within the next half hour.

Mathews looked at his watch … just after five. He decided to wait and, taking the paper cup of coffee the Pro offered him, went out to find a deck chair. Hardly had he taken his first sip when the two men for whom he was waiting came into sight.

He caught them before they got to the Pro's hut, and they agreed to answer his questions. "I won't hold you up long,' he said, 'I just want to know a bit more about the people you saw dog walking out on the course, especially the man with the walking sick; I'm desperate to know what he looked like so I can identify him.'

'We've discussed seeing this guy this a few times,' the man answered, and we even thought of ringing you, but somehow we just didn't get round to it and, anyway, what we had was so flimsy. We couldn't see or can't remember anything about what he was wearing … something pretty indistinctive anyway. As to height and weight; he was about six feet, at a guess, around fourteen or fifteen stone, and bald. There can't have been a hair on his head if the way it was shining in the sun was anything to go by.'

'He was bald? are you sure?'

'I'm sure, we're both sure; we discussed it.'

Mathews offered his hand, which they took as his 'goodbye'. He had what he wanted; a confirmatory description of the man who'd all but killed Lucy Groves.

Now all that was needed, was a name to put on a well - built six footer, who was as bald as a coot.

D. I. Groves's flat in Frensham Terrace

Midday

Connie, having agreed to meet Reynard and Furness at Lucy's flat; had said she'd bring the spare key with her.

They all arrived at the same time and, once parked, Connie unlocked the door and let them into what Reynard later described as being like one of those places featured in Sunday supplements.

'Crikey!' said Furness, genuinely bowled over by what confronted him

Reynard was more circumspect. 'Very nice,' he said.

It wasn't huge, and it didn't have much of a view, but it *was* superb; not a thing out of place and so tidy it seemed more like show piece than a home.

Connie started giggling when she saw the looks of surprise on the faces of the other two, for she hadn't realised they'd not been there before; hadn't cottoned on to the fact her sister kept work and play so entirely separate.

'You like it then?' she stated, rather than asked.'

'Reynard nodded but, as the sight of so much perfection began to sink in, he could feel a sense of sadness coming over him. Beautiful as this flat was, it wasn't a home. It wasn't a place where a visitor might find items lying around, as they'd be in his house … dishes on the draining board, clothes draped on chairs, newspapers in a pile ready to be dumped. It was almost too perfect.

Delving into Groves privacy gave Furness a sense of guilt, but to Reynard it seemed more like betrayal. 'Come on,' he said, 'we'd better get on with it. You take the bedroom, bathroom, and kitchen … I'll have a look in the living room.'

'And I'll make us all a cup of coffee.' Said Connie. 'I've been here loads of times, as you might imagine, but I can't remember ever seeing anything that might be related to the attack on her. And I don't think I've ever seen anything connected to her work, though she hardly ever mentioned that; not to me anyway … so what can it be?'

Both Reynard and Furness had finished their search and found nothing by the time the coffee arrived. Neither had come across a single thing they could associate with the event that had taken place at Crackstone Manor, and were talking about their next move, when Reynard realised the display of artificial flowers, that had caught his eye when they'd first come into the room, was standing on a wooden box to give it extra height.

He got up from the sofa and lifted the bowl off the box.

Straight away he knew what it was - a Victorian table top escritoire - one not unlike a similar piece he remembered in the home of one of his aunts. Typically, it had a hinged lid that was inlaid with dark green leather, and it had corners and locks made of brass. Was this where his second in command kept her private stuff? There was nowhere else.

'Your coffee'll get cold, Superintendent.' Said Connie, have you seen something?'

He nodded. 'the correspondence box under the flowers, the Victorian one, what does your sister keep in it?'

'Oh that old thing … we used it to keep card games and dominoes in it … Happy Families … that sort of thing. I'm not sure where she keeps the key though.'

As Connie was speaking, Reynard put his hand on the box's lid. 'It's open,' he said.' No need for a key.

Inside there was all manner of correspondence, most of which was in one or other of the manilla folders. He could see they bore titles covering most of the key elements of her private life: the top one was marked CURRENT, and the others, lying beneath it, bore their own self-explanatory titles: CAR, BANK, INSURANCE, LEASE, FAMILY, JOB, HOLIDAYS. He put the current one aside and took a quick glance through the others, finding nothing with a connection to the attack.

In the folder marked CURRENT there were invoices for things she must have recently bought, plus a gas bill and a reminder her household insurance premium was due. There was also a letter from a solicitor in Wimbledon that sounded so mysterious he sensed it had something to do with the incident into which they were enquiring. He showed it to Connie, and asked if she knew what it was all about, but she said 'No … Lucy hadn't mentioned it to her.'

Here,' he said, to Furness, handing him the letter, 'Have look at this, and tell me what you think.'

Holland and & Quick
Worple Road, Wimbledon

Dear Ms Groves,

We have been given your name by our associates in Australia who, having traced you with the assistance of Heritage Hunters (UK), have asked us to contact you.

We are not privy to the reason for their unusual request, only that is associated with a bequest of some sort. If you turn out to be the person they are seeking, it could be to your advantage. This is a genuine enquiry, and we are a long established legal practice. Please feel free to check our credentials by any means you wish before you answer.

Yours Faithfully,
Harold E Quick

Once Furness had read it, he photographed it, after

which Reynard put everything back as he'd found it and, thanking Connie for her assistance, they returned to the office. On the way, Furness asked him if Groves's phone had ever turned up. There'd been no sign of it in her pockets when she'd been found, or in her desk when they'd looked there. The tracing app, that was on every official phone, must have been 'down' for it wasn't working. Everyone seemed to be relying on somebody else to find the important instrument but, as so often occurs in circumstances like this, when there is so much going on, the matter had been put to one side and then forgotten. Not by Furness though, he'd been intending to ask around to see if it had turned up for the previous two days but had just never got round to it. 'Now,' he thought, 'might be a good time to start.'

'What's that?' asked Reynard, at the wheel and driving back to their HQ.

'I was wondering if D.I. Groves's phone has turned up yet Guv because, if it hasn't, I've an idea.'

'Go on.'

'Well I've been wondering if the guy who threw the golf club into the trees, didn't throw her phone as well.'

Reynard didn't go as far as to jam on the brakes at Furness's simple question, but he did pull the car into the side of the road rather sharply, and started banging his hands on the steering wheel. 'Idiots, idiots, idiots,' he shouted, 'what a lot of useless bloody fools we are … of course that's where it is … let's go and look for it.'

They didn't find it of course, but, luckily, somebody else had already done so for, only a few hours after the club had been retrieved, two small boys, out rabbiting, had come across it and, on the insistence of their parents, handed it in.

When Reynard got the news of it from Sergeant Hatton at the front desk, he beamed. Maybe at last they were going to get something to work on. His joy was short-lived though, for when he put the phone in a small plastic bag, charged it up and turned it on, nothing happened … the screen was blank.

'Take it up to the canteen and try sticking it in the oven for a bit,' someone suggested. But it was too important to risk doing that, even if the plastic bag didn't melt, so he gave it to a man he knew in forensics, 'a wizard with computers and phones'. Maybe he'd be able to sort it out.

And he did so, and after checking it for finger prints and finding none, Reynard got it back. Fiddling with it for a while, he was surprised to hear Groves's voice. It was on a video recording she'd made for Connie showing a brochure for a Spanish hotel she was suggesting for a holiday.

He went through everything else he could find on the phone but, apart from the video, there was only one thing he thought might be relevant … a text message written four days earlier, addressed to the same law firm she'd heard from. The saved copy of the text, by which she'd replied, said she'd be in touch once she'd had time to think about their interesting letter.

He rang Connie to ask what she knew of it, and if she'd got a letter, but she said 'No' … so he took a chance and rang the solicitors directly. The response he got was predictable; 'they were sorry but, because of a 'confidentiality clause' they could reveal nothing without Ms Groves authorisation. Reynard explained that she was in hospital, but the solicitor wouldn't budge.

At an apparent dead end yet again, Reynard decided it was time for a Grand Forum, a meeting that would necessitate the attendance of every member of the team. He only called for a Grand Forum if the case, or cases, they were working on had ground to a halt. Everyone in the squad had to attend, no matter what. Everyone had to hear, and then discuss, every bit of information collected in relation to the case or cases involved … on this occasion … the attack on D.I. Groves, Mr Townsend's murder, and the Millennium Cars 'steal to order' operation.

Everyone would've been there, even without the reminder D.S. Reynard delivered to each of them by text, late that night.

C.I.D. H.Q.

8.00 a.m.

By the time he arrived they were all sitting, waiting. 'My Goodness,' he said, 'this must be a record!'

The coffee and biscuit precursor they'd been enjoying since around seven thirty, had already got everyone in the right mood, and so it was with an air of great expectation they pulled out their notes and waited for Reynard to begin.

'Gentlemen, for the last three or four days we have been collecting information regarding the three cases we are currently pursuing, and we've been quite successful in building a deal of perspective on each. What we haven't done though, is get our minds around what we've collected, so we can work out what happened to cause the attacks on either Mr Townsend or D.I. Groves … or what Millennium Cars are up to. This morning then, we are going to pool and our information, stir it up, and see if there's a way ahead. … Right?'

All the faces were blank; what the hell was he talking about … wasn't it obvious what they had to do next … assemble the facts, build the stories leading to the incidents, identify the guilty persons involved, and lock 'em up?

'Let's take the attack on D.I. Groves first,' said Reynard, 'we don't know much do we? Only that …'

Furness, speaking on behalf of them all, if the expressions their faces was anything to go by, butted in. Surely, we know about this incident, Guv? We have the weapon, we know what the attacker looks like, and with such a good description of him it'll only be a matter of time before we nab him.'

Reynard rocked his head from side to side, to signify his doubt … and then he said. 'So what about motive? If we don't establish one, we'll never really know what prompted the attack, and if we don't know what moved him to do it, how do we know he won't do it again … not to D.I. Groves obviously, but to some other totally innocent person. Discovering why this villain committed either crime is just as important as discovering who he is. In fact, I'll go farther than that; one might lead to the other, knowing why he did it might guide us straight to the perpetrator.'

Riggs was about to leap in, as usual, but at the last minute he changed his mind and kept quiet. Best was also inclined to question Reynard's thinking, but daren't. It was Mathews in the end who spoke up. 'O.K. Guv, you clearly have some plan in mind … what is it?'

The smile he got in return was reward enough, so much so, he nearly missed Reynard's next few words.

'I thought I knew D.I. Groves as well as anyone else. I

brought her into the squad five or six years ago and we've worked together in total harmony since day one. We must have spent hours and hours together in this very room and we've driven thousands of miles sitting side by side as we went about our business. Never once did she say anything to me that led me to think she had worries of any sort. Yet ... yet ... when I went to her flat yesterday, and for the first time saw how she lives, I was extremely surprised. D.I. Furness will agree with me I'm sure, that flat we went to was an eyeopener, a pristine over tidied residence that looked as though it was not being lived in. It is being lived in, of course, and by D.I. Groves, as her sister Connie confirmed.

'So ... what's wrong with being tidy, Guv?' asked Best, 'My place is totally disorganised because I like it that way.'

Reynard nodded 'it wasn't the tidiness that puzzled me, though that *was* a bit unusual ... not like any of your places or mine. No, it was the fact I've never been inside before, not that she'd ever refused me entry, no, it was more that inviting me in has never cropped up. The upshot of this surprise side of her nature has led me to believe the attack on her might just as likely to have arisen because of something we don't know about her in her private life. Maybe I'm barking up the wrong tree. Have any of you ever been in D.I. Groves's flat?'

His question brought no response; it was clear Groves had successfully preserved her privacy even from her closest friends and workmates. But why?

Riggs, of course, had the answer. 'She's hiding from something that happened in the past, I reckon.' he said, 'But then again, she's hot on the trail of the Murphys so maybe tidiness has nothing to do with it, maybe it's them attempting to shut her up that brought her injuries.'

Everyone spoke at once then and, when everything had quietened down again, Reynard set them all off when he told them about the letter, and the suggestion contained in it that she might be about to receive a bequest from an unknown person.

'A bribe?' asked Mathews. 'Something to buy her silence regarding something she knew … about Millennium Cars for example.'

'If it is,' answered Reynard, 'she either refused it, or she never took it. 'Anyway, it was being handled by a solicitor, which is not how the Murphys work. The idea of a bribe or inducement coming seems unlikely anyway so, as far as this investigation goes, and, until we can ask D.I. Groves personally, let's leave Millennium Cars and the Murphy family until we know more.

In the meantime, ask around to see if the description of the attacker we've got, a big bald man, is known to any of your contacts.

One other thing before we move on … I see there's a text on my phone from Sergeant Hawkins of S.O.C.O. saying the forensic boys think the part print on the golf club is too small to make any worthwhile pronouncement regarding its ownership. Another similar part of one might confirm its probable ownership and help you to find him/her ... but half prints, on their own, won't stand up in court as a means of positive identification.'

'We've not got far, have we?' said Best. 'a half print that's useless, a nice clean flat ... and a description that'd fit half the men in Brighton. Where do we go next, Guv?'

'For the moment ... only as far as Mr Townsend. And, unless I've been reading your reports wrongly, we haven't got far with our enquiry into his misfortune either. You've all read the reports of interviews, and talked to your share of the people who might be involved - residents, staff, etc. And you've all seen round the place especially Mr Townsend's room. So, what do you think? What's caught your eye? Be ready to speak up when your turn comes ... alright?'

'Alright.' They echoed.

'Fine ... I'll go first again. This death's a murder; stabbed in his chest with a deer's foot paper knife could hardly be an accident, so what else ...?'

'Excuse me Guv,' It was Best. 'it wasn't a deer's foot; it was a goat's foot. My uncle brought one like it back from South Africa a few years ago. He got it in a street bazaar in village in near Durban ... it's amazing what you can ....'

'Did he?' said Reynard, all but silenced by Best's thoughtless interruption 'Very interesting ... but not relevant.'

'I know.' said Best, continuing to dig a hole for himself

… 'everyone thinks those knife handles come from deer or antelopes but they don't. Goat meat's very popular in South Africa you know, and it's cheap … according to my uncle.'

Reynard, almost beside himself with rage at the irrelevance of Best's comment, suggested he might bring his uncle in one day to give them a talk on the subject. 'But not now Constable, please … we've a murderer to find first.'

Everyone, except Reynard and Best, was grinning by then, but they got back to Mr Townsend's death in a hurry when Reynard slapped the table with his hand.

'In the real world,' he began, 'It is obvious to me that most of the people we've spoken to, be they residents or staff, actually knew very little about Mr Townsend and never had occasion to say much more than good morning or good afternoon to him. In fact, he was a loner, a solitary man who neither had, nor apparently needed, friends. An unmarried man, an ex-headmaster who, I was told, seemed happy enough living in comfort at Wyckham House, alongside Mr Rueben Platz, his only friend.

He'd been resident in Wyckham House for a long time, Mr Townsend, in fact he'd been there longer than anyone else and, of those interviewed, most agreed he'd been grumpy and rude. Such an attitude,' Reynard suggested, 'is often used as a defence by people who are actually reticent. It is my belief that, though I never met the man personally, his being so withdrawn was no more than his secretive nature taking charge. Mr Platz virtually confirmed this when I was talking to him yesterday. Doctor Neilson confirmed as much too i.e. that, in her view, Mr Townsend was simply a person who didn't need anyone else.

None of the people I spoke to could provide an explanation for his murder, and I was left with the distinct impression his killer entered his room without going through the house or passing any of the windows in rooms with people in them. The kitchen's different, being at the back of the building, its windows face the fire escape steps, the ones down which he probably escaped. Fingerprints found on a garden vase standing on the fire escape indicate he'd pushed it to one side when he raced along the fire escape and descended the steps I've just mentioned. Also, I think it's possible, and D.I. Furness agrees with me, the killer probably *entered* the building by the same route i.e. by going up the fire escape and walking into Mr Townsend's room through his French doors. What d'you say … come on speak up?'

Nobody said anything so, aware the men in front of him had lost their concentration and were beginning to drift, Reynard switched to questioning them.

'Everyone O.K. with what I've said so far?'

Best answered. 'No Guv,' he said, 'we might know what sort of a guy Mr Townsend was; and we might know how his killer got in and out … but we've no idea *who* he is.'

'Precisely, said Reynard, 'so let's find out.'

Best shook his head, 'I'm damned if I can see how we're

going to do that; we've no sightings, and there was nothing found that he might have left behind or discarded as he left.'

Reynard shrugged his shoulders, raised his eyebrows, and glanced round the room, stopping at the team's latest recruit. 'You haven't said much lately, D.I. Mathews … what do you think?'

'I think we're rushing backwards and forwards too much, Guv. We're darting here and there, madly hunting for clues, instead of working out what we need to know, and then going out and finding it.'

The surprise answer might have annoyed Reynard; for anyone could see it was a criticism of the way they were tackling the investigations. But what Mathews had said didn't upset Foxy at all; he was far too experienced not to see the man was right. They *were* rushing backwards and forwards and they *were* getting nowhere fast. 'Fair enough,' he said, 'so what do you suggest?'

Furness and Best couldn't believe their ears when they saw Reynard capitulating, but Riggs, eyes glazed, and away in a mindset of his own, continued to remain expressionless.

The years Mathews had spent in the 'C.I.D. back office', manipulating senior officers to his point of view must have taught him a trick or two though, his suggestion of a new approach by coming at their problems from a new angle, for instance, was one of the methods he'd used, perhaps unconsciously, for years. There was no malice in his comment, and he hadn't actually seen or meant it as criticism; it was just a suggestion as far as he was concerned. But it had struck home with the one man who could take an opposing point of view and use to his advantage ... Detective Superintendent 'Foxy' Reynard, who simply said 'O.K. Inspector, go ahead.'

'Thanks Guv, I suggest we concentrate on the Townsend murder for the moment and leave Millennium Cars out of it; they won't go away, and D.I. Groves, assuming she's still in a coma, is safe enough where she is for the next few days. If we all concentrate solely on the killing at Wyckham House ... we might get a result.'

Reynard looked at Mathews with new eyes; this guy who'd only been slotted onto the team to make up the numbers, had a brain ... and brains need encouragement. 'Yes, I agree, you've a point D.I. Mathews,' he said, 'a good point ... and I hope I'm not too proud to take it on board. We'll do as you say, concentrate our efforts on the Townsend killing, get out into the field, stir things up a bit, and see what happens. Except for me that is; I'll mostly stay here and keep 'the brass' and the press at bay. Now, as to specifics ...'

The meeting finished mid-morning, by which time Reynard had informed D.C.S. Bradshaw about the new approach, issued a press statement saying progress with regard to the murder was being made, and called the hospital to be told there had been a slight setback to the planned withdrawal of Groves from the coma they'd been keeping her in, and that her situation would continue to be reviewed daily.

Furness and Best, the two longest serving member of Foxy's team, who always worked well alongside each other, went back to Wyckham House for a second talk with Susie Knight, Rueben Platz, and the ladies whose rooms abutted, or were opposite to, Mr Townsend's: Marianne Rudd, Betty Forward and Hilda Goulding.

Mathews and Riggs were put together hopefully to confirm the route, in and out of Wyckham House, the murderer had taken, and to re-interview Doctor Neilson and the two young Kurdish domestics who, Reynard was convinced, were hiding something.

Everything had taken on a new momentum. Now all they needed was luck.

The staff room at Wyckham House

12.50 p.m.

The interviews with the three ladies with rooms adjacent to Mr Townsend's were finished. Nothing new had emerged, no information over and above that already secured during their first interview had been presented, and the fresh air of enthusiasm, launched at the meeting earlier in the morning, was showing signs of wilting. Summing up the three additional reports, Best reckoned Mrs Goulding had heard nothing during the afternoon that was different to normal, i.e. the faint hum of traffic, the distant noise of a radio or television, and the occasional sound of a door opening or closing.

Mrs Forward's memory of the period was much the same as that of Mrs Rudd, though she said that, on reflection, she might also have heard voices raised some time after she'd got back to her room after lunch.

Furness was onto her like a flash; here was something new that might well be connected to Mr Townsend's death. But, despite close questioning, all Mrs Rudd was able tell them was that, while she didn't recognise either of the voices, and couldn't make out what was being said, she was sure it wasn't long after she'd got back to her room after lunch.

When asked why she hadn't mentioned this at her previous interview, she said she hadn't heard what was being said and didn't want to get too deeply involved.

'You can understand it though can't you Dessie,' said Best, 'she was scared she'd be next if she let on she'd heard something.'

Furness gave him non-committal grunt. 'Silly old bat! If they're all holding back, we'll get nowhere. Think of it … she said she heard the voices after she'd got back to her room following lunch. That'd be around half one … didn't someone else; Mrs Forward, I think, say she and Mr Townsend had gone upstairs to their rooms together. She also said she'd asked him into her room to watch a video clip her daughter had sent from America, but he'd said 'No'. Maybe the killer was already in Townsend's room, maybe he was a housebreaker, a thief, taking advantage of everyone being occupied with their lunch and got caught by surprise when Mr T turned up earlier than expected.'

'Come on,' said Best, 'you're letting your imagination run away with you, you're building a picture like a pyramid that's upside down; you've a tiny little bit of evidence supporting a bloody great big speculation. No, let's stick to the facts … let's find out what this Forward woman has to say, see if she heard the voices as well.'

But Betty Forward said she'd hardly heard the voices when they asked her, and couldn't tell them whether they were those of men or women. Satisfied she had no more to give them, they then spoke to Mr Platz. He had nothing to add to what he'd said before either ... that he hadn't heard a thing. But when they pressed him, he said he did remember Mr Townsend coughing. 'It's the walls you see, the outside ones are concrete or brick and you wouldn't hear an army tank moving through them. But the interior walls aren't much more than partitions and, if you're that way inclined, he said with a wink, you can hear quite a lot through them. Not that much ever came through from Everett's side except his coughing, especially at night. I've complained to Dr Neilson time and time again but she does nothing.'

'And on the day Mr Townsend was attacked?'

'He was coughing for ages that afternoon, and louder than usual. I like a nap after my lunch, you see, but I couldn't get to sleep with his cough, cough, cough. I got up in the end, to listen to the News headlines at three, and he was still coughing then. I should have mentioned it before, I suppose, but I didn't think it important.'

'And it may not be Mr Platz, on the other hand it at least tells us he was alive at three so he must have been attacked between then and five thirty when he was discovered. That narrows it down a bit, so thank you. If you remember anything else, call us. And, one final thing, just for clarification, your room's on one side of Mr Townsend's … who's on the other?'

'Oh.' Said Platz, 'That'd be Mrs Goulding, but she won't be much help; she's as deaf as a post. Betty Forward's opposite mind you; she might have heard something.'

'We spoke to her; and she said she'd heard voices.'

'Did she? … I'm not surprised; she always seeing things and hearing things … she's batty.'

The conversation dried up when they realised they were in danger of being caught up in an 'in-house' squabble and soon, having made their way to the kitchen, they were talking to the Kurdish girls. Furness had suggested they ought to be seen there; a place where they'd be surrounded by familiar things, in the hope they'd feel less intimidated than if they'd been brought to the office. That it had been a good idea to do so quickly became evident as the girls, more assured, and much more relaxed than before, began to open up. They loved their jobs they said, in badly fragmented English, jobs that made their long and wearisome trek across Europe, three years earlier, worthwhile.

'You got lucky when you wound up here.' Said Best. But his accent had clearly defeated them. Fortunately, he cottoned onto the reason for the blank look they had on their faces, and he reduced his rate of talking so they could make him out.

Playing them as fishermen play fishes, Furness, and especially Best, began to see they were getting through. Ten minutes, a cup of milky coffee and an exchange of names later,

Furness reckoned he might risk putting a few more pertinent questions to them. 'So you were worried we might be from immigration eh? That you might be in trouble because you'd no proper work permit. Well we're not that lot, we're policemen, and we're only here because of Mr Townsend's death.'

The older of the two girls, Citra Kamin, who seemed to have quite a good command of English if it was spoken slowly, and if simple words were being used, said they knew this now, as Doctor Neilson had told them. She also said their visas were current, that the doctor had obtained short term ones for them, and she offered to get them from their room in the attic if he wanted to see them. But Furness said 'No', that wasn't necessary as Doctor Neilson had already shown him photocopies. With that tricky issue out of the way, and with Furness becoming aware of some sort of bridge building between them, he decided to risk moving onto the real reason for his visit, i.e. to determine whether either girl had seen anything usual on the afternoon Mr Townsend was murdered.

'You see,' said Best, pointing behind them, 'none of the windows other than these in the back of the house, whether they're upstairs or downstairs, have a view down the garden to Rodean Close, which is the route we think the man who killed Mr Townsend used to come in and go out.'

Citra, who, a minute earlier, had seemed confident and reassured, blanched, while Kemala, the younger, shyer girl, hung her head to avoid eye contact, and began to shake.

Do we have two guilty people here? Best wondered, 'two kids who are frightened out of their wits by something or someone they saw that afternoon. Had they spotted someone through the kitchen window, someone who'd have been invisible to anyone else looking out of any other window in the house. And, equally important, had that glimpse of whoever it was running down the garden, been between three and five thirty?

Furness could almost see Best's thought processes working and he decided to slow him down. 'Any chance of another one?' he asked draining the last of his coffee and handing Citra the mug.

She didn't answer him, but she did take the mug and walk over to the percolator.

'Are those the fire escape steps?' Best asked, standing at the sink, tapping the edge of it with his fingertips and looking out of the window. 'The ones he came flying down?'

Before she could stop herself, Citra said 'Yes.'

Grinning at his reflection in the window glass, and half expecting her answer, Best now knew what he'd suspected from the beginning, and he stopped tapping the edge of the sink and gripped it instead. And then … he slowly turned round to face the other girl, Kemala, who seemed to be on the brink of tears. 'And did *you* see him as well?' he asked.

He got no answer … she'd run from the room.

Citra glared at him 'You bloody big bugger.' She said,

racing after her friend.

Furness all but collapsed he was laughing so much. Of all the reactions Best words might have provoked, what she'd come out with was likely to stay in his mind forever.

Best was amused too, but he tried not to show it and, when the girls came back a few minutes later, he was almost inclined to put his arms round them.

'We did see a man' said Citra, 'he came down the steps very fast and ran to the lane at the back.'

'A big man?' asked Furness.

'Bigger than me … bigger than you.'

'What was he wearing?'

'She shook her head, 'I can't remember.'

'What was the colour of his hair?'

'I couldn't tell … he had a light blue woolly hat on.'

'Now Citra, and think carefully before you answer. Have you ever seen this man before?'

'No, I have not seen him before … No.'

Prior to leaving, Best walked down the garden to a small gate, partially hidden by overgrown shrubbery. When he turned round, he could see how well the killer had chosen his entrance and exit routes; there were only two places where he might have been spotted: on the fire escape or on the stretch across the lawn.

Furness had been having a few last words with Doctor Neilson while Best was in the garden and, in response to her asking, he'd told her what D.S. Reynard had asked him to say … that she should leave the room untouched and locked until further notice in case an additional search was required, and that she should not let the key out of her possession other than to a police officer. She didn't like it, but she agreed.

Reynard's Office at CID HQ

2.15 pm

Lunch in the canteen was over by the time they got back, so Furness and Best grabbed a sandwich and a paper beaker of tea from the dispenser and went back to Furness's desk to write up their morning's work. By two thirty they'd been finished, with everything ready to present to the others at the next meeting, which, they expected would be some time later that day.

'Now what?' Asked Best.

'Those girls still know more that they're letting on, I reckon we need to find a way of shaking their tree a bit, and see what falls down.'

'Governor won't like that,' said Best. Bullying a witness'll get right up his nose.'

'So ... let's not tell him. What he don't know he can't cry over. I learned that a long time ago.'

'There might be another way.'

'There might be another Christmas. Alright what are you

suggesting, short of torture of course.'

'Follow the two girls, find out where they go after they've finished work. Try to discover who their pals are.'

'You mean check to see if they go to meet the guy they saw running from Wyckham Manor. That'd be stretching it a bit, but you're right in one sense … they definitely know more than they're letting on. Where'd they come from again?'

'Turkey, the area the Kurds live in. Doctor Neilson told me they were refugees in their own country … whatever she meant by that.'

'Well they're refugees here now as well, but I'm not so sure we're what they were hoping for.'

As they'd been talking, they'd moved from Furness's desk to the white Incident Board at the back of the room and Furness, a black marker in his hand, had printed the victim's name at the top of it. Below it he'd listed the names of the people who, it had been agreed, seemed to have the closest or most recent contact with him. Heading the list was Doctor Neilson; below her were Susie Knight, Mr Platz, Mrs Forward, Citra Kamin, Kemala Bhutto … and A.N. Other, the man who'd been seen on the fire escape steps and the most likely to be the guy they were after.

'Are you sure about all this lot?' asked Best.

'What d'you mean 'sure'.'

'Well not all of them are actual suspects, are they? I

mean there'd really only be one name at this stage if we're trying to show suspects … and that'd be that of the mystery man on the fire escape. Let's start eliminating as many of the others as we can once we're know they're definitely not directly implicated.

'O.K. Well, take the doctor for example … she was in her office all afternoon and plenty of people said they'd seen her there. And, though she's no motive we could find, it's possible she might have gone up to Mr Townsend's room and stabbed him while everyone else was in the dining room. Even so, I think we should leave her in for the moment.'

'O.K and we should leave the two Kurdish girls in as well. We don't know half enough about them yet.'

'Yeah, but I reckon we can drop all the others except the man on the fire escape and ….'

'So we're back to him and the girls and the doctor, in other words.'

Furness took the board wiper and removed all the names he'd just put up except the those of the Kurdish girls, the doctor, and the 'fire escape man' - the guy with no name - who Furness had decided to represent with a large question mark.

'We didn't get far did we Dessie?' Said Best. 'Wasted afternoon; the Governor won't be pleased.'

'Look, mate, we got confirmation there was a man on the fire escape, and that he probably entered and left the crime scene through Mr Townsend's French doors. The girls confirmed that was likely when they admitted to seeing him as he came down the steps and ran up the garden. On that basis we can rule out any involvement by other residents. We're only chasing one rabbit and that's good; this morning we didn't even know for sure how many rabbits there were.'

'O.K. so we've narrowed it down a bit. What next.'

'If it was for me to decide, I'd go and shake that tree I was talking about, but it's not me … the man who makes those decisions is standing right behind you. Good afternoon, Guv.'

Best swung round. 'Ah boss,' it's you. he said …'What d'you think … should we have another go at the girls or not?'

'We'll wait until D.I. Mathews and D.C. Riggs join us before making up our minds about that. O.K?'

Even as Reynard spoke, Mathews and Riggs came into sight, and soon the team was settling in Reynard's office watching Riggs doing his duty at the coffee machine.

Furness, at a nod from Reynard, started; and he quickly up-dated the others regarding the findings he and Best had made together with their conclusion that no one in the Wyckham House was directly involved in Mr Townsend's death but that the two domestics, Citra Kamin and Kemala Bhutto, might have been in an indirect way. Their belief this possibility might turn out to be the truth, and their conclusion that the girls' stories ought to be more fully probed, brought nods from Riggs and Mathews, but Reynard remained unmoved.

When Furness saw this, he was surprised and came to a

standstill, thinking Reynard was disapproving of his suggestion. But he needn't have worried, Reynard was only playing tricks by purposefully unsettling everyone. What he was really doing was ensuring the whole squad would be working in unison. It was essential, he reckoned, that to get a result, a concerted effort by all of them working as one was needed, not a maverick pursuit of something Riggs had dreamed up, for he was prone to that; flying off on a mad chase of his own and leaving everyone else wondering what the hell was going on. This investigation would only make progress if they stuck together, Reynard reckoned, and, satisfied he'd made his point without uttering a word, he asked Furness what he was actually proposing to do but, before he could begin to answer, Riggs was at it again, butting in and trying to steal the limelight.

Reynard shut him up promptly, and waved Furness to carry on; which he did by suggesting the Kurdish girls should be followed to see who they met.

With that settled and with Furness and Best authorised to keep probing at Wickham House, the meeting turned to Mathews and Riggs's report of their findings around the outside of the house, and in its garden.

Mathews started off by saying they'd walked all around the exterior of the house and found, as expected, the only way a person could approach or leave it unseen from ground level, was to ensure they kept well within wedge shaped area visible from the kitchen window. Upstairs, the area out of sight was slightly smaller, not that it mattered on the day Mr Townsend was killed, because there was no one up there at meal times.

The timing of the killer's movements, when he left, needed to be precise, and they had to be completed during the half hour to forty minutes the residents were having their tea. If he'd got in while they were at lunch, he'd know he daren't risk leaving until teatime, suggesting the voices Mrs Goulding heard may have been an argument that eventually led to the stabbing. Having killed his victim, the killer must have then waited half an hour to be sure the residents all were downstairs in the dining room, for it was only when they were tucking in, that he'd dare to risk leaving.

Riggs, who'd kept strangely quiet while Mathews was explaining their mornings work, suddenly seemed to wake up at that point and, when Mathews paused, he stepped in.

'I think it was just bad luck for the killer that he was seen, irrespective of whether the girls recognised him or not. If they did, they may somehow be further involved, so it might be that what D.I. Furness and D.C. Best have suggested regarding following them, will sort that out. I think they should do it if they see the opportunity.'

Reynard's eyebrow shot up. 'Oh … right! So you're the one who decides what should be done now, are you?'

Riggs, in full flow, didn't hear his governor's comment, and carried on. 'As to the escape; once out of the garden I reckon the man must have run into Rodean Close. We did the same and, when we went out there, we had some luck. A man, who was cutting his hedge, told us a car had been parked outside his house for the best part of two hours the day of the murder, partially blocking his gate. He'd hung about in his front garden with the intention of remonstrating with the driver when he returned for his car. But his wife had called him in for phone call and, when he went out again, the car had gone. He hadn't associated what he called this 'little annoyance', with the police presence he later heard was seen at Wyckham House, and had no idea a murder had taken place. When we pressed him, he said the car was a black 2013 Toyota Camry and that, while he hadn't taken its number, he'd noticed the final three letters on the plate were the same his own initials - CTV.'

Looking pleased with himself, Riggs ended his talk by saying 'I reckon we did quite well Guv … what d'you think?'

'Yes … you all did.' Reynard replied, but, before he got a chance to add an appropriate qualification, Riggs was off again. 'And that wasn't the only thing we got Guv, not by long chalk … we found this.' As he was speaking, he pulled a piece of paper from his pocket and gave it to Reynard, who took it and, turning to Mathews, asked him if he was 'in on this as well.'

'It's not trick Guv, but I think you'll find it *is* a surprise. Why not let Wonder Cop explain; it was his idea that produced it, and it might bring a new dimension to our case.'

At soon as he said 'Wonder Cop', Furness and Best burst out laughing; even Reynard began to grin. Riggs didn't seem to mind either, it was as if it hadn't registered that Mathews was 'taking the Mickey', and he started grinning too.

'So where did this come from?' asked Reynard, having quickly cast his eye over what was clearly a letter, in his hand.

Riggs had an answer ready; obviously he'd rehearsed what he was going to say so it had more drama. 'I knew we were missing something from the first day I went there, Guv. The shock of seeing Mr Townsend stretched out dead, and covered in blood, must have skewed my thinking, but late that night, when I got home, I realised what was wrong ... there was no old paperwork anywhere; no letters, no bills, no reminders or sales literature ... nothing before the current month stuff in the file we found under his chair. Now being tidy's understandable, but so tidy there was nothing to see ... no ... I couldn't believe that. A man like Mr Townsend, an educated man, a school teacher, could never go through life without accruing a great deal of paperwork. Even if he dumped most of it when he moved to Wyckham House he'd have got a whole lot more since ... like you and I do. So, apart from the current stuff where's the rest? I decided not to say anything about this to anyone until I'd checked again, which I did, with the help of D.I. Mathews, this morning. When we'd finished gathering what we needed to work out how the killer got in and out, I got the key you'd left with Doctor Neilson and went to check the room again ... and I ... 'er we ... spent an age before giving up, and we'd found nothing other than the file of current paperwork we'd already seen under his chair. When I mentioned this to the doctor, as I gave her the key back, she suddenly clapped her hand to her mouth, and I realised straight off she'd forgotten something she ought to have told us.

I was right too; a two car garage built at the side of the main building in the style of a coach house, has been cleared out and is now used by residents to store things they haven't space for in their rooms; things with which they can't bear to part. Mr Townsend, she told me, had a few large suitcases, half a dozen cardboard boxes and a filing cabinet stored in there, and she came with us to point them out.

The boxes were full of stuff from his teaching days, the cases were packed with clothes and bed linen, while the filing cabinet, a three drawer one, had old photographs in its bottom drawer, back copies of The National Geographic Magazine in its middle drawer, and file after file of paperwork, up to five years old in some cases, in the top one.

In one of the files I found what appeared to be a number of letters and photocopies of letters, all obviously part of some correspondence he's been having with a firm of solicitors in Wimbledon at the beginning of this year. I have them here; perhaps you'd like to look at them and tell me what you think.'

'Fair enough.' Reynard answered, 'But I'll read all three out so everyone can hear. The first's addressed to Holland and Quick a family law practice in Wimbledon. It says …

Dear Mr Quick,

I write in response to your telephone call two days ago, asking me to permit you to submit my current address to an Australian law firm also specialising in tracing bloodlines (an issue that often crops up where intestacy is involved, I believe) and I reply as follows. Provided you let me know who is making the request, and if you guarantee strict confidentiality regarding the whole issue, I am happy to confirm I live at the above address, which is my permanent home.

Yours faithfully,
Everett Townsend

The second letter is from an Australian law firm, clearly the one to which Mr Townsend referred in his letter. It's called Parsons and Ogelvie and it's signed by one of the partners - Gareth Parsons.

Dear Mr Townsend,

Firstly, let me thank you for allowing our associates in Wimbledon to forward your address to us.

We are dealing with the preparation of a new will for one of our long standing clients and it is just possible you may turn out to be one of the beneficiaries.

I realise this letter will raise queries in your mind but, I'm afraid, as I have undertaken to conceal both our client's identity and the reason for his benevolence, I am not in a position to provide any explanations other than to say the gift, should you qualify to receive one, will be our client's way of 'making amends'.

As the gifts may be of considerable value, I am sure you will understand that positive identification of potential beneficiaries is necessary. To this end, our client has insisted a DNA test be undertaken by all aspiring beneficiaries.

Would you be prepared to undergo such a test? If you are, send an email to us and we will arrange for a testing kit to be posted out to you. On receipt, do the test according to the instructions and return everything back to us. Should we not hear from you within three months from today, we will assume you do not wish to proceed.

Yours Faithfully,

Gareth Parsons

Solicitor

As Reynard finished reading, he raised his eyes and looked at his colleagues; every face had astonishment written on it. 'That letter's going to give us something to think about, isn't it?' he said, putting it down and picking up the next one, which was short. 'It just says the package has arrived safely, and that once the all the potential beneficiaries' results have arrived, they'll be sent out to a laboratory to be checked against a master. And that those exhibiting sufficiently close similarity to the master will be included in the will. Those who don't, won't.' He finishes by saying the results ought to be available in a month, and that those under consideration for inclusion will be informed of them.'

'So, what d'you make of it, Guv.' Riggs asked. 'Pretty astonishing stuff.'

'You can say that again,' added Best, who was still struggling to take it all in. 'It doesn't sound real to me.'

Reynard turned to Furness. 'Your turn. Inspector, and say something a bit more constructive if you can.'

'It's a family split isn't it?' Furness answered, 'One that took place years ago. There must be thousands like it but not with the same end result. I reckon it's going to be Mr Townsend's brother … or maybe even his sister, who shot off to Oz all those years back and upset everyone. Now, with his, or her, conscience pricking, he, or she, is planning to leave Mr T and a few others a load of dosh as a sort of apology.'

As Furness sat back, a satisfied grin on his face, all eyes turned to Riggs; usually the first to jump in, he was now going to be the last. What was troubling him?

Reynard raised his eyebrows and leaning forward almost challengingly whispered 'Yes … Constable?'

'No Guv, let D.I Mathews go next I'm still thinking.'

'Thank God someone is.' Said Reynard pointing to Mathews who asked if he could read the letters again before giving his view.

'O.K.' said Reynard, 'let's have another coffee, and then we'll go back and hear what D.C. Riggs has to say. When he's done, I'd like D.I. Mathews to wind up this session by summarising our discussions.'

The others turned to Riggs, who'd passed on the coffee, hoping to be entertained when he came up with his answer. Mathews was grinning openly in anticipation of it, but Riggs, ignoring, or maybe not even noticing, the looks that were coming in his direction, took a deep breath and began. 'I agree … it *does* look as though it's Mr T's brother … or sister … is the benefactor. And, being his brother is more likely, I reckon, than being his sister. Men often make a mess of things and then run away from them; women don't seem to, though I can't say why. So, yes, I go for the man in Australia also being called Townsend.

Doctor Neilson must have some details of 'our' Mr Townsend and, if we take what we know to the Births and Deaths Registry, we might find out quite a lot about the Townsend family including the first names of his parents and siblings. We can then check the census records and see who went missing or died. One of the missing ones, I reckon, will be Mr Townsend's brother and, by using our contacts within the Australian Police Force, we ought to find him and tell him what's happened.

After that, if we can zero down to the period when the brother emigrated, and match that to where 'our' Mr Townsend was living at the time, we might uncover the issue that set them apart. Mind you …' said Riggs, hesitating when he realised he'd drifted from the real issue by shooting down a side track that might relate to Mr Townsend's inheritance but had little to do with his death.'

'Yes, go on, Constable,' said Reynard, who'd spotted the error and was curious to see how Riggs would get out of it.

'The main thing for us of course,' said Riggs, who'd obviously read Reynard's thoughts, 'is nailing the murderer. We've plenty of other clues we've collected … now it's up to us to put them together and see what sort of a picture we get. Regarding Mr Townsend, we've finger prints on the pots and the fire escape handrail, we've sightings by the Kurdish girls in Wyckham House, we've the man who lives in Rodean Close, and we've a few numbers on the chief suspect's car number plate. As to the attack on D.I. Groves, we have the putter with which she was struck, and we've her mobile telephone on the SIM card of which Forensic have just rung to say they're looking for prints. And, of course, we've Mr Dussek's evidence and that of the two golfers

Most important of all we have her two sisters who are privy to D.I. Groves's very unusual personal life, particularly during her early years. Surely there's a common line somewhere. Yes of course there is … both victims appear to have been in touch with the same Aussie solicitor regarding what look like similar inheritance issues. D.I. Groves was hardly attacked by

Mr Townsend, and she definitely didn't kill him. We're looking for third party. No doubt whatsoever … a third party who might have wanted the other two parties out of the way.'

'It's going to be a late night,' said Reynard, 'put the percolator on again while I update D.C.S. Bradshaw. We don't want him breathing down our necks until we have something to worthwhile to say. When I come back, we'll have to set about re-thinking our whole position and re-organise ourselves to meet the challenges that've just been identified.'

As soon as Reynard left, heading for D.C.S. Bradshaw, the others began to postulate. With everyone talking at once, they raised so much noise D.I. Crowther, in the next office, not only got to shut them up, he banged his fist on the window between them so hard, he nearly broke the glass.

The investigations had really not been going anywhere up until then; but finally, it seemed, a brighter side was appearing. 'Think of it,' Riggs said, 'this new information has given us a motive for *both* incidents, a motive that might be money driven … a possible unexpected bonanza for Lucy and Mr Townsend, that has somehow gone wrong.'

'He's right.' Mathews said, 'We've been stuck for a motive in both cases, now we have one that they both seem to have.'

'So what do we do next?' asked Best.

Mathews held up a hand to get everyone's attention and then carried on. 'We must calm down, and check through our reports, again noting where there are connections we didn't spot earlier. We have to marshal the facts we've got, and work out what's missing.'

'Bang on, you have it in one.' Said Reynard, slipping into the vernacular as he came back into the room. 'It's just a big jigsaw puzzle with loads of bits we have to fit together.'

Mathews smacked his thigh with his hand. 'You're right, Guv. The new data in these letters D.C. Riggs has unearthed is another piece from the jigsaw; now it's up to us to put 'em together. What d'you say? He asked, turning to Riggs.'

Riggs hesitated a moment, and then it all came out. 'What I say,' he said, 'is that you're a bunch of hypocrites.'

The response was so unexpected, and so untypical, it had to be questioned, and Reynard took it on himself to do it. 'What's eating you, Constable?' he asked.

'What's eating me, Guv, is that whenever I come up with an idea you criticise me for rushing headlong into it. Time and time again you ridicule me for jumping in without looking. And now, here's you lot all mad to chase up this solicitor chap so you can to find the guy who gave the bricks to the man who lives in the house that Jack built. That good enough for you?'

'Blimey,' said Best, but nobody else uttered a word and it took several minutes for a more normal atmosphere to emerge.

'So.' said Reynard, who had wisely kept his mouth shut until then. 'Where do you suggest we go from here.'

Furness, the next most senior in the team after Reynard,

and the second in command of it, answered him. 'We start again with the things we know are factually correct and see where they take us. Get every damned thing we know to be true down, and try fitting the various elements together. And I think we might leave it until the morning as well … so we can get a fresh start.'

Everyone was feeling uncomfortable and tired so there was no dissention to the suggestion and, by five thirty they'd all gone except Reynard who, with a fresh mug of coffee in his hand and his chair tipped back, was reviewing the curious end to the day and Riggs part in it Was he as suitable for future promotion, as he'd previously thought. That he had an amazing instinct for seeing truths others missed was undeniable … which might make him a good detective … but what sort of a man manager would he make if he kept shooting off at tangents on his own?

'Ah well,' he thought, as he reached into a drawer for a chocolate Hobnob biscuit, 'it won't be my problem.'

DAY FIVE

Reynard's Office at CID HQ

8.10.a.m.

Riggs was already there when Reynard arrived, and he greeted his boss with a smile. He'd been in since seven and, together with Mathews and Best, who'd also got in early, he was noting down all they'd found about the attack and the murder.

'You look as if you've been busy if all those bits of paper are anything to go by. What are you doing?'

'It's not just me Guv, we're all here except D.I. Furness who's just gone up for some breakfast.'

'Stuffing himself and leaving you lot to get on with it?'

'Ah no, Guv. He was in first, at six, but by leaving his pad so early he was here before the canteen opened. He'll be down in a minute.'

'Good, I see you have everything under control, so I'll watch for a bit. By the way … I've been on to the hospital and D.I. Groves is doing OK. They might lift the coma in a day or two if she keeps going as she is.'

'Thank Goodness for that,' Riggs answered, but it's still a great mystery isn't it, Guv?'

'Oh yes, it is but, lucky for her, mysteries are what we specialise in, aren't they?

Mathews and Best were about ask him about Groves when he said he'd been to the hospital but, when they heard what he said to Riggs, they got back to what they'd been doing.

Ten minutes later, he appeared at their desks and asked what they were planning … Mathews explained.

'Those letters D.C. Riggs found yesterday, Guv, I think we all agree, have changed everything. For the first time we've a whiff of motives which, to everyone's surprise, look like a possible reason for the attack on D.I. Groves and the murder of Mr Townsend. The letters have indicated a monetary aspect relating to the two cases and, if Riggsy is right, we need to know whether we've the same financial issue in both cases, or whether each has its own separate, but similar, justification. That's what we have to discover. We need to check that this curious way of a man easing his conscience is all part of one man's 'wipe the slate clean' plan or, much less likely but not impossible, part of two similar plans.'

'It's one plan for sure, it has to be; the coincidence of two like this arising at the same time is so unlikely we can forget it.' said Reynard, who was much impressed by the gratifying change of atmosphere compared to that which had been in evidence at the end of the previous evening's meeting.

He thanked them all for pulling together again, but nobody heard; they were too engrossed in what they were doing.

By ten, they'd amalgamated the lists each had made individually. and they were editing them to cut out duplication.

By eleven, with coffee percolating in the background, they had their final list and were putting together a plan for their next move. Half an hour later, by common consent, Riggs presented it to D.S. Reynard and D.C.S. Bradshaw who, attracted by the early morning activity, had joined them.

'O.K.' Riggs began. 'Finger's crossed, we might finally be on the right track to solving mysteries surrounding the attack on D.I. Groves and the murder of Mr Townsend. Yesterday, when I found the letters we've now all seen; I didn't immediately realise their significance. It was only when D.S. Reynard read them out that I saw a potential link between the two cases. The coincidence of both our victims being in touch with the same solicitor regarding what he hinted might be a money issue, and for that issue not to be the same one, is most unlikely.

On the way to coming to this conclusion we've noted that, in the case of Mr Townsend's death, we know the following: He died between three thirty and five fifty when the residents were in their rooms, the 'on-duty' staff member, Susie Knight, was in the staff room, the two domestic staff were in the kitchen, and Doctor Neilson, the proprietor of Wyckham House was alone in her office writing up the accounts.

The three thirty time I've mentioned was determined by Mr Platz, saying he heard the noise of a series of coughs coming through the wall separating his room from Mr Townsend's, plus the possible sound of voices within the same period being heard by Mrs Betty Forward and Mrs Marianne Rudd.

The five fifty time was the earliest anyone, having had their evening meal, might return to their room.

Observations on the site determined that anyone going in or out of Mr Townsend's room via the hallway, interior stairs, and the landing would almost certainly been seen by someone as those common area places are invariably busy, even during meal times.

Anyone entering or leaving Mr Townsend's room via the French doors, the exterior fire escape, the back garden and the gate that opens onto Rodean Close, during the above time bracket, could only have been seen from the kitchen.

Our conclusion, is that Mr Townsend's killer *did* enter and leave by this route. And that he might only have been seen doing so by anyone who happened to be in the kitchen.

The supporting evidence being an unknown car with a part remembered number parked in Rodean Close for two hours within the period specified above, a part unidentified finger print on a garden pot on the fire escape, a conversation the victim had with Mrs Forward in connection with a video clip she'd received from her daughter, and one of the Kurdish employee's admission that she'd seen a man running from the garden while the residents were at their late afternoon 'sit at table' meal.

Our broad conclusion is that a man drove to Rodean Close, parked his vehicle, entered Wyckham House via the back garden gate, crossed the lawn, climbed the fire escape, entered Mr Townsend's room through the French windows, argued with him, killed him, and then went back to his car having only possibly been seen by a domestic servant working in the kitchen or someone in Rodean Close.'

When Riggs finished reading, he looked up from his notes to see how they'd gone down; everyone was smiling. 'Shall I go straight on, Sir?' he asked the Super.

Bradshaw, highly impressed by Riggs's extremely professional presentation despite his relative inexperience, nodded. 'O.K.' he said, 'let's hear the rest.'

Riggs cleared his throat, nervously, and started again. 'Right ... well ... one thing I didn't pick up, Guv and, nor has anyone else as far as I know, is that if the killer locked Mr Townsend's door from the inside before he left, how did Susie Knight get in?'

'With her master key.' said Furness.

'I don't think so,' Riggs replied, 'if there was already a key in the lock she wouldn't have been able to put one in from the other side, the corridor side; not even a master key. No, take it from me, there was *no* key in the lock when Susie Knight arrived the *first* time and found him dead. It must only have been when she arrived at the room for the *second* time, with Dr Neilson, that she needed the master key to get in.'

'So, what are you saying Constable … that Susie Knight is lying, that she's trying to mislead us in some way?'

'Ah no, Guv. When she burst in and found Mr Townsend lying on his bed covered in blood it must have given her a shock, I mean really nasty mind-numbing shock, I'm sure she didn't intend to lie or to confuse us. However, it does mean we'll have to adjust our reconstruction of the event to include the possibility … maybe even the probability that the killer, on hearing her footsteps on the landing's wooden laminate floor, hid in Mr Townsend's en-suite bathroom … or even under his bed. When Susie Knight came into the room, she'd have had no idea he was only a couple of feet from her and, when she shot off downstairs to get Dr Neilson, he must have taken the opportunity to come out of his hiding place and escape via the fire escape, the garden, and Rodean Close … as we've already established.'

Reynard sat back in his chair with a grin on his face; Riggs, irritating as he could be on occasions, had done it again; he'd found out something everyone else had missed. 'Well done again, Constable,' he said, 'you get the lollipop; I reckon your surmise re the door being locked or not locked is correct but I can't see it changes much from our perspective so let's move on to our other investigation … the attack on Inspector Groves.'

Riggs nodded. 'We have less to say about the attack on her, but what we have is good solid stuff. All we need is more. Inspector Groves who, I happen to know, because she told me, has started to take golf seriously. And, as she said to me only last week, if she was going to play golf, she was going to do it properly. With this knowledge in mind, I think she was trying to slip in a hole or two, at the club she's recently joined, before going D.S Reynard's retirement party.

We don't know what happened to her on the fourteenth tee except that she was found lying there unconscious and bleeding, by two men out on a training run at round about six o'clock, and she was taken to hospital in an ambulance one of the runners called on his mobile.

A very large number of people from the golf Club, and the Hotel, to which it is affiliated, were interviewed the next day, but it soon became apparent none had seen anything suspicious late the previous afternoon and early evening.

The next day a man called Dussek, telephoned John's Street nick to report seeing a man throwing something from a lay-by, into some trees near the golf course. He'd heard about the attack and wondered if what he'd seen had anything to do with it. It had of course, as we found when we discovered what the man had thrown, was a golf club.

We've collected some evidence that seems to support this from the club itself, a putter, on which several of D.I. Groves's undamaged partial fingerprints were found. Forensics, on closer examination, spotted a blurred half thumb print with a scar running across it on the shaft's rubber grip. I think I mentioned this before. It could have been missed when the attacker wiped the club before jettisoning it. In addition, after being pressed, Mr Dussek gave us a sketchy picture of the guy who threw it, the most significant element of which, was his certainty that he was big, tough looking, and bald.

Secondly ... Two men playing a few late holes on the course D.I. Groves was attacked on also saw a man broadly of this description. He was in the distance and walking away from the direction of the fourteenth. In his hand, they said he had what they thought was a walking stick but we now think it could have been D. I. Groves's putter. Two women walking their dogs also saw a man who might have been the attacker.

We haven't made much progress with this latter case, unfortunately, because we have so little to go on. We have no one who witnessed anything associated with the actual attack, bar the people mentioned above, and only the putter, which is still with forensics, to help us. Mind you we do also have a phone, found in the woods which, we know from finger prints on the SIM card, belongs to D.I. Groves.

The discovery yesterday of a letter in her flat, plus a large amount of personal information her sister Connie gave to D.C. Best and D.S. Reynard ... details of a life of which they knew nothing, have only gone to show us how little we knew of our friend and colleague. It was as though she was an iceberg with only a seventh of her visible and the rest hidden out of sight.

'And that's about as far as we've got, Sir.' Riggs said, turning to address D.C.S. Bradshaw. 'If we squeeze forensics a bit more, we might get something else, but otherwise, it'll be down to hard graft and, thank God, we've never shied away from that.'

Bradshaw nodded in Riggs's direction and then, grabbing Reynard's arm, he pulled him closer. 'You've got a right little flyer in that boy, Foxy.'

For a moment Reynard didn't answer but then, putting his hand to cover his mouth, he replied; 'I know that, Sir. D.C. Riggs is as sharp as they come, too sharp sometimes; but he's shaping up nicely.'

'A bit of a Prima Donna though … how does he fit in?'

Reynard smiled. 'With difficulty, but we manage.'

After the Chief Super had gone, the whole squad got down to discussing the next move. Reynard was in charge again, nobody seemed to mind, and they progressed quickly.

'What do you want me to do about Millennium Cars, Guv?' asked Riggs, 'only I'd like to continue being involved in that case, even though I expect most of my time's going to be tied up with the other two.'

'Millennium will have to wait, you'll be on the other stuff as you say but, before we divide up the responsibilities, we must decide on our plan … suggestions anybody?

Everyone started talking at once at that; what had seemed to have gone cold was bubbling again and they all want to be there when it boiled over.

'O.K. Hold it, hold it, we started with the most junior member of this squad ... let's hear from the most senior member now ... D. I. Furness ... what have you to say?'

'Me, Guv? I'm not the most senior ... you are.'

'Aha, you're wrong there, Mister; I'm *not* the most senior any longer ... my pension kicks in today, and surely none of you is suggesting an old aged pensioner runs this team of ... what was it again? Oh yes ... this team of Wonder Cops!'

Furness shook his head 'Oh no, wait a minute, you're not escaping that easy Guv, you can't play Foxy with *us*, and get away with it; we know you too well.'

'In that case let's make a start. Have any of you got anything you think we've missed? No ... well I have ... we need more from S.O.C.O. and forensics, we need to know a lot more about the bald headed man, the old Toyota Camry car he was driving, and whether those Kurdish girls do actually know him or not. We need more finger prints from Mr Townsend's room because we've none, bar the one on the pot outside it, and his own and the staff's, at the moment. We need to have the handrail to the fire escape checked again; and what about the back gate? And, finally, we need much more about those letters.'

'No chance of my having a few days off then?' asked Riggs, with the straightest face he could assemble.

'None whatsoever, Constable a lot of what we have to do is down to you, and I'm not letting you slope off, while we clear up the mess.'

'Just asking!' said Riggs.

The upshot of the deliberations that followed was that the team would continue working in pairs, with Reynard keeping the press and 'the brass' at bay, maintaining an eye on Groves's progress in hospital, and acting as go between to ensure everyone's efforts were coordinated.

By lunchtime a plan had been agreed and, after grabbing a bite to eat in the canteen, Furness and Best were soon on their way to Wyckham House again; Mathews was heading for the forensics lab; and Riggs, given the responsibility of re-checking D.I. Groves's flat, was driving along the coast road, humming to the tune playing on his car radio.

Every member of the team had started to sense the key to solving their cases was about to be exposed which, in turn, was giving them a powerful new impetus. Once they knew and understood the motivation behind the attack and the murder, they reckoned they'd soon know the whole of both stories.

Nobody mentioned Millennium Cars.

After the others had gone, and he'd checked with the hospital to be told there was no change in Grove's situation but that they were very hopeful, Reynard sat back in his chair, closed his eyes and began to think. On another day that process might have sent him off into a world of his own where he'd not only ask the questions, he'd answer them too. Not on that occasion though; the jesting with Furness relating to his retirement had suddenly brought reality to his situation. Previous conversations, even with Cathy, had never quite rung true; he couldn't be retiring, it must be someone else who kept on repeating 'when I'm retired'; it couldn't be him.

He might have stayed there all afternoon, thinking of the past instead of the future, but his dreaming was disturbed when his mobile phone began to blast out the new call music Cathy had insisted he install on it in advance of his retirement. Of all the people in Brighton who might have been at the other end of the phone, it was Barney Truscott, the petty and relatively harmless conman Reynard had known for years.

'Ah … Mr Truscott,' He said, 'I've knocked on your door a few times in the past, what is it this time?'

'It's a bit delicate Superintendent, family stuff. I'd like to have chat with you sometime, soon if possible.'

'Sounds interesting. Can it wait few days, I'm snowed under at the moment; I'll text you when I'm free.'

'Oh … pity … I need to see you urgently. You won't regret it. Oh yes, by the way I meant to say … I heard that girl sergeant of yours has got herself into a bit of trouble. She should have steered clear of those boys, they're a bad lot.'

'That sergeant is an inspector now, Barney, you don't mind me calling you that do you?'

'Not a bit Superintendent, but don't expect me to start calling you Foxy; I've reputation to keep up.'

Reynard was still smiling, long after the call finished. 'Barney Truscott,' he kept saying to himself 'now there's a man who might know something. Maybe I *should* see him.'

He called Riggs who was standing looking thoughtfully into the distance. 'Come on Constable, I have a call to make. I've got to go and see Barney Truscott; he has something on his mind and, if it needs following up you can do it because I'll be at home with my feet up'

'Ha … you mean you'll be retired?'

'Yes, but I want to see our present cases wound up before I quit. I'm using up un-taken leave at the moment but, when that's gone, I'll go. Mind you if we find we have a third person involved either as an additional victim, or as the perpetrator, I might ask if I can stay on until all the linked issues are joined up too.'

As Riggs shoved the papers he was reading into his desk, Reynard picked up his phone and dialled.

'Hello …?'

'Ah Mr Truscott, Barney, look I find I'll be driving past the end of your road shortly so, if you're still at home, I could drop in. If you can't see me today, I'll probably not get another chance until late next week. What d'you say?'

'I'm busy as well at the moment,' Superintendent, 'but I could be home fairly quickly … yes … I want a word in your ear, and it's urgent. Shall we say around twenty minutes?'

'We certainly can ... twenty minutes. O.K?.'

144, Peabody High Row

5.05 p.m.

Barney Truscott had had to down his pint faster than he normally did, and he belched as he rose from his regular seat in the snug and made for the door leaving his cronies sinking their own drinks and blaming everyone for everything.

Hurrying, he got to his little house well in time to ensure there was nothing visible in the hall or sitting room to raise unwelcome attention. His activities, always in the doubtful fringes of honest trade, had often been the justification for meetings with Reynard in that room

Today was different though; it was Barney Truscott, 'concerned father', who was to be to the fore, for Barney was worried about his son, Ronnie.

Once Mrs Truscott, a timid little soul called Doris, had let Reynard and Riggs in, in response to their knocking on the solid brass, and probably stolen, lion's head effigy, she led them through to the back kitchen, and disappeared.

'Thanks for coming Superintendent,' Truscott said,

getting up from his favourite chair. 'It seems funny asking for your help after the years I've spent trying to avoid it, but I have problem and I can't solve it without creating further damage to the relationship I have with my boy Ronnie.'

Reynard smiled encouragingly and, declining the hand Truscott was thrusting his way, sat down in the corduroy covered chair he'd just vacated. 'You've two, haven't you, Barney?' he said, 'And what are they now ... twenty, twenty five? I remember them as kids; always had the best bikes, the best pedal cars and scooters, the best anything on the street. What are they up to now, working in your little empire, I suppose? Or are they pushing their own boats? This is D.C. Riggs by the way, all six foot nine of him. He's about the same age as your two. So what can I do for you ...it's a bit odd *you* looking for *my* help.'

'I know it is,' said Truscott, 'but I'm desperate, and I've been wondering if a word or two from you in the right quarter mightn't solve my problem.'

'By landing it on me instead ... no chance.'

Truscott laughed, and turned to Riggs. 'Is he always like this? Here's me, an honest citizen looking for help, and what do I get ... two fingers. Now that's not right.'

Riggs smiled and, entering into the spirit of the exchange, turned to Reynard to endorse Truscott's request, saying; 'He has a point!'

'Alright, fun over ...what is it Barney.'

Truscott cast his eyes to his right and then to his left as though he was making sure they weren't going to be overheard. Then, pulling a rickety old dining room chair to Reynard's side, and indicating to Riggs that he ought to take a chair too, he began to tell them of the problem he had.

'I've these two boys, Superintendent,' he said, 'and you'd be hard put, to find two who were more different.

One, Rocky we call him, though his name's Rockwell - a daft idea of my wife's who wanted her maiden name to be remembered, and Ronnie, who's a couple of years older; he's the one I'm having the problem with.'

'Go on.'

'He's got in with a bad lot, Superintendent, a real bad lot. And I don't know what to do without making matters worse. The problem is while Rocky has managed to haul himself out of the life me and Doris brought him up in, and is training to be school teacher, Ronnie's going the other way. He's trying to work his way into a 'grab what you want and to hell with everyone else' existence. You'll know what I mean when I tell you he's getting thick with the Scortons, and they're flippin' animals.'

'Tough. But what d'you think I can do?'

'Trip 'em up, catch 'em with something small that'd get Ronnie a First Offender's Act and keep him out of jail, while giving him a wake-up call.'

Reynard shook his head; Truscott was off his head

asking for that sort of help; if anything went wrong Ronnie could be much worse off; he could even be serving a sentence. And that's assuming Norris Scorton didn't discover what had happened, for if he did, he could squash Barney Truscott out of existence as easily as he'd swat a fly. All he said though, was 'You're joking.'

'I wish I was, Mister.' said Truscott, turning to Riggs from whom there was no response other than an amused smile … which was no surprise … to grass up your own son in the hope of saving him from destroying himself was barmy.

'Yes … well … we'll pretend this conversation never took place, shall we?' said Reynard, 'you'll have to find another way out of your difficulty, because we can't help you. We're not risking our necks trying to solve your problems. But good luck; I hope you find a way to get rid of your difficulty. Not that I'd be involved anyway; I'll be retired at this time next month.'

'Will you … Mister Reynard?' said Truscott, hoping that by addressing him in a more deferential way he might change the policeman's mind.

But Reynard shook his head again. 'Good try Barney, but we have to go.'

Truscott grabbed Reynard's arm. 'That's them in the photo on the mantlepiece,' he said, 'Rocky and Ronnie as schoolboys. It seems like yesterday. And that's Ronnie as well … with his new pals … more's the pity.'

Riggs picked up the photograph of three men. 'Which

one's your lad? They're a tough looking bunch.'

Truscott pointed to the man in the middle. 'That's him, that's Ronnie. The one on the right is Declan Murphy, his Dad has a garage out on the A23 near Morpeth Road. The other guy's called Harry something, sounds like a kind of soup ... nasty bit of work, he's got a bit of Arab in him if you ask me.'

'A kind of soup? What're you talking about? 'I heard a new gang had started up, but I didn't hear anything about soup.'

'It's the man's name,' said Truscott. 'Harry Chowder ... something like that,'

'I've heard about that lot too,' said Riggs, 'and that one of the Murphys was involved; but I didn't really believe it. Old man Murphy's topman in that area of the town; I can't see him allowing it. Maybe I'll sniff around.'

Keen to get on once he knew they were there for nothing of particular importance, Reynard flung an arm round Truscott's shoulder. 'Stick to your seconds and factory rejects Barney, and keep your nose out of trouble or I'll come back and haunt you.'

Truscott laughed. 'O.K. ... shake hands then. It'll be the end of an era when you're retired ... I might have to start thinking of hanging up my boots, myself.'

Reynard took the hand and shook it. It was a genuine farewell and, although they'd tangled for years with neither coming out on top, it was over.

'Draw?' said Reynard?'

'Draw.' Truscott replied.

DAY SIX

C.I.D. HQ

8.am

Riggs caught Reynard as he entered his office. 'That was a good bit of fun we had with your friend Barney Truscott last night, Guv; he's quite a character isn't he.'

'Oh Barney's alright,' Reynard replied, 'he's the king in his own world and especially in his own house, poor Doris has quite a time with him. But he's got problems if one of his boys has got himself into Norris Scorton's mob. I can see he'll have trouble on the horizon with one son a teacher and the other a crook.'

'Talking about the boys Guv… I was going to tell you last night, but you shot off so quick I didn't get a chance. I've seen that Harry chap before; the dark haired chap in the photograph. He's one of Scorton's men but he's in with the Murphys too.'

'Really? What makes you say that ... and who did Barney say he was'?'

'He's a pal of young Michael Scorton's apparently, and part of this new mob which, as far as I know, consists of Scorton's son, Michael; Murphy's son, Declan; and this Middle Eastern looking guy. I saw him recently, though at the time I didn't know who he was. He was driving a big guy with a broken leg around, a man I subsequently learned was Norris Scorton.'

'You didn't know Scorton?'

'No I didn't, and I wouldn't recognise Murphy senior, if I saw him; which I can't because he's still in jail.'

'Where did you come across Scorton?'

'It was the day I went to have a look at Millennium Cars. I'd hardly parked, when this big guy with surgical boot came out of the showrooms on crutches. With him was the man in the photograph on Truscott's mantlepiece, the man he said was called Harry Chowder.'

'So, what have you heard about this new gang?'

'Nothing much, except to say there are three powerfully connected guys in it, and they're supposed to be setting up to take over Murphy's 'steal to order' car thing.'

'He won't like that; Murphy senior won't.'

'Well he can't do much about it, he's still inside, got at

least another three months to do, I think. Once we have the D.I.'s attacker and the big guy who killed Mr Townsend locked up I'd like to have a go at sorting this new gang before they get too well established.'

'Yes … well … one at a time eh?'

'Riggs smiled. 'You're the boss, boss.'

As Reynard and Riggs were talking, and the other members of the squad were filtering in and taking their customary seats, Sergeant Hatton from the front desk appeared at the open door. 'Got a message for you Superintendent,' he said. 'from a chap at the golf club where D.I Groves was attacked. He wants to know when her car's going to be picked up because it's parked in an area that is going to be resurfaced tomorrow. I told him we'd get someone to collect it this morning … is that alright.'

Reynard, a man who seldom forgets anything, stared at Hatton blank-faced. 'God dammit, when the call from Wyckham House telling us about Mr Townsend's death came through, getting someone to pick up D.I. Groves's car went right out of my head. You two had better go,' he said, pointing to Best and Riggs, 'we'll get around to our morning meeting when you return.

Riggs was on his feet immediately. 'Keys, Guv?'

'Ah, yes … keys. They'll be in her handbag and I know it's in the bedside locker in her room at the hospital; I put it there myself. You'll have call and collect them when you're on your way. We'll reconvene here at what … eleven? Make sure you're here on time, we have a lot to get through.'

Reynard's office

11.00 am

Everyone was seated when Reynard came into room. 'Thank you.' He said, when Riggs handed him Groves's keys. 'Any difficulties?'

Riggs turned to Best. 'Will you tell him, or shall I?'

'No, you do it.' Replied Best, 'You'll only keep butting in if I do it, you always do.'

Manufacturing the best look of innocence he could, Riggs drew in a big breath, smiled and, with a dramatic flourish, pulled an envelope from his pocket and handed it to Reynard. 'There y'are Guv,' he said, 'it's Christmas.'

'You can stop all that nonsense, Constable; just give me the facts.

Mathews and Furness, clearly enjoying the pantomime, kept quiet. As did Best, though he was grinning widely.

'Yes, Guv. When we got to the hospital I went in for the keys. They wouldn't let me into see the D.I. but they told me she was fine and that they were probably going to let her come out of her coma within the next couple of days. They brought the hand bag out for me pick out the car keys; a bit pointless really, they could have done it themselves as they were the only ones in the bag. The letter was lying on top of them and I lifted it out first so I could get at them. It was then, with the letter in my hand, that I noticed the Australian Stamp on it and somehow knew it was important to our investigation.

I stuck it in my pocket and only opened it and scanned through it as we drove to the golf club to pick up the car. If you read it yourself, I think you'll quickly see, as I did, how it seems to confirm there is a believable connection between two of our present investigations; those of the D.I. and Mr Townsend. Here, Guv, see for yourself.'

Reynard took the letter and opened it out …

Holland & Quick
Solicitors
Worple Road, Wimbledon

Dear Ms Groves,
 I write on behalf of my partner, Mr Joseph Quick, who is indisposed and in hospital at the moment.
Two weeks ago, you wrote to us in answer to his request for a meeting, and suggested a date later this month. I conveyed this information to Mr Quick yesterday, and he has now asked me to reply to you saying the date you suggested will be

convenient to him, and that he looks forward to meeting you.

In your response you also asked Mr Quick if he would outline the reason for seeking this meeting, other than that it might be to your financial benefit. I will try but, unfortunately, it will not be easy as we are bound by Rules of Confidentiality.

Two months ago, we were contacted by our agents in Australia, a legal practice not unlike our own. They asked us to find a person, probably living in Brighton, with whom their client has been out of touch for about forty years. We get many such requests, some of which have a financial dimension like a will, or similar form of bequest.

Given time, we usually manage to link the parties together and, hopefully, we will be able to do this in your case.

Yours faithfully,
William B. Holland
Partner

When Reynard had finished reading, he handed the letter to Mathews, who held it so both he and Furness could read it.

'Blimey!' said Mathews, letting Furness take it. 'Riggs is right; this letter confirms what we've been thinking … that the cases *are* tied together; who'd have thought that when we started?'

Furness was obviously still having difficulty in uniting

the cases in his head and suggested they got something on the Incident Board so they could get a better idea of where to go next. Reynard agreed and was about to stand up and take the black marker when Riggs leapt to his feet. 'I'll do it Guv.'

Reynard glared at him and then said 'No', this is a job for D.C. Best. He's neater and more ordered.'

Anyone but Riggs might have been upset by Reynard's obvious move to dampen him down, but Riggs didn't seem to notice, and handed Best the marker.

At the end of the session, an hour later, an overall picture of what they were dealing with was beginning to emerge. There was unanimous agreement that their two main cases were going to wind up being as being two elements of one issue; and that that issue was inheritance. Each case involved a man in Australia and the possibility he was about to leave money to people he believed he'd hurt in the past. The fact two such similar situations existed was very unusual. However, neither had anything to indicate the Australian was the same man in both instances, or that D.I. Groves and Mr Everett Townsend knew, or had ever known, each other. Best suggested they telephone the man who'd written to D.I. Groves, Mr Holland, in Wimbledon, and ask him if there were other beneficiaries involved and, if there were, could he name them.'

'He won't go for that.' Said Reynard, 'He'll hide behind some sort of confidentiality clause, they always do. Mind you Constable … having shot down your idea down, it might be worth contacting the Australian Solicitor, to see if he's in touch with Lucy Groves and Everett Townsend.'

'And then what?' asked Mathews. I go along with asking, but surely the information we already have and the evidence we've collected so far ought to be tested first.' We started on a list of what we know and need to find out, let's get cracking on it and start pulling the threads together.'

'Absolutely,' said Riggs, grabbing the black marker pen and advancing to the Incident Board.'

Reynard sat back with a bemused smile on his face.

'Right.' Said Riggs. 'We can split the work between the four of us, leaving the Governor controlling and coordinating everything from here by phone. Supposing I try tracking the big bald guy, from when he ran off through the garden and, D.C. Best, would you look again at what we have leading up to the moment he stepped off the fire escape. With such information it's possible we might be able to classify him as a suspect, and interview him. Under cross-examination you don't know what might come out. Now as to …'

Reynard held up finger. 'Anyone have anything to say? … D.I Mathews? … No … D.I Furness?'

'I don't like the idea of getting stuck into Townsend's death and forgetting Lucy, lying there in intensive care.' Said Best, 'What about her attacker? They should be given equal attention.'

Reynard, who was enjoying the 'not so subtle' way Riggs

was leading the discussion, and had decided to intervene before they found themselves taking sides, held up a finger again and asked Riggs what he had to say to that.

Untroubled by the remarks the others were making, or maybe not even hearing them, Riggs was so engrossed in his own ideas he just ploughed on. 'I reckon that you, Inspector,' he said, pointing to Mathews, 'have the best temperament to talk to Lucy's sisters again … see if you can find something we missed earlier, that sort of thing.'

Furness seeing the way Riggs was working his way round the room, said nothing for the moment. Better wait and let the young fellah make fool of himself, let him learn that teamwork solves cases, not prima donna performances.

Riggs didn't proceed as expected though … he flattered. 'What d'you think Dessie?' he asked Furness, 'You're my boss, next to the Governor, have I got it right? Have I've covered everything … I hope I have?

Before Furness could answer, Riggs was off again. 'I was going to suggest I went to the records office to get all that information we discussed last night: birth certs, death certs census details and so on, but I'm no bloody good at that sort of thing whereas you are, I've seen you doing it before. I reckon you've a better chance of digging something up than I'll ever have … would you take it on?'

Furness couldn't decide what to say but, in the end, and laughing as much at himself as he was with Riggs, he said he'd take on the records office and he didn't need help.

It was ten by then; time for Reynard to report to the Super, which he did before spending the rest of the morning sorting out the hundreds of memos, letters and reports that were crammed into his filing cabinets and cupboards - a life time of written stuff in which nobody would be interested in a couple of month's time.

On the spur of the moment and, as none of his team had returned from their morning's investigations, he went to the hospital where, to his delight, he learned Groves had started to slowly come out of her coma and would soon be transferred from the intensive care unit and put in a in a private room. He asked if he could see her but they said it was too soon, and that it might be possible the following day. He resolved there and then he'd have her assailant in custody before he next saw her.

Reynard's office
1.30. p.m.

They were all back except for Furness and he turned up while the coffee was being poured. From the expressions on their faces, everyone must have had some sort of success.

Reynard spoke first. 'Before we get into the detailed information you guys have been gathering all morning, let me tell you D.I. Groves is out of her coma and well on the way to recovery. By tomorrow or, more likely, the next day, I'll be able to visit her and to get her recollection of the incident which nearly took her from us. And, all things being equal, you may visit her on the day after that. Now I don't know about you, gentlemen, but, as I see it, this gives us a target. We must have a suspect in our holding cell and responding to our questions by then or, better still, on his way to prison to await trial. So … who's going to start. I'm cracking the whip this time D.C. Riggs, so you can get the proceedings under way. How did *you* get on?'

'How did *I* get on? How did D.I. Furness get on you mean, Guv; he did all the work, I just carried his bag. No, while he went to the county library, where the births and deaths information is available on-line, I went to the West Sussex Records Office and checked the censuses. It's something I've never done before and it takes a while to get a hang of it.

Luckily for me a young student archivist was on hand to aid anyone in difficulty, and she helped me dig out what I wanted to know and to summarise it. So here goes … based on a phone call D.I. Furness made to me from the county library, and information Doctor Neilson from Wyckham House gave me, I was able to find Everett Townsend on the 1951 census return. He was four years old at the time. Also, in the household in 1951, were his parents and his older brother Oscar.

In each of the next censuses right up until the one taken in 2001 Everett continued to live at the same address though his brother and both parents did not; they must have died or left the area for they didn't appear on any of the later censuses either.

In the 2011 census, as I've just told you, Everett was living at the address alone and, from this information, I think we may reasonably allow that while his brother might have died, it's more likely he'd moved away. Assuming it was the latter, it now seems he could be the man in Australia who is bent on making the bequests about which we know.'

'Fantastic.' Said Reynard, 'a great bit of detective work. And what did you discover D.I. Furness, on your trip to the county library?'

'Guv, I got a lot of stuff on the births and deaths of the descendants of Leonard Townsend, Everett's father, but none of it was as useful as the 'info' D.C Riggs has just given you, which I'm happy to endorse.'

'Can either of you suggest where we should look next ... we need much more ... the year Oscar emigrated to Australia would be a help; the incidents that are now giving him a guilty conscience must have occurred around then.'

Riggs was obviously having similar thoughts and set out to provide Reynard with an answer. 'From what D.I. Furness gleaned at the library, Guv,' he began, 'he was ... No, no, you tell them, Dessie; you were the one who dug it all out.'

Furness gave a nod and opened his note book. 'It seems, from what I gathered from the register of births, Guv, that Leonard Townsend had a much younger unmarried sister, named Margery.'

'She'd be what ... Everett Townsend's aunt?

Furness nodded, 'Correct, and when I learned that, at 93 years of age she was alive and well, I rang D.C. Riggs, who was still at the Records Office and, with the help of the archivist he told you about, and a couple of phone calls, he found her.

She's living, on her own, in sheltered living complex just outside Worthing. Riggs and I are going to call on her tomorrow morning at ten. Her name's Margery Townsend, and what she has to say, assuming her memory hasn't gone walk-about, will be very interesting.'

'That's *your* mornings settled then,' said Reynard, 'what about you D.I. Mathews and D.C. Best ... how did you get on?'

Mathews answered for both of them. 'We decided to split up; I went to talk to those two girls again, and D.C Best followed the route the killer took after he left the house and ran to his car in Rodean Close. Before leaving though, we had a good long chat in the canteen, going over what we already know.'

'I hope you didn't spend all morning gossiping; its action we want now.' said Reynard.

Chancing giving his boss a disapproving look, Mathews ignored the taunt and carried on. 'It's the relationship between the two cases that was bothering us, Guv, we reckoned there was more for us to find if we looked carefully.'

'For instance?'

'For instance, we know the two girls saw the man running out of the garden and, though their description was vague, in a loose sort of way it matched the description both Mr Dussek, and the two golfers, gave of the man on or near the golf course… 'the big man with a bald head.'

'There's plenty of them in Brighton.'

'With knotted handkerchiefs tied round them! Yes, but the point is … if we're talking about these two sightings being of the same man, we're saying he was both D.I. Groves's attacker *and* Mr Townsend's murderer. We're not talking about two cases with a common perpetrator any longer … we're talking about one case during the course of which two crimes took place. Furthermore, if that's right, we can put all the information we've gathered into one pot. Solve one mystery; solve both of them. We continued this conversation on and off all morning but we did a lot of other stuff too: I went to talk to the two girls. The fact a few days have elapsed since they were last spoken too, meant they'd had more time to get their stories right, though clearly it hadn't done much for their nervous state when interviewed by a policeman.

I saw them separately, of course, and kept things as low key I could. The first thing I spotted, was how jumpy they got when I said we weren't interested in their immigration status for they clearly didn't believe me. There's not much doubt they're illegals though, irrespective of the paper work they gave to Doctor Neilson when she engaged them and, to a degree, I played on that. By the end of our chat it was clear Citra Kamin and Kemala Bhutto had both seen the man *and* recognised him, despite the woolly hat he was wearing to disguise his baldness. I again assured them I wasn't from Immigration, which of course just re-ignited their fears, but it also prompted the best answer I got all afternoon. Kemala whispered it. 'He works at The Sea Of Marmon … he's a bouncer.' She said.

'Cripes, that dump,' Riggs burst out. 'I wouldn't be seen dead in a place like that. If you're looking for sleaze, that's where you'll find it. It's one of Norris Scorton's joints.

Reynard began to rub his hands together; here were signs of a decent break through at last. What he said though, was. 'Is that it then … how about the rest of the story?'

Riggs answered. 'That'll be down to me, Guv, I followed the bald man's route out of the garden, and I spoke to the householder whose garage had been blocked by the Toyota Camry. But I got nothing new from him so I set off to come back here. On the slightly roundabout route I purposefully took I passed the Millennium Cars garage. Standing on the forecourt, amongst the other cars for sale, and with a price of £4,000 marked on its windscreen, was a Toyota Camry. I looked at the number, and then drove past and read it again, though I had already anticipated what it would say … the last three letters, Governor, were C T V. It was the bald man's escape car.'

Reynard, a huge smile on his face, felt inclined to clap. He didn't of course, he summed up the new position. 'Well done gentlemen; I knew we'd get there eventually. So, what have we? We've the identity and possible location of the man who, we believe killed Mr Townsend. Now we know our two crimes are two aspects of the same case, can we also say we now have D.I. Groves's attacker in our sights too? I think not; not quite yet anyway. We have to prove to our satisfaction that what we thought were two crimes committed by two men are, in fact, two crimes committed by one man. Right?'

'Right.' They all echoed.

'And tomorrow?'

Furness was the first to answer. 'Tomorrow, Guv, me and Riggs'll be seeing Margery Townsend, and I reckon we'll be back here by late morning.'

'And I thought I'd chase Forensics to see if they could find any correlation between the part finger print found on the golf club. and the part prints found on the fire escape and plant pot at Wyckham House.' Mathews added. 'This would consolidate our belief the same guy's involved in both cases.'

All eyes then turned to Best, who often seemed to wind up suffering from Reynard's jesting. This time it was no different and they were all spluttering when Reynard said; 'And what about you Mister Best! Going out on your yacht ... or have you better things to do?'

Best, frequently ragged by the rest, was actually a good detective; he just wasn't as flamboyant as Riggs, as deliberating as Mathews, or even as experienced as Furness ... but he was thorough, damned thorough, and he all but floored them with his reply. 'I'm meeting Connie for coffee,' he said, 'I might even take her for lunch!'

Reynard's home in Malvern Gardens

8.00 pm

They'd finished their supper and were sitting watching the television when the land line telephone rang. Reynard picked up the handset; guessing the identity of the caller immediately.

'Hello?' he said.

The response was a message, delivered in a monotone, by a muffled voice.

'There'll be new stock delivered tomorrow, to a building in a cul de sac near where that girl was hurt.'

'Say that again, slowly.' said Reynard.

There was no reply, but Foxy knew who'd called him. Barney Truscott … who else?

DAY SEVEN

Shangrila
Sheltered village

10.10 a.m.

Furness and Riggs got a considerable surprise when Margery Townsend opened the door and invited them in. They'd been half expecting a fragile old lady with a shawl round her shoulders and maybe stick in her hand but, instead, they found themselves facing a tall, fit looking, silver haired woman in a track suit with a grin on her that contrasted very nicely with the look of shock on theirs.

'Er ... Ms Townsend? Asked Furness, doubtfully.

'Call me Margery,' she replied, 'but come in. 'You must be the policeman who rang me last night ... this is very exciting.'

'I'm not so sure I'd call what we're here about exciting, Madam ... 'er Margery, but yes, it *was* me who rang you. I'm Detective Inspector Furness and my colleague is Detective Constable Riggs.'

She stood aside to let them in and then, pushing past them, led them into tiny sitting room. 'It's a bit cramped,' she said, 'but there's only me. Take a seat and tell me why you're here. As I said last night, I already know about Everett's death; my solicitor told me three days ago. We used the same solicitors you see, Everett and I, all our family are with Fellowes; we have been for generations. Steven Fellowes rang me himself and told me you'd probably come calling. Would you like some tea … or coffee maybe? I have it all ready because, knowing the complications in our family, you're likely to be here for some time.'

Riggs, who could normally be relied on to jump straight into a conversation without thinking, was strangely silent when she said that, but Furness politely said 'yes, coffee, that would be very nice, thank you.'

The unit they were in seemed to consist of just three rooms: a bedroom, a bathroom, and a kitchen/living-room … all in all a very appropriate set up for an old person living on their own. The furnishings were classic and comfortable, and Furness couldn't help thinking it was the sort of place that would suit his widowed mother if she could afford it.

'I see you're sussing me out!' said the woman, much to Furness's embarrassment … and Riggs's amusement. 'Well look away! It's bit like living in a cage but I'm happy here; it's just right for an elderly spinster like me who prefers her own company to that of those who, in good faith, try to help, but actually get in the way. If that sounds ungrateful, I'm sorry. Anyway, the coffee's ready now so let's start … why are you here?'

Furness sat forward in his chair and began by telling her that the investigation into her nephew's death had uncovered the very complicated set of relationships that had existed, and continued to exist, within the Townsend family for many years. To help them understand all this, and to judge whether or not it had brought about Everett Townsend's death, he continued, they needed assistance, and who better to give it than Mr Townsend's solicitor, Mr Steven Fellowes, and it was he who had suggested they contact her.

'That's good enough for me.' Said Margery, 'what d'you want to know?'

Again Riggs sat back, seemingly, if unusually, satisfied to let Furness take the lead, which he did; 'Assume we don't know anything about your family and the bust up that led to your nephew Oscar's departure for Australia back in the seventies. 'We need to get a picture of how the other members of the family reacted to his apparently unexpected departure and, of course we need to know what problems he left behind him because, I believe, nobody ever heard from him again.'

'Until recently.' Said Riggs, suddenly coming alive.

Furness was furious; he hadn't intended to say anything about the inheritances until Margery had given the information they wanted so, not waiting to see if Margery responded to

Riggs's interjection, he asked her again if she'd give them a resumé of the Townsend family's history.

'I thought you'd ask for that,' she said, 'so I've made a few notes and, if you don't mind, I'll read from them, keeping what is a very long and complicated story as brief as I can. I should also warn you that my memory is not what it used to be and some of what I'm going to say may be slightly wrong … Is a that alright?'

'Don't worry about any errors it'll be just what we need.' replied Furness, opening his note book and pulling a pen from his pocket. Riggs did the same but, while Furness's notebook page was still blank, Riggs's was covered in the notes he'd made the night before.

Margery began her treatise with her brother, Leonard Townsend, a hard man who spared neither himself nor his family in anything they did, a man who dominated every part of the lives of his wife, Lily, and his sons Oscar and Everett. He made their lives miserable. Any comment Margery made in defence of Lily or the children was dismissed by him with the comment that she ought to 'mind her own damned business'.

Oscar, Leonard's eldest son, came off worst … every time he showed any enterprise he got stamped on. Leonard liked bossing people; it was as simple as that. And, with such a timid wife, he got away with it. But when he tried to control his sons, he found resistance. Not from Everett, the youngest; he was totally compliant, but from Oscar who had a temperament so like his father it was inevitable they'd fight. And they did, Margery told them, with fists on one or two occasions.

Around the time of Oscar's seventeenth birthday things came to a head between him and his father. He wanted to leave school, get a job and make his own way. When his father got wind of it, he exploded. Oscar's response was inevitable; he walked out, and no amount of counselling by his aunt, or threats by his father,
could make him change his mind. With a kit bag containing his clothes, and two ten pound notes he'd taken from his father's wallet, he set of to conquer the world. He was in for a shock; the world wasn't in the mood to be conquered ... especially by a youth so full of himself he was bound to trip.

He joined up with another maverick, and they recruited third who manoeuvred to get jobs for each on them, labouring on a building site.

'For a while,' Margery told them, 'I lost touch with him too, but one day he came knocking on my door. He'd left his two workmates and moved in with a girl he'd known at school, a youngster who'd also left home under a cloud. Their home was a bed/sit she was renting, with a kitchen in a cupboard, and a bathroom shared with three others. It didn't last of course. One winter cooped up in such a small place without even a radio for company was never going to be enough for a boy with ambitions like Oscar. The girl, Doreen Makins, wasn't troubled any more than Oscar had been when they broke up; she went back to live at her family's home … all forgiven. The only trouble was … she was pregnant. He never went back to *his* family home, and didn't seem to care that his mother was broken hearted. 'I told him,' said Margery, 'over and over and over again'. But he wouldn't give in; wouldn't even meet his Mum, and under no circumstances would he even go for a drink with his brother Everett. Once he'd made the break, it seemed, he was never going to go back. Oddly, he appeared to exclude me from the from his list of people he didn't want to know, and he visited me quite frequently. I used to pass information to Lily, but I doubt if anything ever came to Leonard's ears, or Everett's for that matter, and it didn't seem to trouble him, Everett that is.

And then, one day, Oscar, having permanently abandoned Doreen and the child she'd had, told me he had new girlfriend, a young medical student, a foreigner, and he was going to move in with her. I met them in the town occasionally; she seemed nice enough, and I wished them well, but it didn't turn out that way; it didn't last long. She got pregnant you see, and he didn't want that. It got right round to the day the baby was born, in the Royal Sussex Hospital, and what did he do? He took off again. Not a word to anyone, not even to me, who'd stuck by him all along. He went up north somewhere but he came back a year or two later and moved back in with this foreign woman and the young toddler she'd had by him. I thought everything was going to be alright for them at last. It nearly was but, eventually, he broke loose again and shot off to Australia, leaving his 'wife' and child behind. Such a procession of disasters, and all packed into twenty four years, for that's what he was the last time I saw him.

I got a card from him a few weeks after he'd left to say he'd landed safely, but I never heard from him again after that, and I have no idea in the world where he is now.'

Riggs got to his feet. 'I'll put the kettle on.'

Margery nodded, but Furness was too busy with his notes and didn't answer.

As the kettle began to boil Riggs, who'd remained totally silent throughout Margery's long account of life in Leonard's branch of the Townsend family, finally made a comment. 'Fantastic.' He said. 'That was absolutely fantastic Ms Townsend, … you've given us plenty of stuff to get our teeth into.'

Margery, pleased to have such praise piled on her, told him they could come any time if they need more.

'Thanks,' said Riggs, 'Actually there is one point that puzzles me. You've told us a lot about Oscar, and we're certainly interested in him, but you've hardly mentioned Everett, and he's the one who was murdered. Why's that?'

'I think it must be because I was closer to Oscar than I was to Everett. I trod a wild path myself when I was young, and I also constantly fell out with my parents … I haven't always been the dowdy old lady I am today.'

Furness laughed, politely.

'There were men in my life too, plenty of them, I think my mother must have been constantly on edge in case I came home one day to tell her I was 'expecting'. I never was, though I sometimes wish … but you don't want to know all this surely; it's not relevant.'

'It might be. We'll only know when we have all the facts. So, back to Everett, you've hardly mentioned him. What sort of a man was he? Did he have any enemies, any people he'd fallen out with?'

'Everett, you're joking; he couldn't fall out of an open window. He was a nonentity, a studious nonentity … did what he was supposed to do … hadn't an ounce of originality in him. And he didn't like me because of the way I'd sided with Oscar. I haven't spoken to, or even seen, him … in years. I'm sorry he died in such a horrible way, obviously; but, other than that, all I can say is he was dull, uninteresting, and selfish.'

'Selfish … that's new.' Said Riggs, joining the conversation for the first time.

'You don't want to know this.'

Riggs cocked his head to one side and gave her a quick smile. 'Oh but I do, Ms Townsend.'

She shrugged her shoulders and then carried on saying … 'It was all over the house, you see … our family home. When my parents died, I got nothing … my brother, Leonard, got the lot and, in due course, he passed it on to Everett, who didn't give me a penny of it; there's greed for you. I've always paid my way and, to be honest, it's sometimes been a struggle, while Everett's never had to want for anything with all the money he got after Leonard died … but did he offer to help me out? He did not. Oh, I shouldn't have been surprised; after all my grandfather ignored *his* daughter, my aunt Gertrude, and left everything to my father and then, a generation later, my father did the same blinkin' thing; he ignored me and left everything to Everett.'

'That was because you'd fallen out with him.'

'It was not! No, it was because I'd never fallen *in* with him, or for his ideas for my future. I wasn't going to be another puppet; I wasn't going to let him pull *my* string.'

'I see … Crikey, that's amazing … thank you Ms Townsend.' Said Riggs, with a depth of feeling that had Furness very impressed. Talk about her father, pulling her strings; Riggs was doing it too … and without thinking!

They left shortly after that, and headed for the office, bursting to tell the others of their extraordinary morning with Everett Townsend's aunt. But they were first to get back and none of the others was around.

While Furness and Riggs were talking to Margery and Best was chatting to Connie, Mathews was chasing Forensics regarding the finger prints. He didn't have much success.

There was enough correlation to say it was highly

probable the prints had all been made by one man, but not enough positive imagery to convict him on.

It was a great disappointment, and he was about to leave, when he turned back and asked the technician what was the lowest percentage of a print that would be considered necessary to define its owner. 'Sixty or seventy percent I'd say,' the technician answered. 'But you only have one of that size, the one found on the flower pot. There's nothing to compare it to, so we're no farther on. All the rest, including the one from the handrail of the fire escape, would be seen as indicators rather than proofs. 'It's a pity,' he said, 'but you'll just have to keep looking.'

'Yeah, O.K.,' Mathews replied, 'did you second check the phone that was handed in, the one found near the trees where the golf club was discovered.'

'No,' said the technician, 'nobody asked me to. I did it once and thought that was it. Anyway, that's a different case.'

'Not anymore it isn't, it's just a different incident in the same one. You should have been told last night. Any chance you could have a quick look?'

The technician looked at his watch. 'A quick look only, otherwise it'll be this afternoon.'

Mathews was on his way twenty minutes later, with news that would bring a smile to Reynard's face, but it was still a bit soon to go back so, with time on his hands, and having spent much less of it at the forensic lab than he'd anticipated, he decided to give The Sea of Marmon 'the once over'. But when got there, there was no sign of movement, and it was beginning to look as though he'd made a wasted journey when one of the paired entrance doors opened and man came out. He was big and he was bald, and Mathew could hardly contain himself.

Two units down from the club, there was a newsagent's shop. The big man went in, only to come out again a few minutes later with a newspaper under his arm. He stopped for a moment just outside the shop door, as if he was deciding whether to go back to the club or continue on into town. In the event he went back to the club, but it wasn't before Mathews had whipped his phone from his pocket and taken two photographs.

With no excuse to enter the club, even though the doors were open, and thinking D.S. Reynard wouldn't be too pleased if he just barged in, he settled for second best and went to the newsagent's shop. And was he glad he did? The young Pakistani assistant, the only person on the premises at the time it appeared, was only too glad to talk and, under the promise of ensuring he'd be O.K if the bald man found out, he gave Mathews enough to fill two pages of his notebook.

Twenty minutes later, Mathews was back in the office re-writing his scribbled notes. He wanted to be well prepared for the four o'clock session.

Since three, Furness and Riggs, had also been back in the building. They were in the canteen, comparing notes of their meeting with Margery Townsend, when a phone call came from the technician in Forensics to say he'd checked the SIM card again and found a couple of smudged prints that weren't of much help and another, a crisp and clear partial one with a scar on it, at first glance not dissimilar to the one found on the putter, that might be useful even though it wasn't complete.

Reynard's office,

4.00 p.m.

The only one missing when it got to four, bar D.S. Reynard, who was having a beer and sandwich snack in The Marquis of Granby pub with his boss, D.C.S. Bradshaw, was Best ... and he was in a good mood too, for he'd been having lunch with Connie.

It had been a suggestion of his, an excuse, to visit Lucy's flat again, to maybe find one more little thing that would tie the two cases together ... but it turned out to be more than that for, as he'd stood at the front door wating for Connie to open it, the postman had arrived with a small package. It was addressed to Ms Groves, the postman told him, and it was covered with Australian stamps. He'd offered to sign for it as he was about to go into the flat, but the postman wouldn't give it to him. Had it not been for Connie opening the door. it would have gone back to the sorting office. She'd signed the receipt and, as soon as they got inside the door, she handed the package to him.

At that moment, just as Best was about to tell them what

it contained, Reynard, walked in.

''Ello, 'ello, 'ello,' he said. 'Started without me. I'm not retired yet ... what's going on?'

'Nothing's going on, Guv,' Furness replied, 'we're just mucking about with 'the jigsaw'. It seems we've all had a bit of luck today and came in earlier than usual to swap notes. When I got here at half two, the others were already well dug into the coffee and biscuits.'

'And celebrating ... O.K. who's first?'

'Me if you like, Guv,' said Riggs.

'Fine ... fill the percolator!'

'May I join you.' Asked D.C.S. Bradshaw who, attracted by the clamour of voices, had come over to Reynard's office and was standing in his favourite place ... just inside the door with his back to the wall.

'You may Sir,' said Reynard, by then in his swivel chair ... this might be quite good ... I sense drama ... look at 'em ... they've all got something up their sleeves.'

When the meeting eventually settled down, Reynard pointed to Furness. 'Right ... tell us about your visit to Mr Townsend's aunt; it must have been quite interesting.'

It took all of ten minutes for Furness to acquaint them with what he'd found out about the family, one which, he told them, was 'an unbelievably mixed up mob.'

When he'd finished, the questions it provoked came thick and fast, and none of them were more penetrating than those raised by Reynard who, having heard all about the family from Connie a day or two earlier, seemed to be winding himself up for a grand finale that would seal his career.

When Furness had finished, Reynard turned to Best. 'You're next, tell us about your chat with Connie.'

'Briefly?'

'Well I'm not expecting a lecture.'

Best nodded. 'The most important thing that happened, Guv, was the arrival of the postman with this package; as you'll see, it's addressed to D.I. Groves.'

Reynard took the small cube shaped parcel and tore off the brown paper wrapping to reveal a cardboard box with what looked like medical equipment in it. Lying on top of the parcel, as he took it, was a letter. It had a slip stapled to it, indicating two attempts to deliver it had been made seven days earlier, and before the attack on Groves. He opened it, quickly skimmed through it, and then began paraphrasing it out loud so everyone would be in the picture …….

'A young man, from Brighton, some fifty years ago, it seems, having fallen out with his family and friends over the direction his life was taking, emigrated to Australia; where he's lived ever since.

He's currently in his seventies, in poor health and, as he's never married, or had had any other relationship of substance in Australia, he's got no strong affiliations there to worry about. Accordingly, he's going to re-write his will leaving half his estate to a local charity; and half, in equal shares, to the three, blood line connected relations, he believes he most hurt when he left England. The share each of them is likely get will be considerable and, to ensure it goes to the people it's supposed to, searching checks to confirm their identity are to be carried out. The most significant is a DNA test. Prospective beneficiaries must take this test to confirm their relationship, and subsequent eligibility for inclusion in the distribution once probate has been granted.'

'You will have received a DNA confirmation kit with this letter,' it goes on, 'and, if you wish to be considered as one of the bloodline beneficiaries, you must carry out the test according to the instructions on the pack, and the return it to us. In the event you are unwilling or unable, for any reason, to provide us with the necessary information, the money and/or assets that might otherwise be passed to you will be shared equally between the remaining persons involved.'

'Hello!' said Riggs. 'We heard something of this before, remember? It was mentioned in a letter we found in Everett Townsend's filing cabinet in the garage at Wyckham House, or maybe it was in that old Victorian writing box thing in Lucy's flat. Such a palaver over one man's estate. He must be worth a few bob though. Maybe …'

'Hang on, I haven't finished.' said Reynard, holding up a hand to halt Riggs's interruption. 'Apparently there are to be no negotiations over the details of the distribution. 'If you **do not** wish to be included,' the letter says, 'please let us know. If you **do** wish to be included, please carry out the test according to the instructions and return everything to us. We hope to hear from you by email, confirming you have completed the test and posted it to us by recorded delivery.'

'Is this for real d'you think?' asked Best.

Reynard nodded. 'I do,' he said, 'And did you spot the interesting bit … 'If, after three months, we have had no response from you, that which might have been to your benefit will be re-distributed. What d'you make of that?'

Riggs, who'd almost been jumping up and down he was so keen to have his say first, said. 'It's practically the same, word for word, to the letter we found in the filing cabinet in the garage at Wyckham House? But are these letters genuine or some sort of scam? Can we believe what they say? It could even be some sort of stupid leg-pull.'

Reynard shook his head; he was as surprised as anyone. 'Ah no; this letter looks genuine enough to me. But then so did the other one. So where's this leading us?'

'Don't ask me,' said Riggs, 'but, assuming it is what it looks like, we have a very nasty prospect in front of us.'

'What's that?' asked Best. Reaching for the letter to read it himself.

'What indeed?' Reynard added, passing it to him. 'What Constable Riggs is implying is that if, according to the letters, there are to be three bloodline beneficiaries, and we assume D.I. Groves and Mr Townsend are two of them, who's the third? Is there more violence to come? Will there be another murder? We've a problem here, gentlemen, and it's getting bigger by the day.'

'There wouldn't be another murder, if the third beneficiary is the person we're already looking for in connection with the other two incidents.' Said Riggs, grinning.

'What! Oh my God you're right.' Reynard replied, 'Of course you're right, and it's the damned will that's doing it. Let's see that letter again, Constable.'

Holding it by his fingertips as if it were poison, Best handed it back. 'Here y'are Guv, the murder weapon.'

Reynard took it grim-faced and cautiously, and quickly scanned through it until he came to the paragraph laying out what would happen should one of potential beneficiaries predecease the benefactor. 'Here we are!' he said … 'In the event you are unwilling or unable, for any reason, to provide us with the necessary information, the money and/or assets that might otherwise be passed to you will be shared equally between the remaining bloodline persons involved.'

'It's an open invitation to murder, and someone's taken it up.' Said Reynard. Now we're motoring. We have a candidate - it's a Last Man Standing job – the longest survivor gets the lot. All we have to do is find who he or she is and make the arrest. Sounds easy enough but I bet won't be … where do we start?'

'Governor,' it was Mathews, 'you never gave me a chance to tell you what I found.'

'Later, Inspector, we can get to that later. Right now we must concentrate on this letter and what it's telling us.'

'Whatever you say, Guv, I was just going to let you know about a man called Dag Pasha.'

'Dag what?'

'Pasha it's a common Turkish surname, I've just looked it up. And Dag means mountain.'

'Inspector,' said Reynard, flushing with exasperation. 'We're not interested in Turkish mountains today, or Turkish delight; we're looking for a blasted murderer.'

'Who might be called Dag Pasha.'

'Alright, you win. Who the hell is *he*?'

'I thought you'd never ask, he's the man who killed Mr Townsend and attacked D.I. Groves.'

Reynard started at Mathews, a long, unblinking eye to eye, challenging stare. Was Mathews trying to be funny? If he was … 'O.K. tell us.' He said, 'it looks as though you've got one over me this time. Well done. Now give us what you know. Who is he for a start … the big bald guy we've been looking for, I assume? And how did you find him.'

Mathews smiled. 'As you know, I was to go and ask Forensics to re-check the finger prints for a matching pair. Well it didn't take long; the tech guy who was doing the comparisons told me only one of the prints he got was big enough to use when looking for matches so, having come to a standstill regarding the prints, I decided to see what the night club the Kurdish girls told us about was like from the outside. I'd hardly stopped the car in a vacant slot opposite it, when this big bald headed guy came out the front door. I knew in an instant he was the man we were looking for so I took a few camera shots.'

'I can't believe what I'm hearing this. How on earth did you find out his name … did he come over an introduce himself? No, sorry, scrub that, you did well. Maybe *very* well.'

'I asked a young lad working in a mini market a few doors away.' Said Mathews, 'He told me the big fellah's name. D'you want to see a picture of him?'

'You have the photos with you?'

'Just a few screen shots on my phone … but if they're good enough for the Kurdish girls and the man in Rodean Close to confirm he's the one they said they saw. It might even jog Mr Dussek's memory, as well as that of the two golfers who saw the man with what they thought was a walking stick but which we now believe was more likely to have been D.I. Groves's putter being held upside down … which reminds me …'

'You've more … ?' asked Reynard.

'Not much. It was just a thought that provoked it …'

'Oh for God's man … what? You're worse than Riggs for stringing it out.'

Riggs eye brows shot up, 'Me. What have I done?'

But Reynard didn't react; an argument with Riggs, even a

fun one, was one thing he didn't want right then … not when he was getting the taste of a major breakthrough. 'Go on …'

Mathews started grinning; he had everyone's attention by then, and he was going to make the best of it. 'It was the golfers saying the man had what they thought was a walking stick, and our belief it could just as easily be putter that was being held upside down.'

'Go on.'

'If we're right, then the most likely place to find a finger or thumb print will be on the head of the putter, not on the shaft or the rubberised grip, as the fingerprint guy in Forensic probably assumed. And, when I asked him if that's what he'd done, he said 'Yes'; when the club had been found in the trees and sent to them, they had indeed concentrated on the shaft. After my call they looked again, and they found a decent print on the back of the putter's head. It matched the one found on the fire escape's plant pot so, as I see it, we now have a joined-up picture showing that this man Dag killed Mr Townsend, and attempted to kill D.I. Groves. In both cases, he either committed the crime for his own gain, or did it for someone else. I favour the latter, not because I have any information that points that way, but because of the unlikeliness of a man, who has probably only been in this country a few years, having any involvement in rows, fights, or disagreements, that took place before he was born. We have another person to find yet Guv … the person, man or woman, involved in those incidents that took place so long ago; incidents that have now sparked off the violent crimes we're investigating.'

Reynard looked at Mathews admiringly. He'd thought it ridiculous that an officer from another division, who was also nearing retirement, should be brought in to temporarily fill the gap once he'd gone. Now he could see why it had been done; Mathews's analysis of the current position in the two cases, and his suppositions regarding the future, were about as good as he could have dreamed up himself. All he said though, as the rest of them stopped chattering and settled down, was … 'Bull's eye!'

None of them offered a comment, they were all as stunned as Reynard and stood back in case they made a fool of themselves.

Riggs, of course, was itching to have his say, and he didn't have long to wait. 'Are you going to give us an assessment of D.I. Mathews views, D.C. Riggs?' Reynard asked, 'Or are you going to sit there all day with your mouth shut. It's not like you to be quiet.'

Riggs smiled … he knew he was being teased and quickly worked out that an attempt to upstage a colleague would not go down well.

Reynard felt he could see the struggle in his young colleague's head, and he could have helped him out. But that would never have been Foxy's way; he'd much rather see a learner 'have a go' than 'play safe, so he sat back and listened.

Finding Jessica

'I may have been' quiet Guv,' Riggs finally said. 'but I haven't been asleep. D.I Mathews is right; he has to be, based on what he's seen and reported to us. But that's not all; in my view there's more to come.'

'Put a lid on it Riggsy,' Best whispered, 'you're going to make a fool of yourself.'

It was well meant piece of advice, but once again it was ignored; what would Riggs come out with next?

They soon found out!

'I know you all think I'm being presumptive.' he said, 'and I am, I admit it. But if I see a gap I can plug, I'll plug it

'So ... what have I missed out?' asked Mathews, who clearly didn't like being challenged. 'You've targeted the killer at the expense of finding out who set it up. We'll never get to the bottom of this case, these cases, until we know who the paymaster is. Yes, I agree with the idea a contract killer might be involved but, while we have to catch *him*, we also ought to be nailing the person who set it all up. After all, in law they're equally responsible. O.K. ... look, I did find out a bit more but I wanted to do some research on it before I said anything.'

'Oh great,' exclaimed Riggs, 'how long will it be before you share what you know with the rest of us?'

Reynard, his elbows on his desk, his hands clasped and his steepled fingers tapping against his lips, glared at both of them ... competition was good, fighting was not, and 'holding back' to get a dramatic effect was absolutely taboo. His silent admonition seemed to have been enough, for Mathews got a grip on himself and answered Riggs's question.

'While I was in the corner shop, I took the opportunity to ask a few questions about The Sea Of Marmon, and what I was told was illuminating. The club is owned by three young men. Two of whom you'll have heard of, and one's a newcomer. They've set up a company, well I'll call it a company, but I doubt it's a PLC. They've set it up, the guy from the shop told me, to own and operate a series of late night drinking clubs. The Sea Of Marmon is their first.'

'Oh … just a minute; you're talking about young Declan Murphy and Barney Truscott's son, Ronnie aren't you? Said Riggs, 'They're into something with a third guy. You remember Governor … the photo Barney took from the mantelpiece.'

Reynard nodded, 'I do, the third man was smartly dressed in a dark suit. He'd a black well shaped beard and a sort of Middle East look about him. I'll remember what he's called in a minute … yes … he was named after a soup, wasn't he? Yes … got it; Harry Chowder. And, hang on, didn't Barney tell us they're running Declan's old man's 'Steal to Order' car racket … not that we've ever been able to prove he had one! The drinking clubs must be a new thing. Yes, interesting, but where does it get us, and, are we shooting off down a side alley chasing a bunch of 'learner gangsters' like these young men?'

'I don't think so.' said Furness, 'We've agreed this Dag man is the person most likely to have killed Mr Townsend and, anyway …' he tailed off, 'we don't have anyone else.'

'I agree.' said Mathews.

'Me too.' said Riggs.

Best stuck up his thumb.

By then it was nearly eight o'clock and Reynard suggested they ought to go home and think about what they were going to say at the next day's meeting. 'It'll be an important one,' he told them, 'we're going to set a trap.

'What'll we catch though?' asked Riggs, who just *had* to have the last word.

DAY EIGHT

Reynard's Office

8.00 a.m.

They were all there, except Reynard, with the notes they'd jotted down at their homes the night before in their hands. The coffee was percolating, the biscuits, two packets of them, a special indulgence, were opened. Everyone was waiting for Reynard to arrive, which he did ten minutes later due to the length of the catch-up conversation he'd been having with his superior ... D.C.S. Bradshaw.

'The Chief Super's laying down the law on expenditure I expect,' said Furness; 'it could take all morning.'

But it didn't, and soon they were where they'd been the previous evening; deciding on their defining plan.

Reynard started the meeting by saying 'I assume you've all got different ideas as to how we should tackle this next phase. Good; let's have 'em out in the open and see what we've got. D.I Furness would you like to kick off?'

'I will if you want Guv, but, as we've been discussing our different views and ideas since we came in this morning, and, as D.I. Mathew really set us on this track in the first place by what he told us last night, I'd feel happier if he got us going. We can chip in if we've something to add.'

'Yes ... whatever.' Said Reynard, in an unusually conciliatory tone, one he wouldn't have use used in the past, but now, with his retirement looming, well ...

Mathews cleared his throat and launched into his assessment and his suggestions for action. 'I got lucky yesterday;' he said, 'almost every question I asked produced an answer ... first at Margery Townsend's place, and then at The Sea of Marmon. I'm not going to try to repeat every word that passed, nor will I attempt to list all the information that was brought to the table yesterday; I'm just going to try to put it all together and then suggest our next move.

My first thoughts are regarding the persons we now see as key to our investigations, people on the 'guilty' or 'potentially guilty' side of the equation. I will not be repeating our thoughts on innocent witnesses, be they hostile or friendly, though I might include the information they gave us.

Our enquiries have brought us to the point where we see five people as being the most likely ones to have been involved in the killing of Mr Townsend and the attack on D.I. Groves; Dag Pasha, an Iraqi who fled his own country to take refuge here; Harry Chowder, a Middle Eastern gentleman with a yet unchecked pedigree; Ronnie Truscott, son of a well- known local petty criminal Barney Truscott; Declan Murphy Junior, also son of a local man, a shady customer who has a motor car sales business and, inevitably, Norris Scorton's son, Michael. All have doubtful, if unproven, criminal tendencies. Alright so far?'

There were nods all round.

'O.K.' Mathews continued, 'We can rule out Declan Murphy senior, he's been in prison since before the crimes we are investigating took place, although we can't rule him out completely, as he may have commissioned someone else to carry out the actions from which he'll profit. For the purposes of this exercise though, I'm leaving him and his son, Declan Murphy Junior, to one side. Similarly, for the moment, I'm doing the same with the two Scortons. If these families are involved, they'd never have done any of the 'dirty work ... they'd have got someone else to do it. And, before anyone says they might still be just as guilty, in law, I agree. But, right now, we have to catch the actual people who committed the crimes. If, on the way, we discover the Murphy's and the Scortons really are involved ... we can go for them later. And that brings us to the other man, Ronnie Truscott; an ambitious chap who has wormed his way into the Scorton family, and is now doing the same with their gang. This man, I believe, is one we need to watch in the future; but probably not in our present cases, so I'm leaving him to one side as well.'

Which leaves us with two villains ... Dag Pasha, the

almost certain killer of Mr Townsend and attacker of D.I. Groves; and Harry Chowder about whom we know little, though we suspect he may have been involved in both crimes; possibly by paying Dag Pasha to carry them out.

I had a chat with a … 'er … 'er … 'gentleman' I know. last night, a man who seems to know what's going on in criminal circles in our area, and, incidentally, he told me that Margery Townsend's recollection of our Middle Eastern man's name, is not correct. He is actually called Hari Choudrey. And he is not from the Middle East, as we thought, but from Brighton, his father being one of the town's tearaways back in the sixties, and his mother, a Lebanese medical student, the daughter of a prominent businessman in Beirut. She was studying at the Brighton and Sussex Medical school at the time.

Before Hari had learned to walk I believe, than his father, Oscar Townsend, disappeared, leaving his mother to raise him.

Her family cut her off with a hefty amount of money and, when that ran out, she had to manage on her own, 'temping' in a nursing home, bringing up young Hari, and continuing with her studies until she qualified and got a decent job.

She's still working part-time in the Family Practice in which she's been a partner since it was formed … an embittered, lonely, and not much loved woman. But she's a damned good doctor and her patients swear by her.'

'Ye Gods ... you've been putting in the hours Inspector,' said Reynard 'how did you manage to come up with all this stuff?'

Mathews laughed, 'After my supper last night, I went round to call on my sister.'

'Really, and she told you all this did she?'

'She and her husband; he owns the mini-market, two doors down from The Sea Of Marmon, the one that employs the young Pakistani I told you I spoke to yesterday, and he gets all the gossip and tittle tattle from people who work in the club; they're in and out of his shop all day.'

The look of astonishment on Reynard's face brought grins to those of the others; it had been a long time since anyone had surprised him so much. But it wasn't *his* reaction that stopped the conversations, it was that of Riggs, who said 'Bloody hell that's it ... *he's* the third one ... yes of course he is; it all fts. The Aussie who's trying to salve his conscience by giving his money away is Hari Choudrey's father ... Oscar Townsend.'

Nobody said a word, they were totally taken aback at what now seemed obvious.

'You can have two spoon-fulls of sugar in your coffee today, Constable Riggs,' said Reynard, 'and well deserved. You too D.I. Mathews, thanks to your enterprise in joining the dots, we seem to be on the right track at last. Question is what do we do next that doesn't forewarn them to the extent we lose them.

Hari Choudrey and Dag Pasha are our targets from now on. We'll have to forget about the rest for the moment and concentrate on these two boyos ... any ideas?'

Best stuck up a finger. 'I don't know about ideas, Guv, but has anyone else come to the same conclusion I have ... if Hari Choudrey is Oscar Townsend's son, then he's also Everett Townsend's nephew.'

Furness let out a long sigh then, almost as if he was afraid to say so, he asked the others how they thought Lucy might be involved.

That stunned them; the thought of her mixed up with crooks of this sort was absolutely beyond belief.

'So what are we to do ...?' asked Reynard, hopefully.

Riggs responded 'For a start,' he said, 'I had the easy bit at Margery Townsend's yesterday, I'd have got nowhere without D.I. Mathews's input, I'd like to acknowledge that even though he'll kill me for saying it. The information, regarding Choudrey and his background he picked up, gets us straight to the heart of our case though ... doesn't it? The missing links, Choudrey and Pasha, are our culprits. What we have to do now is find a way of getting them here without alarming them to the extent they make run for it. They only came into our sights yesterday, and we know very little about them. Here's what I think ... Pasha is a distinctive looking big bald man and, if he's been anything like close to the crime scene in our area, we ought to know of him, but we don't, so either he's just turned to crime, which is a bit unlikely, or he's just moved onto our patch. I favour the second possibility; people don't turn to violence without a reason. Not unless they're mad and I don't think he's that.

We called in to Wyckham House on our way home last night to talk to the Kurdish girls and we got bit more from them, which didn't mean much at the time, but now … after what we've heard today, seems more significant.'

'What did they tell you, for Goodness's sake?' asked Reynard 'Don't keep stringing it out.'

'Like you do, you mean?' whispered Furness, a comment which, thankfully, went unheard.

'So.' said Riggs, with exaggerated patience, 'The older of the two girls, who might by now be regretting suggesting she'd only recognised Pasha as the bouncer at The Sea Of Marmon, apparently knew him quite well … knew he was actually much more than a bouncer … that he had authority at the club and was all but in charge of it on a daily basis. And, if you didn't get to see her when you were at Wyckham House,' he went on, 'I can tell you she's a very pretty girl, and it was no surprise to me when, last night, she told us Pasha had tried to date her on more than one occasion. She'd turned him down, and his reaction had been, she told us, to grip her by her arms and shake her. She'd been terrified by this and she hasn't been back to the club since.

When, later, she saw him running in the garden, she convinced herself he'd spotted her at the window and decided to keep as far out of what was going on at the house as she could … just in case he came round to shut her up. All a bit dramatic I know, Guv, but it's easy to see why she lied when she was so frightened. What it does show is the ruthlessness of this man Pasha and, if we can nail him for injuring D.I. Groves so badly, we'll have done good day's work and … if we can nail him for Mr Townsend's death as well, we'll have done a better one. What it comes down to, in my opinion, is finding any excuse we can, to get these two guys safely banged up. Bring 'em in 'for questioning' first, and then worry about arresting them for the crimes they've committed when we have the full facts.

What we need to do is dream up a legitimate reason to collar them, to get them off the street while we set about proving them so guilty, they never get out. The trouble is, D.I. Mathews and I haven't been able to think of one. So, if any of you have come to the same conclusion as us i.e. that Choudrey and Pasha are the ones we need get hold of, tell us; and together we can work out how to go about capturing them.'

As Riggs flopped back in his seat, exhausted from the effort of expounding everything he and Mathews had agreed he should say, Reynard stood up.

'Half hour break,' he said, 'Be back in your seat by ten thirty, we're going to put this to bed before lunch. I've an inkling of an idea, bearing in mind all we've heard this morning. We can tease out the details when you come back.'

Detective Superintend Reynard's office.'

10.30 a.m.

The air of anticipation was palpable, everyone was sitting on the edge of their seat, when Furness said; 'There's just one thing, Guv, it's something that's been puzzling me all morning and I'd like someone to explain it before we get going on a plan; something I can't understand. Can *you* tell me, can *anyone* tell me, how Lucy has got herself caught up in this vendetta between Oscar and Everett and Hari. *They*'re members of the Townsend clan but, as far as I know, she's not. But then I began to think about all those strange 'goings on' in her family … the ones Connie told us about. Are they what's tied her into this mess? Are we now saying she's a Townsend as well; that, unknown to us, and maybe to her, she's also part of this weird and murderous crowd who keep doing such awful things to each other? Surely not? There has to be an explanation.'

Best raised his hand, and was about to say something, when Reynard stopped him. 'It sounds as though you've been exercising your minds, gentlemen … I have too so, before we go any farther, I have a suggestion to make. It's a gamble but, if it comes off, we'll get 'em all in one swoop. A couple of days ago

D.C. Riggs and I paid Barney Truscott a visit. It was, if you remember, at his request. He's worried that his son Ronnie is getting sucked into the 'steal to order' racket the Scorton and Murphy boys have got going. He went on to hint that he wouldn't be averse to seeing his son get a rap on his knuckles if he got caught red handed, with the rest of the gang, should they be apprehended in the middle of an operation. I was bit surprised, but I got his point.'

Best looked at Riggs and raised his eyebrows … what was coming next? Had the Governor got something up his sleeve? They leaned forward, willing him to tell them what he had in mind, but he didn't; he just smiled.

Best groaned … the boss was up to his old tricks. 'What on earth could be coming?

Only Mathews, new to the team, fell for Reynard's favourite tactic; and held back his question until he could hold it no longer, before asking … 'what's this got to do with us?'

Reynard, lips clamped, eyebrows raised, and his fingers ruffling his hair, gave him a Stan Laurel smile. 'We're going to spoil a party I've heard will be taking place tomorrow night. We're going in, sirens screaming, headlight flashing, loads of coppers and we're going to nab 'em all. Every man Jack of 'em will be spending the night in John's Street cells. How does that sound?'

'It sounds fantastic, Guv but how …?'

Reynard tapped his nose and winked.

As they moved on to discuss Reynard's disclosure, doubts about Groves's connection to her assailant and his cohorts began to creep in. How could she be related to that crowd? She bore no physical resemblance to Hari or Everett Townsend, she'd never been to Australia, and, anyway, her pedigree was known. Connie had already gone to great lengths to explain all the complications that defined her half sister's childhood. The fact she was the daughter of a man called Wilding, who was killed in a car accident when she was eight, was just one of them. Nothing she had subsequently said had contributed to the knowledge they already had; now, as Reynard told them, it was a question of *making* something happen. Maybe 'the party' Reynard had mentioned was the catalyst for which they'd been waiting.

'So what is it, Guv … this 'party' you're talking about?' asked Best.

Reynard smiled, teasingly, and then he told them … 'It's like this, gentlemen,' he said, 'I happen to know a luxury car, stolen a week ago, is going to be handed over, two days from now, to a driver from the continent who will take it to France on the Dover/Calais ferry. A large sum of cash will almost certainly be handed over, there and then, in exchange for the vehicle. You'll appreciate I can't tell you how I know this, but I can assure you my information is rock solid.'

The location where the handover is to take place is close to Crackstone Manor Golf Club and almost certainly in a single storey semi derelict building, situated at the end of a blind ended lane just off the A23. We'll have support from a detachment of uniformed colleagues; and D.I. Crowther's team will erect road blocks, on points yet to be decided, at a signal I'll give. This may be the best opportunity we'll get to catch all the people we're after in one go. Any questions?'

'I have one, Guv.' Said Furness. 'this is a trap to catch as many as we can of those involved in the car stealing racket D.I. Groves has been working on for months … and that's fine, but what about Mr Townend's murder? Surely it ranks higher in importance than the theft of a car.'

'Under some circumstances, yes; it would. But, bear this in mind … at the moment we believe the car thieves are also Mr Townsend murders. All we need is for them to turn up for the handover and we'll be killing two birds with one stone.'

'Fair enough, Guv.'

'And there's another thing I found when I was looking at a blown-up Google map of the locality … good parts of the blind ended lane must actually be visible from the golf course. This made me wonder if that might explain the attack Dag Pasha made on D.I. Groves. Supposing he was at this derelict building, for instance, and he spotted her, through the hedge, walking about, taking the occasional swings with her club but remaining on the tee much longer than most golfers would, and supposing that led him to think she was spying on him … and the barn. Would that be enough to make him think of doing something about it?'

'Blimey Guv, that's a lot of supposing.' Said Riggs, hurriedly adding 'but you might be right.'

The more I think about it,' said Reynard, 'the more convinced I am, that that's what happened, and it'll give me a great deal of pleasure if I can collar him near enough to where he got hold of Lucy's putter and hit her.'

There were no other queries and, after detailing the arrangements for the next day, the meeting broke up.

As they left the building to go to their cars, everyone was experiencing a new tingle of excitement, though that of Detective Constable Riggs was tempered with a tinge of doubt. Something was missing, something important he feared, but what? 'The Governor's on the right track to catch the car thieves - no problem about that. But how did that tie in with the money the man in Australia seemed so keen to give away? It didn't.

Back at home half an hour later, and with his evening meal out of the freezer and into the microwave, Riggs had returned to his concern that, somehow, they were missing something. It was a doubt that niggled all evening and only as stared at himself in the mirror while brushing his teeth, did he realise what it was ... and it wasn't to do with stolen cars or golf clubs ... it was to do with Lucy. Quick as they'd been in finding *how* she'd been attacked, which would probably be confirmed by the events of the next day, they still didn't know *why* she'd damned nearly been killed that fateful afternoon.

He was inclined to telephone Reynard, but thought better of it … shooting down his boss's plan was one thing … doing it when he had no alternative to suggest was suicide.

He spent an age racking his brains for an answer that would stand up, but he couldn't think of one and, when he eventually drifted off to sleep. it was two a.m.

He woke just after three and, still half asleep, went through to have a shower. He turned on the water, ran it until the hot came through, and stepped into the cubicle. In that first exquisite moment, when power driven jet of hot water hit him, he realised what the last piece of the jigsaw might be, and he whooped … and whooped again. Luckily, the walls of basement flats in converted sea front Victorians are thick and not one of his neighbours was disturbed.

As he dressed and gulped down some milk, which would have to serve as his breakfast, his head was churning and, by sifting through what he'd heard from different sources over the previous few days, he'd managed to reduce the number of his concerns down to just one … why was the Governor working on a theory there was another, not yet apparent, reason for Dag Pasha's attack? Should he raise his concern immediately, he wondered? That might upset the governor's plan, which was probably well advanced if the activity he could see going on was anything to go by, or should he wait until it had been successfully completed?

He flipped a coin ... Wait.

The old barn, Crackstone home farm

4.00 a.m.

Everyone was in place and no one was in sight when a dark green Land Rover turned off the A23 and slowly made its way up the lane to the old barn. It was still dark but the first streaks of day were already showing on the eastern horizon, and it was cold.

When the Land Rover pulled up at the barn's door three men got out. Reynard, thirty yards away and well hidden by a dense growth of hazel branches, slightly parted two of them to get a better view as a man who, by his appearance, could only be Hari Choudrey, got out of the front passenger seat at the same time a huge man and small one got out of the back. Were they Dag Pasha and the pick-up driver from the continent? The Land Rover driver, who remained in the vehicle until he'd turned it round, was seen to be Ronnie Truscott when he eventually got out and joined the others, who were tugging at the creaky old doors of the barn. When they were sufficiently open, the four men went in, pulling them shut behind them.

Reynard uttered a sigh of relief; the idiots had just made their capture easier, and he signalled his men to move in and secure the door. With no windows to the barn the thieves were trapped. Fortunately, they realised this and, cursing themselves for being so inattentive to the details of their own plan, they gave in and walked out, one by one, to be handcuffed and taken away.

The road blocks weren't needed, and the whole operation was stood down by four thirty a.m., with D.I. Crowther's borrowed men, and everyone else, bar Reynard's squad, on their way back to HQ by five.

It couldn't have been easier … the whole operation had taken just under forty minutes.

The car that the thieves had gone to collect and then hand over, turned out to be a 2015 shiny black BMW X5. And the leather holdall the Belgian, as they later discovered, was carrying, had twenty one thousand euro in it.

A good mornings work, but all to do with the car stealing racket the young crooks were operating, and nothing to do with Australia or inheritances.

Riggs was right, but he wasn't the only one; Reynard also knew exactly what was missing.

Interview Room One.
John's street Police station Brighton

2.00 p.m.

The four men were awaiting their fate as, one by one, they were wheeled into the Interview Room to be grilled by Reynard and Furness. The rest of the team; Mathews, Best and Riggs, were watching them through the two-way mirror wall.

The Belgian driver was taken first. He had little to say; he'd been given a job and he was in the process of carrying it out. He was a contract driver and no more. He spent his whole life picking up and dropping off vehicles. Sometimes, if he was working for a prospective purchaser, he might be asked make cash payments to vendor. This was one of those instances, he said. The money in his holdall was money to be paid to Mr Choudrey once he'd taken delivery of the BMW but, as he had not at that stage taken delivery of it, he still had the money for it in his holdall. Reynard didn't believe a word he said and Choudrey was remanded in custody so his claims could be tested.

'It won't be the end of the world if he just gets sent back to where he came from.' Said Reynard.

They saw Ronnie Truscott next; he wasn't anything like what they'd expected, based on how he'd looked on the photograph he and Riggs had seen on his parent's mantelpiece. He was not so robust in stature for a start, or so threatening in attitude as they'd believed him to be, and he crumpled at Reynard's first question after the mandatory caution had been read to him. 'Did you strike and severely injure a woman with a golf club the other day, a woman who was driving practice balls, just a few yards from the barn we found you in this morning?'

'No.'

'Who are Kontinental Kars?'

'They're 'er ... me and the other two lads I was with.'

'And you sell cars to buyers on the continent?'

'Sometimes ... look, you'd better ask Hari, he deals with all that stuff.'

'Ah, Hari. So he's the car man, which makes you what?'

'I run the club we own; The Sea of Marmon.'

'Oh very posh ... own a club as well do you? Anything else? And what about that big baldy guy who was with you ... does he have a position in this amazing double enterprise of cars and clubs. There's a lot of money in cars and clubs I hear, loads of it ... if you have the nerve.'

Furness, who had been silent until he worked out Reynard's tactics and saw that humbling Truscott and frightening the life out of him was the way he way heading, piled in with a few questions of his own. 'Mr Truscott, where did that BMW motor car you and your fellow directors were on the point of selling come from.?'

'Hari deals with all that.'

'But you are a director of Kontinental Kars I assume?'

'Well not really … it's more a title, Hari's the director.'

'Do you have shares?'

'Yes, my share's five percent.'

'That's not what I meant, Mr Truscott but never mind because I don't think you know what you've got yourself into. Does Norris Scorton know what you're doing?'

At the mention of Scorton's name, Truscott visibly shrank; it looked as though Norris Scorton didn't know much of Ronnie's involvement with the stolen car racket, or was pretending he didn't, and that could spell trouble for the young man who clammed up immediately and refused to answer any more questions. In consequence, and like the Belgian before him, he was escorted to a holding cell, where permission to detain him was sought from a magistrate, and the DPP's office was informed.

In the observation room meanwhile, Mathews, Best and Riggs talked quietly as they waited to see how the next two prisoners fared under cross examination. These two were the ones in whom they had the greatest interest.

Dag Pasha was brought in first and, after taking the seat

that was pointed out to him, he slumped against the wall and started picking his nose.

The caution was read out to him, but he seemed to have no interest in it, or the two detectives sitting opposite to him; D.S. Reynard and D.I. Furness.

'Now Mr Pasha,' Reynard began, 'you are going to be charged with the theft of a motor car, namely the B.M.W. that was at the barn where you were detained; have you anything to say about the part you played in its theft, and its probably destination. You were going to sell it to this Belgian man for the cash he was carrying, weren't you, you and Hari Choudrey and Ronnie Truscott? Twenty one thousand euro … it's a lot of money.'

'Nothing to do with me.' Pasha mumbled, moving from his nose to his ear, which he then proceeded to massage between his fingers. He never once looked Reynard or Furness in the eye; he ignored them completely.

Reynard banged the table with his fist. 'So, what were you doing in the car with the other men if you had nothing to do with selling it?'

Pasha glowered back at him but said nothing, the 'acting dumb' response hadn't surprised Furness at all; it was just part of the ritual of shouted questions and silent answers that often occurred when a hardened criminal found himself face to face with the police. In fact, Furness and Reynard were waiting for him to come out with 'No Comment' and, when he didn't,

Reynard continued questioning. 'Come on,' he said, 'You *were* selling that car weren't you? Why was it kept hidden in the barn? Could it be that you were hiding it? Hiding it because you'd nicked it, stolen it for a customer on the continent like you've done before. We know what's been going on; it's one load of crooks stealing for another load of crooks in a different country, isn't it?'

After about five minutes of quick-fire questioning Reynard suddenly changed tack. 'we've got your finger prints Mr Pasha, you weren't as clever as you thought. And, before you tell we couldn't have them because you never touched the car … I'm talking about a golf club, the golf club you hit a police officer with … injuring her so seriously she's still in intensive care. *Now* what have you got to say?'

Pasha still sullen faced continued to remain silent, causing Furness to turn to Reynard and say; 'He thinks we don't know.'

'Y'mean about his car … the old Toyota Camry, the one with a number plate that ends with CTV? Or maybe you're talking about his finger prints all over the place at Wyckham House, not to mention on the putter he was seen carrying as he left the golf course at Crackstone Manor. The same club he was later spotted throwing into the trees beside the lay-by. Oh yes … and there's the telephone those kids found near it; it was the policewoman's too. Yes, Mister Pasha, we have witnesses who are prepared to swear they saw all these things.'

It was enough, as soon as the questioning had turned from car theft to killing, Pasha knew he was in trouble, and he too changed tactics.

Emerging from silent defiance, and speaking for the first time, he asked for a solicitor.

'It's your right,' said Reynard, quietly cursing.

As Pasha was led back to the cells Furness punched the air; 'One down, Guv, and one to go. That bloody man gave in with less trouble than I was expecting. Huh … I wonder if Hari Choudrey will do the same?'

Before Reynard got chance to give an answer, the other members of the team appeared. 'Nice one Guv.' Said Best.

Reynard nodded and was about to ask Riggs for his opinion on how *he* thought the interview had gone when, true to form, Riggs suggested they'd only done the easy bit so far, and that Hari Choudrey would be a different proposition.

He was right; Choudrey was tough, both mentally *and* physically. He'd left school ten years earlier with particularly good grades it seemed, and followed that with solid progress at Brighton Tech during which time he'd kick-boxed his way to the final of the County Championship, won four hundred pounds playing snooker, and had trial for Brighton and Hove Colts. In addition to these notable achievements he'd advanced his standing considerably when, still only a new employee at The Sea of Marmon, he'd caught a youngster scratching his name on Scorton's Mercedes. He'd been in the process of giving the kid a good hiding when Scorton turned up; which turned out to be a happy coincidence for Choudrey, who was only an acting barman in the club; and a happy one for Scorton; who'd been looking for an extra shift manager for weeks, and here was one right under his nose. He offered Choudrey the job immediately. From barman to boss in a few weeks. Choudrey could hardly believe it.

But it hadn't stopped there; his smart appearance and quick-thinking brain had soon seen him higher up the ladder; the connection to Norris Scorton was working out better than he could ever have hoped. And then, one day, Scorton, having taken to Choudrey, asked him if he'd be interested in some 'extra work'.

Reynard only knew part of this of course; but it was enough for him to bear in mind when he got down to cross-examining the up and coming young criminal who, up until then had been below the police radar. Indeed, had not been for Barney Truscott, and the photo on his mantlepiece, the man he was about to interview may never have come in sight.

Choudrey, already in the interview room, stood when Reynard and Furness entered; a perfect example of his rapidly developing hypocritical attitude. 'Thank you Sir,' he said, politely, giving a slight bow and unsettling Reynard right at the start of the interview.

'Sit down.' said Furness, going on to give Choudrey the

mandatory caution.

'You know why you're here?'

'You're curious about the car.'

'Very curious … who owns it?'

'Well, at the moment I do. I was about to sell it to that Belgian gentlemen, who was in the car, once he'd handed over the price I was asking. I believe he had the cash with him.'

'You say 'at the moment' what d'you mean by that?'

'What I told you … I own the car; I bought it from a man I know who's had bad run with his investments and needs cash to pay his mortgage. Lots of people sell an asset if they're a bit short, or, as in this case, if the horse they backed is a bit slow. I do it myself.'

'And you have the appropriate paperwork?

'I do, it's in the briefcase you took from me.'

Reynard held up a hand and then stooped to pick up the attaché case resting against the leg of the table. 'Hang on until I open it.' he said, I need to check what's in it before we go on.'

'Be my guest.' said Choudrey, politely.

As Reynard leafed through the documentation he gradually began to get concerned. The papers looked O.K. so, either they were genuine, or Choudrey had used damned good forgers. He could almost feel the patronising smile that was beginning to light up Choudrey's face.

Inside the lid, secured by an elasticated band was an envelope; it contained a letter and, even before he'd managed to slip it free and open it, he knew from where it had come … Australia. He couldn't stop himself. "Ello, 'ello, e'llo.' he said, 'What have we got here?'

Furness leaned towards Reynard so he could see what he was talking about, and had to stop himself smiling when he realised what was.

'That's just personal stuff.' Said Choudrey … nothing to do with the car. May I have it please, it requires an answer.'

'And so do I.' said Renard 'I require some answers too, this changes everything.'

'It's got nothing to do with the car. I'll talk to you about *it,* but that letter's private.'

They could have argued all day, with Choudrey protesting the letter had nothing to do with the reason he'd been brought in, and therefore couldn't be interrogated about it. And Reynard continuing to question him about it, without giving away the fact he already knew what it was all about.

At five o'clock, two hours after they'd commenced the interview, Reynard suddenly terminated it and Choudrey, despite his protestations, was locked up in the cell next to Pasha. A new and fairly obvious approach was necessary, one that would include searching the homes of Pasha and Choudrey.

Interview Room One

11.00.am

The search of Choudrey's flat, over The Sea Of Marmon, at dawn that morning had only proved slightly fruitful. That of Pasha; a nearby bed sitter, wasn't fruitful at all; his place was spotless and tidy and, when they left, they were content they'd left nothing of use to them except a light blue woolly hat the Kurdish girls might confirm having seen before.

'Have we enough d'you think, Guv?' Best asked, as the whole team set off from the canteen to return to the interview room. When they got there, and before Choudrey and Pasha were ushered in, Reynard explained to the defending 'duty' solicitor that he had unassailable proof of Choudrey's involvement in the attack on Groves and the murder of Townsend.

The solicitor, maybe because he sensed he was on a loser, or maybe because of the arrogant way Choudrey had spoken to him, inferred he wouldn't object … rather he'd concentrate on persuading his client to trade an admission of conditional guilt, in the hope of receiving a reduced sentence. The actual interview, which could have taken many hours, was over in two. Reynard's procession of proof confirming facts regarding the presence of Pasha in Mr Townsend's room, and at other locations in or near Wyckham House around the time of his murder, brought silence. So did the mention of the golfers having seen him on the golf course, and of Mr Dussek witnessing him throwing the golf club.

Reynard would have proceeded to an 'arrest on suspicion' but, before he did that, and while he had Choudrey in custody, he needed to solve the inheritance money puzzle. This, hopefully, would lead to the reason for the attacks on Mr Townsend and D.I. Groves. In that regard, his first priority had to be unravelling the mystery of the letters, and working out the connection between the prospective benefactor, and the bloodline beneficiaries they already knew about... indeed the reason it was happening at all. Pasha, Reynard assumed, wasn't involved in this aspect of the mystery; his actions, unpleasant as they were, were a symptom of it, so he wasn't brought into what Reynard and his colleagues considered to be the definitive interview, one in which all would be revealed.

It was set to start at two p.m.

Interview Room One

2.00 p.m.

'Mr Choudrey, you must now realise we have a lot of information regarding this series of letters, written to you and others, that have arrived from Australia; but we don't have everything, and your cooperation in helping us resolve the last few queries we have may be taken into account when you are sentenced, as you surely will be, for the killing of one person and the injuring of another. We know you got one of these letters from Australia; it's here on the table; I found it in your attaché case this morning. We also know Mr Townsend got one, it was amongst his things, and we know Inspector Groves got one; her sister found it in her flat. Now when I say one letter, in some cases there were two, or even three, indicating to us that 'proof of identity' was necessary for a claimant to get access to his or her inheritance. I presume you're familiar with all this Mr Choudrey, and that you know from whom the letters came?'

Choudrey didn't answer at first, he just continued to stare fixedly at the table top, though he was clearly in two minds as to what he ought to do.

Maybe, thought Reynard, he was weighing up what his

solicitor had told him during the break; that he might get some recognition of his cooperation if he told them what he knew. The problem was; the more he told them, the guiltier he'd look; a difficulty which, up until then, he hadn't resolved.

Furness decided to get things moving. 'Come on Mr Choudrey, say something. Your silence will do you no good. You wanted the lot didn't you. We've seen the letters you all got remember … we know.'

'What'll you charge me with?'

'If you reveal all? Don't honestly know … maybe 'accessory to murder'… we won't be able to influence the charge, but we might put in a good word for you regarding the sentence … if you help us. Or, of course, you might get no relief at all … no lightening of your sentence. It'll be up to the judge, and he'll be influenced by what we say. It's possible he'll adjust the length of time you'll be spending in prison to be in line with the amount of reliable information given to us; but there's no guarantee.'

'Can I have a word, in private, with my solicitor,' said Choudrey, 'a break of a few minutes?'

Reynard nodded and got up from his seat. 'Fifteen.' he said, 'I'll send in some tea.'

Interview Room One

Twenty minutes later

Drinking their tea had taken up more time than arguing what each thought Choudrey would decide to do.

They all had mixed feelings; Reynard and Furness were clearly hoping Choudrey would spill the beans, talk, and chance him not getting too much relief in exchange. Mathews and Best were dead against any sort of bargaining, while Riggs, in his own colourful way, suggested that as it was Choudrey's 'Last Chance Saloon' all they had to worry about was whether he'd come in with his guns blazing or his hands up.

In the end Choudrey said he'd tell them what he knew, having extracted from Reynard, his word that he'd mention the help he was getting to the judge when the case came to court.

The atmosphere in the interview room was tense. Choudrey was fidgeting, as he worked out how much to tell. His brief was praying his client wouldn't shoot himself in the foot. Furness, pencil poised, was waiting to jot down the information as it came out. And Reynard, who'd seen it all before on countless occasions, was hoping Cathy was going to give him sausage and chips for his supper.

The solicitor spoke first, and he handed Reynard a sheet of paper covered in notes as he did so. 'Here are my client's disclosures and recollections, which he asks you to read. Afterwards he will do his best to answer any questions you may wish to raise.

Reynard took one of the copies and handed it to Furness, keeping the other one for himself.

In the observation room Mathews, Best, and Riggs, struggled to find a position from which they could see what Choudrey had written. It wasn't much, so they were left trying to lip read what he was saying in support of what he'd written.

The words and phrases came out like machine gun fire. Delivered in a staccato procession of explosive words, it told Reynard almost everything he wanted to know and, when he paraphrased it later for the benefit of Mathews, Best and Riggs, it came out much as follows ……...

Everett's elder brother, Oscar, had left a trail of disasters behind him when he emigrated to Australia in 1973.

He'd upset his parents because of his waywardness, his abandoning his education, and the 'unsuitable' friends he made. Their subsequent over-closeting of his younger brother Everett, and the way they stifled his social life as a young man, must have prayed on Oscar's conscience for years. He'd felt responsible for Everett being trapped in a life he didn't want, while his own was free of curtailment and full of adventure; and he'd resolved to make sure Everett was compensated.

His parents had expected him to come back with his tail between his legs after he left home for the first time, but he didn't; he'd moved in with his girlfriend, Doreen Makins and, when she became pregnant, he'd abandoned her, leaving her to bring up their daughter, Jessica, who was born on Christmas Eve 1968.

He tried to get a job in northern England after leaving Doreen and the child behind, but the accents of those with whom he worked were impossible to understand. After a couple of years he abandoned that experiment and moved back to Brighton and a Lebanese medical student with whom he'd had a fling when he'd still been living with Doreen. Her name was, and still is, Anita Choudrey. Sometime later, she also had a child … me … I'm Hari Choudrey; Oscar and Anita's son.

I remember nothing whatsoever about my father because he was constantly on the move. He paid my mother and I no attention at all and, eventually, he abandoned us completely and emigrated to Australia. I was two or three at the time. I have no knowledge of his whereabouts; I have never seen or been in contact with him since he left England. I don't know him and I don't want to know him. As far as this legacy business is concerned though … I'll take him for all I can get.

I have sent my DNA test back to the solicitors as requested and I hope to receive a share in his estate eventually.

I swear that all I have written is true.

When Reynard got to the foot of the page, he put it down on the table alongside the copy Furness had been reading.

The solicitor, looking as non-committal as he possibly could, asked Reynard and Furness if they had any questions.

Reynard held up the list of notes he'd made. 'Plenty.' He said. 'And I expect my colleague'll have a few too.'

Choudrey who, up until then had allowed his solicitor to speak on his behalf, pointed to the statement Reynard had just read out and said. 'There's nothing more … I've done the best I can, now it's up to you to fulfil your side of the bargain.'

Reynard slowly shook his head. 'You've got to do better than this Mr Choudrey; you've only given us half the story. Your man killed your uncle … why would he do that unless you told him to, or paid him to? No, we need much more.'

'Like what, for God's sake? Asked Choudrey. 'I had no part in my uncle's death.'

'Alright … so why did Dag Pasha, who works for you, attack Inspector Groves? She had nothing to do with your uncle? This is not going well. I'm going to give you one more chance to rethink you position. Half an hour. You can stay here; I'll go out and have a word with my other colleagues in the next room … and, if we don't get meaningful progress when we come back, you can forget about me talking to the judge. You'll be charged with murder, conspiracy to murder, accessory to murder and GBH. One of them'll stick and you won't see this

Brighton for years.'

When Reynard and Furness joined Mathews and Best and Riggs, a few moment later, they were met with long faces. 'That didn't go down well' said Mathews, 'that clever bastard's giving nothing away.'

Best expressed similar feelings, but Riggs … well Riggs had to say something … and he did, he came out with a typically unexpected remark … 'I've got it.'

'What fifty quid or a toffee apple!' said Best, thinking everyone would laugh; but the only one that said anything was Reynard, and he only said two words … 'Oh … please!'

Suitably admonished, Best sat back and studied his nails, but the rest waited to hear what Riggs had to say; it could be something outrageously daft, or something inspired.

'Here's the way I see it Guv. What that man has just told us is probably all true. It's what he hasn't told us that's interesting and I've had a stab at guessing what it is. D'you want me to tell you? I can forget it if you like.' he added knowing such a remark was all but guaranteed to bring a 'Yes.'

'Go on,' said Reynard, wearily, 'but keep it short.'

Riggs shuffled about on his seat; adjusting his position before beginning. Then, with a piece of card in his hand bearing his notes, he began. 'I've been thinking … yes … yes… that *is* unusual, but this time I'm pleased to say I got something out of it. Everything we need to know we have already; it's just a case of sorting out the bits and putting them together in the right order.

For a start, I was curious find out why Lucy's letter arrived so long after the ones the others got ... and I wondered why that could be? And then there's all that palaver about DNA tests to confirm identity, and the implied threat of disqualification if the sample didn't match the master. Confirm with who ... the benefactor I assumed, though it wasn't specifically stated? I sweated all night, tossing and turning; the night before last that was. I didn't say anything to you guys because what was becoming patently obvious to me was extremely unpalatable, especially for a woman none of us know.'

Reynard rapped the table. . . 'D.C. Riggs you're at it again ... what the hell are you taking about?'

'I knew you'd all think I was nuts, Guv, but I'm not; I have a perfectly reasonable if very unusual explanation that covers all our concerns. May I lay it out for you.'

Furness, Mathews and Best all turned to look at Reynard ... would he give Riggs his head?

'Alright ... Wonder Cop ... tell us.'

'O.K. Guv, we begin by considering the criteria the previously unknown man, we now know is Oscar Townsend, chose when considering the potential beneficiaries, we know about: his daughter, Jessica; his brother, Everett; and his son Hari.'

Best was the first to react. 'What... that can't be right?'

'I think you'll find it is,' said Riggs, quite unruffled; 'all the facts we've uncovered support such a possibility. May I go on? O.K. Now we don't know how Oscar's solicitors got the addresses of these people but they obviously did, because they got the letters sent out first; the ones we've seen.'

'We don't know if Jessica got one, of course, because we don't know her, but I think Hari Choudrey does; he must have tracked her down somehow and found out; he seems to know everything else.'

'But what about Lucy?' asked Best.

'I'm coming to her. After the letters and DNA kits were received, the recipients self-tested and sent the results back to Oscar's solicitor in Australia. Now here's my real guess; I believe one of these people's DNA failed to match the master, which meant that person was disqualified and a new test kit sent to the person who should have got it in the first place; Oscar's daughter.'

'Hang on.' said Furness. 'You have something wrong here Oscar's daughter didn't get it … Lucy did.'

'Precisely.' Said Riggs.

After that all hell broke loose, and the noise of their arguing brought people from the general office to see what the fuss was about. Choudrey and his solicitor, down the corridor in another room, couldn't make out what was going on.

Finally, as the uproar subsided, Reynard, amused at the sight of Riggs in sight of his quarry, persuaded everyone to go back to their seats. As soon as they were settled, he turned to Riggs and asked him if he had any more outlandish gems to disburse. He said it with humour, but he was far from sure he was doing the right thing; letting Riggs loose was like lighting a firework and hoping it wouldn't turn to be a moon rocket.

'There's just one more thing,' Riggs said, 'and, in a way, it's the most important of all. But first… did anyone notice Lucy's date of birth? No? Nobody? Well I did. It's easy to find out from the records office downstairs … she was born on twenty-fourth of December nineteen seventy three. 'So what? I can hear you say …. I'll tell you what … it's the same day Jessica Makins was born and, in a roundabout way, it explains why Lucy was attacked.'

'Keep it simple D.C. Riggs, please;' insisted Reynard. 'and keep it brief.'

Riggs shrugged his shoulders, 'I'll do my best Guv but there's still another twist. Lucy and Jessica were both born on the same day, you can check, and when Jessica's DNA didn't match the master sample taken from Oscar, I reckon the Aussie solicitors asked their U.K. counterparts in Guildford to see if they could find the Jessica who really was Oscar's daughter.

Now I don't know how they did it, Guv, but I'm assured it was all legal. They found the nurse who'd been on duty the day Lucy was born, a retired lady called Allardice. She told them she'd been sick with worry all her life regarding a minor accident that had occurred on the day Jessica was born; she'd accidentally spilled few drops of hot tea on Jessica's mother, when her grip on the tea pot's handle slipped, and the resulting uproar brought the Ward Sister running. Allardice got a severe and disproportionate dressing down as a result of which, later that afternoon, in a moment of extreme annoyance, she went into the special care incubator room, where Jessica and another premature day old baby were being kept, and switched their arm bands.

She'd regretted what she done immediately but, somehow, there was always some about and she never got a chance to change them back.

In the end she shoved her act of stupidity to the back of her mind and hoped it would never be found out. Nor has it … until now. You may wonder how she got away with it; I certainly did. But, apparently, at that stage of its early life, especially if a baby happens to be premature, as these two were, its face was probably red, wrinkled, and squashed looking. Hair apart, Guv, these new-borns are easy to mix up. Even their mothers, exhausted and half asleep, don't recognise them sometimes. I'd have told you last night, but I was waiting for this retired nurse to ring me. She did, while you were all drinking tea at the last interval. So that's how Jessica became Lucy, and Lucy became Jessica, though, as we already know, Lucy Groves was actually born Mavis Wilding; Connie told us. All this is expected to be confirmed when Lucy's DNA arrives in Sydney. And by then, Lucy will know she's in for a handsome amount of cash and another change of name.'

'D'you think this'll all happen?' asked a still slightly unbelieving Constable Best.

'I can't see why it wouldn't,' said Riggs, but there's more. As Everett is 'no longer with us', and Hari can't benefit from the estate of a man he's murdered, or had murdered, their shares will also go to her. Lucy is going to be a very wealthy woman.'

Best, who clearly didn't believe a word of what had been said, and was laughing his head off, suggested Riggs should try lying down for a while.'

'Hear, hear,' said Mathews, 'permanently'.

And Furness seemed inclined to agree.

But Reynard wasn't laughing. Everything Riggs had said, fitted. Lucy would soon be Jessica and he, as things stood, would be sitting at home wondering how to fill in his time.

Three months later

Groves's Flat in Frensham Terrace, Brighton.

The taxi pulling up outside her apartment, had brought only one passenger - Oscar Townsend. Exhausted by the long flight, he was doing his best to stifle a yawn as he reached into his pocket for his wallet.

Unknown to him, Lucy, who'd gauged his arrival time with surprising accuracy, was watching him from behind one of the velvet curtains at her sitting room window.

'She has a fine place if her apartment's in this house,' he said to himself, looking up at the classic lines of the white painted four storey Georgian building, 'I hope she's in.'

, and grabbing the door handle as he stepped down to the pavement.'

'Want some help with these, Sir? Asked the cabbie as he unloaded the bags.

'No, it's alright, I can manage.'

'They're heavy.'

'OK, thanks, take them up the steps then,' said Oscar, plucking a fist full of banknotes from his wallet and handing it to the driver. As he did so, he glanced up.

One of the curtains in the front room window had just moved; someone was watching him.

He pretended he'd not seen anything, and slowly crossed the pavement to the foot of the steps. And there, in a moment of indecision, he again began to wonder if he'd done the right thing in coming back. Was this visit for which he'd had such high hopes going to make matters worse instead of better? Would calling on Jessica solve anything? Was there a risk it might stir all the old passions up again, and make a bad situation worse? Nothing he could say was going to bring Everett back or release Hari from the life sentence he'd been given. He sighed, shrugged his shoulders, grasped the wrought iron hand rail, and started to climb.

Halfway up he halted again, a thousand thoughts still going round in his head, the same ones that had been plaguing him for months. Now was the test … should he carry on up the steps, or go back down and hide himself until he'd finally made up his mind what to do? Whatever he did, he was still going to have to face Margery and, if he stuck to the plan he and Gareth had come up with, Yana and the girl who thought she was Jessica as well. He daren't think what he could ever say to Hari.

It was nightmare scenario and, even at this late stage, he still hadn't made his mind up as to how he was going to handle it.

He glanced up at the window again; whoever had been there, had gone. Maybe he'd been mistaken. Maybe she lived in another flat … one at the back possibly.

Through the tiniest of gaps in the curtains, one that was too small for him to see her, Lucy saw him hesitate.

'Come on, come on …' she whispered; but he made no move to climb the last few steps to her door.

She'd guessed what was going on in his mind, of course. It must have been mirroring what was going on in her own, especially the fact she might have to change her name yet again to benefit from his estate.

Mr Quick, the solicitor who'd been handling the British end her father's affairs had told her she *might* be able to change her name back to Lucy Groves after everything settled, though he'd never heard of such a step being undertaken before. 'We must go with the flow, as far as your father is concerned,' he said, 'what matters to him is that he's found you, his daughter, but at what cost? He's lost his brother and, to all intents, he's his lost son too. His great plan to make things right, has gone disastrously wrong. What was she going to say if found herself opening the door to him? Mourning the loss of her uncle, Everett; and blaming her half-brother, Hari, for killing him … were awful, sad, unbelievable … but she felt no sorrow. How could she when she didn't know either of them, had never heard of them, let alone met them. No … of all the victims in this tragic affair, the only ones she felt real pity for, were the girl who thought she was Jessica Makins only to find out she was Mavis Townsend, and the girl's mother, Doreen, who'd thought the same. 'Anyway,' Lucy said to herself, 'they're not going to be forgotten; I'm working on a little surprise that'll come their way if they've been left out.'

As she'd been turning these thought over in her mind, she'd left the window and was heading for the front door. When she got to it, she knew there was only the thickness of a piece of wood between her and the father she never knew she had.

When his knock finally came, she crossed her fingers and slowly opened the door.

He was taller, than he'd seemed in the brief glance she had of him through the gap in the curtains, and browner under his silver stubble. But the sweat stained battered old Aussie hat he was wearing, and the smile he'd somehow managed to conjure up, were just as she'd thought they'd be.

He lifted his eyebrows and widened his smile.

She hesitated.

'Jessica?' he asked … softly … tentatively.

She paused and then, standing back with the door wide open, she beckoned him in.

Finding Jessica

The towns, villages, and establishments
mentioned in this book
are a mix of the real and the imagined.
All the characters are fictitious.

About the author

Alan Grainger is an Englishman who emigrated to Ireland at the time when everyone else seemed to be going the other way. He got seduced by the lifestyle, married an Irish woman, and never went back. They have three children and seven grandchildren. His business career ended unexpectedly early when his company was taken over, and a whole new world of opportunity opened up. Ever since then, other than when he's watching rugby or cricket on television, he has been travelling, painting, and writing. His journeys have taken him all over the world, provided him with much of the background material which features in his books, and allowed him to choose authentic sets against which he can tell his stories.

The following books written by the same author are available from Amazon, Kindle, and other major online retailers. They may also be obtained by ordering through any bookshop.

The Learning Curves

Divided from his father, and frozen out of his home in Ireland by his new stepmother, sixteen-year-old Jimmy O'Callaghan runs away, resolving never to return. With no one to guide and support him, he finds himself with little option but to learn about life and love as best he can. He's aided in his quest for enlightenment, success, and happiness, by an unlikely collection of worldly people, the sort of people he would never have encountered, let alone befriend, at home in Templederry. Starting off with the few pounds he'd stolen from the till in his father's pub the night before he left, and with little appreciation of how big a risk he was taking, his personality and determination ensure nothing is beyond his reach.

This book is the first of The Templederry Trilogy, all of which are stand-alone stories connected by the characters, and is partly set in the rural Irish town of Templederry, County Tipperary. It is followed by Father Unknown and The Legacy.

Father Unknown

The fragile and sometimes volatile relationship between two brothers, Dick and Roger Davenport, is demolished forever when they find out something previously unknown to them about their beginnings. In the aftermath of the violence which follows their discovery, Dick, strongly supported by his grandfather Archie, sets off in a new direction, one which brings him to Ireland on a journey of more surprising discoveries.

This book is the second of The Templederry Trilogy. It is preceded by The Learning Curves and followed by The Legacy.

The Legacy

When an heir hunter turns up looking for Charlie Cassidy and finds he's been dead for years, he tells Cassidy's son and daughter, he has information which might connect them, through their late father, to an unclaimed legacy. He asks them if they'd like him to process their claim, but they think his fees are too high and decide to do the job themselves. It's a choice they regret when they discover their father was not the man they thought he was.

The Legacy is the third and last book of The Templederry Trilogy. It is preceded by The Learning Curves and Father Unknown

The same author's murder/mystery novels, featuring Detective Chief Inspector 'Foxy' Reynard, are available from Amazon, Kindle, Create Space and other on-line booksellers, or by ordering through bookshops.

Eddie's Penguin

When a young girl's quest to find the father she has never met becomes entangled in a police investigation into a series of seemingly unconnected murders she has no idea the information she digs up will ultimately lead to the uncovering of the last bit of the jigsaw the police are struggling to put together. Detective Chief Inspector 'Foxy' Reynard, who makes his first appearance in this murder/mystery story, leads the team from Sussex CID who finally solve the mystery and the crimes.

Deadly Darjeeling

When Nelson Deep, wealthy tea merchant, is found dead in his study in bizarre circumstances and Detective Chief Inspector 'Foxy' Reynard is called in, a solution seems inevitable. Such an assumption, however, makes little allowance for the dysfunctional and self-centred attitudes the D.C.I. uncovers as he attempts to unravel the strange relationships prevailing within the Deep family.

Deep & Crisp & Even

The body of a young woman newspaper columnist is found part buried under the snow and Detective Chief Inspector 'Foxy' Reynard is brought in. As his investigation into her death proceeds, it becomes increasingly apparent there was more to Rosaleen Sommerton than met the eye

Box of Secrets

When a dead woman is found, sitting in a garden chair in a quiet cul-de-sac in Eastbourne, with no clothes on; and the Prime

Minister's wife chokes on an oyster at a Food Festival at the Royal Pavilion in Brighton, nobody gives any thought to the possibility the two incidents are in any way connected. But they are ... as are some other unexplained happenings ... and it needs all the intuitive and logical skills of Detective Chief Inspector 'Foxy' Reynard of Sussex C.I.D., plus a few truths which have lain hidden in an old box for years, to work out what they are.

Short & Fat & Dead

A short fat man is found dead in the bottom of a grave, freshly dug for somebody else. Nobody knows who he is or why he is there; but Detective Superintendent 'Foxy' Reynard and his team of detectives, working through the evidence they collect in their slightly outdated way, finally bring his killer to justice. It's a British police detective story, the fifth in the series and it's told in the style of many British classic detective novels where even the criminals seem half decent.

Good Intention, Bad Result.

Detective Superintendent 'Foxy' Reynard and his team from Sussex CID have to unravel a complicated web of circumstances to get to the murders of two men more associated with wine and frying than death. A typical 'Foxy' Reynard story, in the style of a British 'Whodunnit'.

Blood On The Stones

Alan Grainger's saga/spy thriller, **Blood On The Stones**, has just been re-launched by the publishers and is available through the sources mentioned above.

It is about two young men, conceived in 1938, when rioting Nazi supporters were roaming the streets of Vienna taunting Jews, who are born and brought up in a remote village in the Carpathian Mountains of Czechoslovakia

The childhood friendship which develops between them as a result of their similar circumstances is strong at the start, but it starts to crumble when new relationships intervene. By the time they reach their early twenties the ties between them which had been becoming progressively weak are finally torn asunder when they fall out over a girl. They vow never to see each other again but, unexpectedly, fate takes control of their lives again a few years later when they find themselves face to face in the course of an attempted royal assassination.

All Alan Grainger's books are available
in Kindle format.

Made in the USA
Monee, IL
31 October 2020